"I can quite see why you must kill me," said the duke. The gun wavered. Then Georgia Baillie spoke: "You must hide in the priests' hideaway. At once."

Behind the mask of the bold brigand, the Duke of Westacre knew there was a frightened girl. He knew too, that she was completely unlike any of the other ambitious, scheming damsels so eager to become his duchess.

Before he realized what had happened, the obstinate bachelor was madly in love — and trapped in a terrifying drama which included a fearsome secret, a hazardous Channel crossing, and a traitorous plot to kill the heir to the throne of England . . . .

Also in Pyramid Books
by
BARBARA CARTLAND

DESIRE OF THE HEART

A HAZARD OF HEARTS

THE COIN OF LOVE

LOVE IN HIDING

THE ENCHANTING EVIL

THE UNPREDICTABLE BRIDE

THE SECRET HEART

A DUEL OF HEARTS

LOVE IS THE ENEMY

THE HIDDEN HEART

LOST ENCHANTMENT

LOVE HOLDS THE CARDS

LOST LOVE

LOVE ME FOREVER

LOVE IS CONTRABAND

THE INNOCENT HEIRESS

LOVE IS DANGEROUS

THE AUDACIOUS ADVENTURESS

THE ENCHANTED MOMENT

SWEET ADVENTURE

THE ROYAL PLEDGE

WINGS ON MY HEART

WE DANCED ALL NIGHT

THE COMPLACENT WIFE

A HALO FOR THE DEVIL

THE ODIOUS DUKE

LOVE IS AN EAGLE

THE LITTLE PRETENDER

THE GOLDEN GONDOLA

STARS IN MY HEART

MESSENGER OF LOVE

THE SECRET FEAR

AN INNOCENT IN PARIS

THE WINGS OF LOVE

THE ENCHANTED WALTZ

THE HIDDEN EVIL

ELIZABETHAN LOVER

THE UNKNOWN HEART

OPEN WINGS

AGAIN THIS RAPTURE

THE RELUCTANT BRIDE

THE PRETTY HORSE-BREAKERS

THE KISS OF THE DEVIL

A KISS OF SILK

NO HEART IS FREE

LOVE TO THE RESCUE

STOLEN HALO

SWEET PUNISHMENT

LIGHTS OF LOVE

BLUE HEATHER

A LIGHT TO THE HEART

SWEET ENCHANTRESS

LOVE IS CONTRABAND

Barbara Cartland

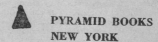

PYRAMID BOOKS
NEW YORK

LOVE IS CONTRABAND

A PYRAMID BOOK

Pyramid edition published August 1970
  Sixth printing, August 1974

© Barbara Cartland 1968

All Rights Reserved

ISBN 0-515-03429-0

Printed in the United States of America

Pyramid Books are published by Pyramid Communications, Inc.
Its trademarks, consisting of the word "Pyramid" and the
portrayal of a pyramid, are registered in the United States
Patent Office.

Pyramid Communications, Inc.,
919 Third Avenue, New York, N.Y. 10022

LOVE IS
CONTRABAND

1

"HELL and damnation, you've beaten me again!' The Duke of Westacre rose from the green-baize table and flung the cards across the room. They scattered over the carpet, the elegant inlaid furniture, and came to rest on the damask-covered spindle-legged sofa.

His companion tipped back his chair from the table and laughed.

'You're becoming a bad loser, Trydon.'

'That's the third night running you have beaten me at écarté,' the Duke replied. 'And I've sworn never to match you again at faro!'

'You know what the saying is, don't you?' Captain Pereguine Carrington asked.

'I do not,' the Duke replied disagreeably, 'and I am confident that I will not pay for the knowledge.'

Pereguine Carrington laughed again.

'I'll tell you for nothing,' he said. 'Unlucky at cards, lucky in love.'

The Duke glared at him, marched across the salon and flung open one of the long french windows which opened into the garden. The night air was fresh and sweet on his face as he stood staring out. A few hours earlier there had been a profusion of taper lights illuminating the flower beds, encircling the water-lily pond, and edging the paths down to the artificial lake. But these had spluttered out into their own grease; now only a few Chinese lanterns swinging in the breeze remained to show that the garden had earlier sported an air of festivity and gaiety.

'Well?' Pereguine Carrington asked from the card-table.

'Well what?' the Duke replied, his voice still disagreeable. 'Do you think I've enjoyed this evening? Gad, Pereguine, I've felt like a fox! I know now what it is

7

like to be hunted. Yes, hunted, by those damned match-making mamas and their puling, wet-faced chits with the dew still on them.'

'They've gone by now,' Pereguine answered consolingly. 'Her Ladyship peeped in about two hours ago. I suspicioned that she wished to bid you good night. But when she saw you were engaged with the cards, with a monstrously ferocious frown on your forehead, she withdrew, giving me only a wave of her hand.'

The Duke turned towards his friend and had the grace to look almost shamefaced.

'I suppose I ought to be grateful to my godmother for taking an interest in me,' he said. 'But the deuce take it, Pereguine, I have no desire to be wed and that's a fact. All this talk about a chatelaine at the castle, a hostess in London! 'Tis I who have to live with the wench, not my godmother! Not those damned trustees that make my life a sheer misery with their eternal talk of what's expected of me.'

'Well, you're a Duke and that's that,' Pereguine said cheerfully. 'In other words, you can't have the strawberry leaves and not pay for them.'

'I never wanted to be a Duke; I never expected to be a Duke! If anything makes me want to fight the whole of Napoleon's army single-handed, it's the fact that he killed my cousin.'

'Doing it a bit brown, aren't you, Trydon?' Pereguine asked lazily. 'Most fellows would give their right arm to be in your position.'

'I know, I know,' the Duke said testily. 'I'm ungrateful—that's what you are thinking, isn't it? Of course I appreciate being a person of consequence after being a poor relation for so many years. Of course I enjoy my property, my position at Court and the fact that people listen with respect to my opinions!'

'You sound like Methuselah—the old rattle-bones we learnt about at Eton,' Pereguine laughed.

'And I feel like him,' the Duke snapped. 'I was perfectly happy until there was all this talk of marriage. "You must have a Duchess!" "A wife is essential for your position!" "You must entertain and a bachelor can't do that!" They nag me all the time—morning, noon and night! And now this ghastly ball with all the girls paraded in front of me as though I were a Sultan picking out a concubine.'

'No, no!' Pereguine said hastily. 'Wrong simile, old man. A concubine is not at all the type of female we met here tonight.'

'I should think not indeed!'

Suddenly the Duke regained his humour, threw back his head and laughed as heartily as his friend.

'Did you see that chit with a white rose in her hair?' he asked. 'I never saw such a vacant face. She looked as if she was moon-struck. Yet my godmother actually suggested she might make me an excellent wife. "You would deal well together," she said. "Her father's lands march with Westacre's on the north." '

'Oh! you couldn't contemplate her,' Pereguine protested.

'I should think not,' the Duke replied. 'But they were all the same, looking up at me when I danced with them, with greed in their eyes. I knew that each one of them was thinking how attractive she would look in the Westacre diamonds.'

'The trouble with you,' Pereguine said, 'is that you are beginning to fancy yourself too much by half.'

'Not really,' the Duke replied. 'The truth is that after two years of pomp and circumstance I am beginning to pull at the bit. Do you know where I would like to be more than anywhere else in the world?'

He got up again as he spoke and went towards the window.

'No, where?' Pereguine asked curiously.

'On the Peninsula, with the rest of the Regiment! You know I asked Prinny if I could go back.'

'And what did His Royal Highness reply?' Pereguine asked.

'He was quite peeved,' the Duke answered. 'Said that if he had his way, what with the casualties and the expense, he would bring the whole damned army home. He wasn't having his Dukes—his Dukes, if you please!—in a position where they might be taken prisoner or shot down like the merest rabble, so that Napoleon could claim another victory! In fact, he was so violent on the subject that I withdrew from his presence.'

'You know Prinny hates the war,' Pereguine said.

9

'I cannot credit that anyone enjoys it,' the Duke answered. 'Napoleon has never seemed more formidable. He has the whole of Europe under his heel and would do anything to crush us.'

'He can't do that as long as Collingwood's there,' Pereguine replied. 'What is it we have now . . . eight hundred and fifty ships under sail? Napoleon will think twice before he attacks us!'

'We have to attack him, that's the answer!' the Duke cried. 'But I am to have no part in it! Instead of thinking of battles I am to contemplate marriage!'

'But the two are sometimes synonymous,' Pereguine smiled.

'When you start prosing you are a dead bore,' the Duke retorted. 'Come, if you are sure none of those simpering misses are lurking along the passage, we'll to bed."

Pereguine Carrington rose slowly to his feet and collected a pile of gold guineas which were still lying on the card-table. He must carry them; for his skin-tight trousers and elegantly moulded coat which fitted without a wrinkle would not have accommodated one of them. Turning towards the door, he stopped and looked back at his friend, who was walking slowly across the room, a frown between his eyes.

'You know what?' he said. 'You expect too much.'

'In what way?' the Duke asked.

Pereguine looked at him reflectively.

'Handsome phiz,' he said; 'a devil of a Corinthian; an unparalleled rider; a dangerous duelist; Tulip of the Turf; a Nonpariel; rich as Croesus; a Duke; and yet you expect to fall in love!'

'Don't say it,' the Duke interrupted. 'Even to talk about it makes me spit. All I want is for females to leave me alone!'

'That's hardly something you practise when you are in London,' Pereguine said. 'That little lady-bird of yours could tell a different tale.'

'Ah, Janita!' the Duke exclaimed. 'She's different, as you well know. If ever there was a bit o' muslin who knew how to make a fellow relax and enjoy her company, it is Janita.'

'Too expensive for me,' Pereguine replied. 'Those chestnuts you gave her are the envy of the Park.'

'She liked them because they matched her hair,' the

Duke answered casually, and opening the door he preceded his friend into the hall.

A sleepy flunkey handed the gentlemen two lighted candlesticks. There was really no need for them as the tapers in the silver sconces were still alight even though they had burned low.

'Good night, sleep tight,' Pereguine said, as they reached the landing, with a note of affection in his voice. 'Things may seem brighter in the morning.'

'I doubt it,' the Duke said grimly. 'If I know anything of my godmother she will be cross-examining me about those unfledged brats before I have hardly opened my eyes.'

'Thank the Lord I'm a commoner,' Pereguine said with a laugh, and went down the passage towards a room at the far end of it.

With a sigh the Duke turned the handle of his own door. He had the feeling that tired though he was he would have liked to go on talking. To his surprise the room was in darkness. For a moment he thought he had mistaken his bedchamber. His valet should be waiting for him; for however late he came to bed there were always fresh tapers, and if the night was cold the fire was kept replenished in the grate.

It was one of the advantages of being a Duke, he found, that he was surrounded by every comfort. There were, in fact, hundreds of people employed to make sure of this.

'I must be in the wrong room,' he thought, lifting his candle higher. Then, as its light illuminated the darkness, he was suddenly very still. Just for a second he remained immobile; then with a speed which showed that underneath his languid exterior was an alertness which came from his training in the Army, he moved from the room out into the passage and closed the door behind him. He hurried down the corridor and burst into the bedchamber of Pereguine Carrington, who, in the act of taking off his satin evening-coat, turned towards him in surprise.

'Hello, Trydon!' he exclaimed. 'I thought you had retired.'

The Duke shut the door behind him.

'No valet?' he asked suspiciously.

Pereguine looked almost embarrassed.

'As a matter of fact, I told the fellow to go to bed,' he said. 'He's getting on in age. He was with my father before

11

me and it seems a bit over the odds to keep him up all night."

'I am not interested in your reasons for having, or not having, a valet,' the Duke said testily. 'Peregine, I have to get away from here.'

'What do you mean?' his friend asked in astonishment.

'I mean what I say,' the Duke answered, putting his candle on the table. 'Otherwise I am trapped.'

'What the devil are you talking about?' Pereguine enquired.

The Duke sat down on the edge of the bed.

'When I went into my bedroom just now, who do you think was there?'

'Old Hardy, I suppose, or whatever that other manservant of yours is called. Who did you expect to find?'

The Duke drew a deep breath.

'Hardy was not there,' he said slowly. 'The room was in darkness, but by the light of my candle I could see who was in my bed.'

'Good Lord!' Pereguine ejaculated. 'Who was in your bed?'

'I think, but I couldn't be sure, mind you,' the Duke said, 'that it was that fair-haired chit I danced with at the beginning of the evening and immediately after dinner.'

'That is Isobel Dalguish,' Pereguine told him. 'She's not too platter-faced, but her mother's a match-making dragon. Freddy Mellington told me she was after him last season and he had a terrible time shaking her off. In fact, at one moment he threatened to leave London. Said they pounced on him whenever he appeared.'

'Well, apparently I've taken Freddy Mellington's place,' the Duke growled.

'Damned difficult situation,' Pereguine remarked.

'I have told you, I am going away,' the Duke said positively. 'Now, and at once!'

'Good heavens, is that wise?' Pereguine inquired.

'You must be a bird-brain if you can't see the consequence of my staying,' the Duke replied. 'I wager that her Mama is lurking somewhere down the passage waiting until I am safely inside the room. Then she will rush in and throw the Cheltenham theatricals.'

'Good, God, I never thought of that!' Pereguine interjected.

12

'But I have,' the Duke said grimly. 'I am not such a cheesecake that I don't realise that in such a circumstance the only decent thing I could do would be to offer for the girl.'

'Suppose you don't go back,' Pereguine suggested. 'Stay the night here.'

'However good an explanation I may have,' the Duke replied, 'there is always their word against mine that I invited the girl to my room. It is, of course, extremely reprehensible that she accepted such an invitation. But doubtless the irreparable damage to her reputation would be assuaged by the fact that she becomes the Duchess of Westacre.'

'I must say you are pretty fly when it comes to the throwdown,' Pereguine remarked. 'Damned if I would have known what to do!'

'If you had any sense you would have done what I am going to do now,' the Duke retorted. 'You will have to lend me your clothes. Lucky we are almost the same size. I always borrowed your things at Oxford because you were better off than I was and you could afford to patronise a more expensive tailor.'

Pereguine waved his hand towards the wardrobe.

'All that is mine is yours,' he said dramatically.

The Duke wasted no time. He changed into Pereguine's riding-breeches, tied with a practised hand a stiff white cravat round his neck and put on his friend's dark grey, whipcord riding-coat, which could only have been cut by a master hand.

'Thank heavens we go to the same boot-maker,' the Duke said, as he eased his feet into a pair of Hessians which had been polished with champagne.

'Here, steady, old boy!' Pereguine exclaimed, 'that's my new pair! I've only worn them once.'

'Buy another pair and put them down to my account,' the Duke replied.

'I certainly will,' Pereguine answered. 'And now will you be kind enough to tell me what I am to say in the morning to Her Ladyship. She left us together when she went to bed, and if you are not to be found the first person to be cross-questioned will be me.'

'You can tell my godmother,' the Duke said reflectively, 'that I had a message which informed me that I was urgently needed elsewhere on matters of military importance.'

'Think she is going to believe that?' Pereguine asked.

'She will if you tell her convincingly enough. You always were a good liar, Pereguine. At least you could always lie yourself out of a tight corner! On this occasion you can do your best for me.'

'I hope I shall be successful,' Pereguine said gloomily. 'I have a good mind to come with you. Where are you going, by the way?'

'Dashed if I know,' the Duke said. 'I think I shall ride across country to Charles Bryant's house. I believe he lives somewhere along the coast.'

'He does, it's not far from that place that Prinny raves about—Brighthelmstone. If you keep the sea on your left you shouldn't have much trouble in getting there.'

'I shan't come back to London for a few days,' the Duke said.

He stood up and looked at himself in the wardrobe mirror.

'Hell! I believe Weston cuts your coats better than he does mine.'

'If you spoil the fit you will have to give me a new coat as well,' Pereguine warned him.

'Try and find something up to scratch from what I have left behind,' the Duke answered. 'Tell Hardy I said so. He won't let you have anything otherwise.'

The Duke took a high beaver hat from a shelf on the top of the wardrobe. Then, as he put it jauntily on the side of his head, he said:

'By the way, Pereguine, you had best give me back the guineas you won from me and anything else you have handy. I may need the soft if Charles is not at home, or I get into trouble on the way there.'

'Everything I possess,' Pereguine answered, 'is in that little drawer on the top of the dressing-table.'

The Duke went to the drawer and gave a whistle.

'Your pockets are pretty heavy at the moment, old boy.'

'As a matter of fact, I took a couple of monkeys off old Buckhaven before supper,' Pereguine grinned. 'It must have been while you were flirting with the ambitious Isobel.'

'Don't talk to me about that girl,' the Duke commanded.

14

'I would like to wring her mother's neck, setting a trap like that. And to think there might have been men not so astute as I who would have fallen into it!'

'You are too smug,' Pereguine smiled. 'One day you will get caught, you mark my words.'

'I bet you a pony I will not,' the Duke asserted.

'Done!' Pereguine replied, 'and within a year.'

"So be it,' the Duke answered. 'You have lost your money though. From this day forward I am going to eschew all women. I have had enough of them.'

'Shall I tell your godmother that?' Pereguine asked mischievously.

'No, let her find out for herself. But, for your own information, no one is going to badger me into marriage. No one is going to nag me any longer. I have had enough! Be certain of one thing, I am remaining a bachelor, and the Westacre diamonds can stay in the bank until they turn black for all I care.'

Pereguine laughed. He was still laughing as the Duke went out of the room shutting the door unusually quietly behind him. The idea of His Grace tiptoeing down the passage for fear he should be heard made Pereguine laugh so much that it was some considerable time before he could compose himself and finish undressing.

In the meantime the Duke reached the stables without mishap, roused a stable-boy, who awoke a groom who knocked up His Grace's head coachman. After what seemed an extremely irksome delay, the Duke was furnished with one of his favourite black stallions, and, having given instructions for the rest of his horses and his phacton to go back to London, he set off over the downs.

Feeling an almost irrepressible relief at leaving the great house and its matrimonial dangers behind him, the Duke put his horse to the gallop. He travelled for over an hour before the dawn broke and the darkness began to lift. He then realised that a heavy sea-mist was obscuring the landscape. By this time he found the lie of the land was descending. He could still hear the beat of the waves on his left, but some of the freshness had gone out of his horse and they were, neither of them, in such a hurry as they had been at the beginning of their ride.

They picked their way carefully past gorse bushes and rough stony patches which might easily have precipitated a fall. The Duke bent forward to pat his horse's neck. He realised now that he had been reprehensibly foolhardy to have galloped in the darkness. A rabbit-hole might have resulted in a twisted fetlock, or, as far as he was concerned, a broken neck.

He was too good a rider not to appreciate the dangers, and now as the wet mist swirled about him he moved more carefully, peering to the right and the left for some landmark to tell him where he might be. He had ridden over the downs, often enough as a boy, but now he realised he was lost, although he knew he was travelling in the general direction he had chosen. The land was still sloping downhill and he guessed he would soon come to one of the many creeks which dissect the south coast.

Suddenly he thought he heard voices. They were not far away and instinctively he reined in his horse and sat silent and still, straining his ears for another sound. Then unexpectedly the wind began to lift the blanketing mist and he heard a voice say in a harsh whisper:

'Ther' be some 'un a'coming.'

'Shall Oi blow a hole through 'um?'

The Duke's hearing had always been very acute. But now, as he held his breath, wondering if he had heard right, a third voice, and astonishingly he knew it to be that of a woman, said:

'Fools! Do you want to bring the Coast Guards down on us? It will be the tubman that Philip said he would send us.'

'Ah, that's who it be,' one of the men answered.

Suddenly and immediately in front of him the Duke saw the man who had been speaking. He was a fisherman, with high boots and a cap pulled low over his forehead. He didn't look violent except for the fact that in his hand he held a pistol, primed and cocked. The Duke had the feeling that, whatever the woman might have said, this man would not hesitate to use it.

'Who be 'ee?' The man's question was sharp.

Almost without thinking the Duke gave the right answer.

'Philip sent me.'

If the man was relieved he did not show it.

'Cum on then, ye be late.'

The Duke followed him, his horse picking its way with

16

some difficulty over the rough shingle which had now replaced the soft grass of the downs. They were in a creek. Now, as the mist lifted, the wind blowing it unevenly across his path, the Duke felt a moment's uneasiness. The creek, hollowed out perhaps by a stream which had long since dried up, was very narrow, and hardly had they entered into it when the banks rose sharply on either side, so that he felt as he followed the man with the lantern that he and his horse were riding into a narrow tunnel.

Then, almost as though they were conjured out of the mist by magic, other people appeared: men, perhaps a dozen of them, all fishermen, and pulled up high on to the shingle, a boat. Now the Duke was aware why they had been frightened of him and why there had to be no noise for fear of the Coast Guards. They would only have had to see the tubs weighing down the stern of the boat, or the bales piled high in the bow, to know these were smugglers. They were, the Duke thought quickly, dangerous men who would not hesitate, were they suspicious of him, to cut his throat and chuck his body into the sea.

'You are late.'

It was the woman who had spoken earlier. Her voice was cultured and the Duke stared down at her in astonishment. She was wearing high boots such as the fishermen wear, and he realised with almost a sense of shock that she was in trousers. She had on a shabby old-fashioned, full-skirted coat, in the fashion that had gone out with the end of the century, and a black handkerchief covered her hair.

'Well, hurry up!' she said impatiently. 'The men are tired and cannot manage the cargo by themselves.'

'No, of course not,' the Duke said. His voice caused her to look at him swiftly with suspicion, but it was still too dark and misty for her to see his face, and as he dismounted she started giving orders to the men.

'Take the kegs up first: they are the heaviest.'

The Duke was not quite certain how it happened, but he found a keg of brandy on his shoulder, and then he was following the other men through a low cave which necessitated their bending their backs, along a winding passage cut through the rocks, up a rickety staircase, and along another passage, rising, rising all the time. Finally a heavy door was flung open and he found himself, as he had expected, in a long dark cellar. Whether it was the cellar of some private house or the crypt of a church he had no idea.

As he headed back with the other men down the passage, down the rickety stairway, which he realised now was held together with rope, he was trying to remember all he had heard of the smugglers' exploits.

There was not a village or a hamlet along the south and east coast of England which was not suspected of being a smuggling haunt. The local villagers and farmers were far too frightened to give anyone away; and, what was more, most of them benefited one way or another from the smuggling activities in their midst.

Another keg was slipped on to the Duke's shoulder. This time it seemed incredibly heavy. 'Next time I drink brandy,' he told himself, 'I shall remember this and be more appreciative of it that I have been in the past.'

Up the stairway, along the stony passages again into the cellar. The third time it was agony to have to bend his back as he moved down the cave which led from the sea. The men with him worked in silence, they did not stop; they all seemed fiercely concentrated on getting the cargo to safety. It was almost impossible for them to see one another's faces, for only an occasional flickering lantern lit the route. But outside the mist had gone and the first rays of the sun were glittering on the smooth sea.

It was as he bent to pick a heavy bale from the bow of the boat that the Duke's foot slipped on the stones covered by seaweed, and he crashed to the ground, tearing his hand against a piece of wire which had come loose from some of the merchandise. He let out an oath almost without thinking, and instantly the woman, whom he had hardly noticed during the carrying, appeared.

'Hush, no noise!' she commanded, then in another tone, 'Are you hurt?'

'Not badly,' the Duke said ruefully, looking at the blood dripping from his hand. He realised that Pereguine's Hessians were not the right footwear for climbing over wet shingle, although it was hardly the moment to say so.

'You have cut yourself,' the woman said. 'This should be your last carry. After that I will see to your hand.'

He picked up the bale to carry it the long, back-breaking

journey to the cellar. He set it down, and realised as he glanced over the merchandise on the floor that it had been a good haul. Someone would make a great deal of money out of this, he thought, as he sucked the blood from his torn thumb on his way back to the boat.

Perhaps the Duke was slower than the other men because he found when he arrived at the opening of the cave that they had all gone, vanishing as silently as they had first appeared. As he stared at the boat, which looked like an ordinary fishing-vessel with some of its nets hanging out to dry, he felt he might have dreamed the whole episode. But there was his damaged thumb and the woman with her high fishing-boots and her ancient gentleman's coat to assure him it was no figment of his imagination.

She spoke as he approached.

'Let me look at your hand. 'Tis a nasty cut and it is dirty. It must be cleaned or it will become inflamed.'

'I'll manage,' the Duke said. 'Is there an inn around here?'

She looked up at him and for the first time he realised how young she was. Her face was grimed and dirty, but her eyes were large and fringed by long dark lashes.

'You cannot go to the inn,' she said. 'Surely you must realise that. The Coast Guards are everywhere asking questions, nosing about.'

'All right,' the Duke said, 'I will move further along the coast.'

'First I must bandage your hand,' she said, almost as though she were speaking to herself. 'Come, follow me, and let us hope no one sees us.'

She turned and walked ahead, as though she took his compliance for granted. Because he was curious he made no protest and followed her.

He longed to ride, but she was walking and he knew he must walk too. Taking his horse by the reins and following on foot, he realised now how painfully his back was aching and he felt almost dizzy from the strenuous work on top of a night without any sleep.

How Pereguine would have laughed, the Duke thought, if he had seen him smuggling kegs of brandy. Then, as they came out of the creek, the Duke saw in the morning sunlight what he had expected to see—a large house, near to the edge of the creek, but protected by the rise of the land and a plantation of trees from the winds which came from the sea.

It was a lovely building, doubtless erected in Elizabethan times, for its warm red bricks were mellowed with age. With its walled gardens on one side of it and its ancient stables on the other, it seemed complete in its immunity against encroachment, either from the sea or the land. A perfect hiding place for smugglers, the Duke thought, either with or without its owner's consent!

The woman ahead of him had reached the stables. There she stood for a moment calling for someone, and as the Duke caught up with her a very old groom, wizened and wrinkled came shuffling from one of the loose-boxes.

'Take this horse, Ned,' the woman said, 'and rub him down. He will be wanted very shortly.'

The groom said nothing and the Duke thought that he eyed him with hostility.

'Follow me,' she spoke sharply.

The Duke followed her across the stables and towards the house. She avoided the front, he noticed, and came to what he imagined was the kitchen door. Entering they marched along a flagged passage and passed through a green-baize door. Their footsteps sounded unnaturally loud and the Duke had the feeling that the house was peculiarly quiet.

The woman opened a door on the right of the passage. It led into a small room; it had once been attractively furnished but was now shabby and worn.

'Wait here.'

It was a command, not a request.

She turned, walked out of the room and shut the door behind her. To the Duke's utter astonishment he heard the key turn in the lock.

2

THE Duke stared at the locked door, his face wearing an expression which those who had served him in the Army knew as one scenting danger. Then he crossed to an armchair, seated himself in it and stretched out his legs.

He was very conscious of the ache on his shoulder where the tubs had rested; and, deliberately suppressing thoughts about his present position, he calculated that a tub—or a half-anker—weighed about fifty-six pounds when full.

He remembered hearing a Member of Parliament say recently that the loss to the Revenue due to the intensive smuggling operations taking place along the coast of Britain was nearly £60,000 a year. He tried to calculate what would have been the profit to the smugglers on this run. He thought that the men whom he had seen only vaguely in the mist and the darkness of the caves and passages appeared to be country types, not the rough kind of brute that he had been led to believe was the usual dangerous and aggressive smuggler. But who in heaven's name had ever heard of a smugglers' gang being led by a woman?

The Duke glanced round the room. Indeed what type of female would engage in smuggling and át the same time, apparently, have the entrée to a house such as this? The kitchen quarters had seemed empty, and he guessed that the owner of the house must be away, perhaps not having the slightest idea that his premises were being used for such nefarious purposes.

The Duke settled himself lower in the chair. If he was in a dangerous position he could do nothing about it. His hand was throbbing, his back was aching. He closed his eyes. He was half asleep when he heard the key turn in the door, but instantly he was fully awake and alert even though he did not move his position in the armchair. The door was thrown open almost violently and bustling into the room came a small, plump, apple-cheeked woman carrying a basin.

'Now, I've told you many a time,' she said in a high scolding voice, 'that I won't tolerate you rapscallions coming into the house. The cheek of it, forcing your way in here! As I've said before and I say it again . . .'

She put the basin down on the table, looked at the Duke as if for the first time, and the words seemed to die on her lips. She stared at him and then, as he did not speak, said in a very different tone of voice.

'I understand your hand is damaged . . . sir.'

The Duke got slowly to his feet.

'It is indeed,' he said. 'And I would be grateful if you would bandage it for me.'

Looking at her he decided that she was definitely either the housekeeper or maybe the family's nurse. She was a type that he could recognise easily enough. He held out his hand towards the basin. He had wrapped the torn thumb with his handkerchief which was now soaked with blood. Just for a moment he wondered if it was one of his own fine lawn kerchiefs, embroidered with his monogram and coronet, or one of Pereguine's.

Then, as the old woman pulled it gently from the wound, he saw with relief that it was plain, unembroidered, and therefore not his own.

'That's a nasty wound, sir,' the woman said, 'and dirty too. For safety's sake you best have a dot of brandy on it 'Tis the way they tell me that Admiral Nelson himself advised to prevent his sailors from getting their wounds afestered.'

She didn't wait for his answer but bustled from the room, while the Duke stood with his hand over the basin watching the blood drip slowly into the water.

When she returned a few moments later, she had a cutglass decanter in her hand and a small elegantly chased wineglass.

'I think the brandy would do me more good inside than out,' said the Duke with a smile.

'I'll have no smuggler drinking on these premises,' the old woman said sharply.

22

She started and glanced over her shoulder, as if she were afraid of what she had said and began to bathe the dirt from his hands. It hurt him so excrutiatingly that for a moment he felt almost faint.

'Now keep still,' she commanded him fiercely, and poured the brandy over the wound.

For a moment the pain was agonising. The Duke gritted his teeth but said nothing. A pad of clean white linen was laid on the wound, and a bandage of delicate lawn torn neatly into long strips was finally fastened into position round his wrist.

'Does it hurt now?' the woman asked, raising her head for the first time since she had begun her task.

'It's better than it was, thank you,' the Duke replied, conscious that the raw spirit was making his torn flesh tingle.

' 'Tis not very deep,' she said, 'but it will throb for a day or two, all the same. Now be off with you! You should not have come here in the first place.'

'I merely obeyed orders,' the Duke protested. 'And I suppose it's no use telling you that I am half famished, having done a heavy job of work on an empty stomach.'

'Hungry?' the old woman asked. 'Well, 'tis not my habit to send a hungry man away from this door. Sit you down and I'll find you something to eat, though it goes against the grain.'

The Duke had the feeling that she was being more severe than she really felt. Her eyes rested on him kindly and he had not forgotten that first reluctant 'sir', which his appearance had drawn from her lips.

She bustled from the room, shutting the door behind her, and he noticed she did not turn the key in the lock.

The Duke walked to the window and found himself looking over an elegantly laid out rose garden centred round a statue. Beyond it the gardens were protected by yew hedges, and beyond them again shrubs and woods seemed to frame the house like a green mantle.

Where did the girl fit into all this? Because she had vanished the Duke was curious about her. He tried to remember what she had looked like, but could only recall a black handkerchief pulled low over her hair, a small face smudged with dirt and grime, and the absurd, out-of-date, full-skirted coat and the high fishing-boots. A young

23

Amazon, indeed, to brave the perilous journey between England and the Continent and the ever-increasing vigilance of the Coast Guards and Revenue officers.

He had thought, when he entered it, that this room must belong to her, but now he was doubtful. There was an inlaid marquetry work-box by the armchair. There was a tapestry-covered stool which must have been worked by skilful fingers. There was a vase of flowers elegantly arranged on a small polished table, the first scented roses of summer mingling with blue forget-me-nots. It was a picture of colour and beauty which only a woman could have arranged.

The door flung open again, but this time without violence. The old woman came in carrying a tray.

'There's eggs and ham,' she said, 'for I have time for little else. If you are looking for a gentleman's meal of meat and fat pigeons you'll be disappointed.'

'I am extremely grateful for eggs and ham,' the Duke smiled.

He seated himself at the table as he spoke, and almost instinctively, as though there was no question about it, the woman waited on him. The eggs, three of them, with thick rashers of home-cured ham, were more delicious than anything the Duke had tasted for a long time. He almost wolfed them down.

'Now what will you drink?' she asked with a twinkle in her eye. 'I am not going to say that I approve of the likes of you drinking brandy, but it's there if you wish it.'

'What about tea?' the Duke asked. 'I wager there's plenty to be had in this house.'

He had the satisfaction of seeing her flush, her rosy cheeks becoming even rosier.

'If it's tea you want, I will get it for you,' she said. 'And without the impudence, if you please.'

The Duke had a feeling he was back in the nursery again.

'Very well, Nana, I would like some tea very much,' he said.

'And who's told you to call me Nana,' the old woman demanded. 'I am Mrs. Wheeldon to the village and Mrs. Wheeldon I'll be to you. Nana, indeed! What's the world acoming to, I should like to know.'

She flounced out of the room with the crackle of her

starched apron, and the Duke threw back his head and laughed. He had guessed right. A children's nurse and still the autocrat of the nursery. And she had fed him because she couldn't see one of her charges go hungry, even though he had behaved badly.

He cut himself a piece of home-made bread from the loaf which he knew had not long come from the oven, spread it thickly with golden-yellow butter and heard his teeth bite crisply into the crust. There was no doubt that hard manual work improved a man's appetite.

He thought with a feeling of superiority of the breakfast which Pereguine would be eating a little later in the morning: a glass of brandy to sweep away the fumes of the spirit he had taken the night before; then he would toy with the wing of a chicken, a cut from a saddle of mutton or perhaps a boiled capon. But after a few mouthfuls he would push away his plate, feeling almost nauseated with the thought of food.

'That's the difference between a hearty life and a Society one!' the Duke said aloud, as if he were speaking to Pereguine himself.

The door opened again and the Duke looked towards it, expecting to see Nana with her brew of fresh tea. But it was not Nana who entered, shutting the door sharply behind her to stand with her back against it. It was a girl—a girl who for a moment the Duke thought he had never seen before. Then he realised almost in astonishment it was the Amazon Smuggler.

Her fair hair fell in soft curls on each side of her head and her eyes were periwinkle blue and fringed with dark lashes. Her face was heart-shaped. She was much smaller than she had seemed in her boots and breeches. Now she was wearing an unfashionable cotton dress, washed and ironed until the colour had faded, but the Duke was not particularly concerned with her appearance. His eyes were on the small dueling pistol which she held in her hand. For a moment they stared at each other. Then, slowly, the Duke rose to his feet.

'Stay where you are,' the girl commanded.

It was the hard voice of command that she had used the night before in directing the smuggling operations.

'Who are you?'

'Is that of consequence?' the Duke enquired.

25

'You are an impostor,' she said accusingly. 'You said that Philip had sent you.'

'And how have you learnt that he did not?' the Duke asked.

'Because a boy has just brought a message to say that the man who should have been with us last night was held up on the way because his horse cast a shoe.'

'That was unfortunate!' the Duke remarked.

'Unfortunate for you,' she said. 'What is there to stop me from killing you? You know too much und I cannot let you go.'

'You don't look bloodthirsty,' the Duke said. 'Certainly not dressed as you are now. I have never met a female smuggler before. Come to think of it, I have not met many smugglers.'

'Do not prevaricate,' the girl said angrily, and stamped her foot. 'You are here under false pretences. Why? What have you to gain from it? Unless you are in the pay of the Coast Guards.'

'I can give you my word of honour on one thing,' the Duke said, 'I am not in the pay of anyone.'

'Then why are you here?' she repeated.

'Shall we say fate sent me?' the Duke asked. 'And the fact that I have sharp ears saved me from having a bullet blown through me.'

'So you heard what was said?'

'Yes,' the Duke replied. 'I heard what was said, and there was really nothing for it, was there, but to agree that I had come from Philip, whoever he may be.'

The girl sighed.

'Was there ever such a tangle? So you were really just a stranger? But why, why then did you help carry the tubs up to the cellar? Why did you take part in what must have seemed to you something wrong and reprehensible?

'Perhaps because I have a peculiar dislike of having pieces of lead lodged about in my body,' the Duke answered. 'Surely you can't complain. I did my part, unpleasant though it was, and you must admit that I have been wounded in your service.'

He made a gesture with his bandaged thumb as he spoke.

The girl lowered the duelling pistol.

'But what am I to do now?' she asked. 'You have seen

things you ought not to have seen and you know too much. You could destroy us all.'

'You could accept my word of honour,' the Duke said, 'that I will never reveal to anyone what I have seen here.'

'How can I trust anyone?' she asked angrily, 'especially someone like you.'

'Like me?' the Duke asked in genuine astonishment.

'A gentleman! A Society popinjay! They are all the same!' she cried sweepingly. 'All they think of is money, money, and grabbing for themselves. If I let you go you will begin to think that perhaps you are a fool not to have extorted some money from me.'

'Do I really appear so impecunious as that?' the Duke asked.

'Gentlemen who are warm in the pocket do not ride about in the middle of the night without a groom. And come to think of it, why the middle of the night? Are you in trouble, sir?'

The Duke's eyes twinkled.

'Perhaps I am,' he said. 'In which case are you prepared to help me?'

'Indeed I am not,' the girl replied crossly. 'I have troubles enough of my own. What I want to know is what I am to do about you? I am afriad to let you go and obviously I cannot keep you here.'

'Then there is nothing for it,' the Duke said. 'You will have to follow your first instinct, which was to kill me. But wouldn't it be more convenient if I moved a little nearer to the sea. I presume that is where you will dump the body, and it will be a fearsome task for you to get me there once I am dead. And Nana said quite clearly she won't have any of those rapscallions inside the place.'

'You are impossible,' the girl said angrily, putting the duelling pistol down on the table. 'You are making a mockery of the whole thing!'

'I cannot conceive why you should be so deadly serious,' the Duke retorted. 'I promise that I am no danger to you or to any of your illicit activities. Let me thank you for my breakfast, express my gratitude to Mrs. Wheeldon for bandaging my thumb, and if your groom has attended to my horse I'll be on my way. You will never see me again.'

'I wish I could be sure of that,' the girl said. 'What is your name?'

The Duke hesitated for just a moment; then, choosing the name he bore before he inherited the title, he spoke the truth:

'Raven—Trydon Raven at your service.'

'I have never heard of you,' the girl said frankly. 'It is not a local name, is it?'

'No,' the Duke replied.

'And you are in trouble. Perhaps you have no wish to bring yourself to the notice of the authorities?'

'None at all.'

'Then I suppose I can let you go.'

'I really think you have very little choice,' the Duke answered. 'Before I leave, may I ask your name?'

There was a little pause. Then the girl said:

'I suppose there is no harm in your knowing: my name is Georgia Baillie—at least, that is my married name.'

'You are married?' the Duke spoke in surprise. He had not thought of her as having a husband.

'Yes I am married,' she answered.

'And your husband allows you to indulge in carrying contraband. It is not an occupation for a woman.'

'My husband knows nothing about it,' Georgia answered sharply. 'He is at sea and he has not been here since we were married.'

'Do you really think he would approve of your behaviour?' the Duke asked. 'I cannot imagine a man of any mettle—and I have the greatest respect for the officers of His Majesty's Navy—allowing his wife, especially someone as young as you, to consort with such dangerous men as I saw you with last night.'

Georgia gave a laugh of sheer unbridled amusement.

'Dangerous!' she exclaimed. 'None of the men you saw last night are dangerous. They are the men on our estate, and I have known them all since I was a baby.'

'Then why . . .' the Duke began, only to be silenced as Georgia put up an imperious hand.

'Do not ask so many questions,' she said. 'Go away, go away quickly. I cannot imagine why I am talking to you like this! Oh, why did you come here and complicate things? I have told you far too much. Promise me, promise me by all that you hold sacred that you will never repeat one word of what you have seen or heard to a living soul.'

She was pleading with him now, her blue eyes raised to

his, her red lips trembling a little with the intensity with which she spoke.

He held out his unbandaged hand and took hers.

'Do not be afraid,' he said. 'I swear to you that everything I have seen and heard since dawn this morning is utterly and completely erased from my mind.'

'You do understand,' Georgia said, her little fingers gripping his, 'that one word would put these men's lives in jeopardy. One word and they are for the gallows or transportation. You would not have that on your conscience, would you? They are decent and honest men, except when life is too hard for them.'

'I believe you,' the Duke said quietly, 'but give it up. It is a mad, crazy risk to take: sooner or later you will be caught. You must be aware of that.'

She withdrew her fingers suddenly and turned away from him.

'I know full well the risk we run,' she said, 'but there is nothing I can do about it—nothing! Now go. I have accepted your word of honour and I cannot believe that you would betray it.'

Her face was turned away from him but he knew that she was trembling.

'Listen,' the Duke said. 'Let me help you. I don't like to think of your taking this almost insane risk. Tell me why you do it?'

Almost before he had finished speaking Georgia rounded on him.

'I shall tell you no more,' she said. 'It is not your business, sir, and gentlemen, whether they are in trouble or not, can do us only harm. Please go, keep your word and forget what you have seen. Forget this house and everything that has happened since you most unfortunately came into the neighbourhood.'

'Very well,' the Duke said. 'I must thank you, ma'am, for your hospitality.'

He picked up his hat from the table where he had laid it on entering the room.

Georgia was standing very stiff and still, and he had the feeling that every nerve in her body was urging him to be gone. Somehow it irked him that he could be so easily disposable.

29

'May I say goodbye to Nana?' he asked, 'or Mrs. Wheeldon, as she prefers to be called.'

'No! I will escort you to the stables,' Georgia said firmly. 'You must not be seen. I'll show you a way to avoid the village and to get on to the road. Are you journeying west or east, sir?'

'West,' he replied. 'I gather that very shortly I shall come to Romney Marsh.'

'You are right in your assumption,' she replied coldly.

The Duke held open the door, and he was just about to pass through it when- there was a clatter of feet in the passage and Nana, pink-cheeked and panting, came hurrying towards them.

'Miss Georgia . . . Miss Georgia!' she cried. 'They are here! I was opening the door to dust the hall and I saw the coach coming down the drive! 'Tis the usual one with all them pesty servants, but Her Ladyship will not be far behind.'

'Coming down the drive? . . . Then there is no time . . .' Georgia began in a flustered manner.

'No time indeed,' Nana interposed. 'They must not find him here. You know how them servants talk, you can't trust one o' them.'

'No indeed,' Georgia said. 'What shall I do?'

'Hide him until it's dark. You will have a chance of getting him away then.'

'Yes, yes of course.' She hesitated, then added almost reluctantly, 'It . . . it must be the priest hole. There is nowhere else!'

She put out her hand towards the Duke.

'Come, quickly, there is no time to be lost.'

'But what is happening?' the Duke asked, bewildered. 'Who is arriving?'

There was no answer to his questions and the Duke found himself being pulled by his hand along the passage. There was an open door and through it they passed into a large square hall. There was an oak stairway, with beautiful carved newels, curving upwards from the panelled hall and a huge fireplace opposite. Georgia had now released his hand and was feeling the panelling beside the fireplace.

Silently, and without even a click, a portion of it swung to reveal an opening. She turned to face him.

30

'The priest hole,' she said. 'No one knows of it except Nana and me.'

'But I don't understand,' the Duke expostulated. 'Why should I hide? Why not say I am a stranger who called here to ask the way?'

'Strangers never come here,' Georgia answered. 'My stepmother's servants would be suspicious at once. They are horrible, nosy, supercilious creatures. They will only stay a day or two.'

'I do not intend to stay a day or two in a priest hole,' the Duke protested.

'No, of course not,' Georgia answered. 'I will get you out as soon as it is safe. Perhaps at midnight. It just depends how late the guests sit gaming.'

'But this is absurd!' the Duke began, only to be interrupted by Nana who was standing on a chair to look out of one of the windows.

'They have crossed the bridge over the lake,' she cried, 'and any second now! . . . Oh, hurry, Miss Georgia, hurry!'

'Oh, please, please do as I say!' Georgia pleaded with the Duke, and almost despite himself he found himself bending his head to pass into the priest hole and heard the panelling close behind him.

'I'm going upstairs,' he heard Georgia say. 'When they arrive, say I have not yet awoken. That is, if they ask for for me, which is very unlikely.'

'I can't understand why they are here so early,' Nana replied, in a worried voice.

The Duke heard her footsteps receding as if she had walked away from the front door and down the passage which led to the kitchen.

He reached out his hand to feel where he was. At first it was very dark; then, gradually, as he stood there, he saw a faint light was coming from one side and he guessed it was an air-vent concealed in the chimney-piece. Gradually he was able to see more clearly and now he observed a very narrow flight of stairs directly in front of him leading upwards. They were just wide enough for a man to climb and slowly, moving quietly, the Duke went upwards.

As he ascended he heard below him the front-door bell clanging furiously, as if pulled by an imperious hand. He thought with a little smile that Nana would take her time in answering it. She would not be at the beck and call of the servants she disliked if she could possibly help it.

Up, up, he went. There was a small landing on the first floor and he realised there was a door there. Another exit, he supposed. He didn't waste his time in seeing if it could be opened from the inside but climbed up still further. Another small landing and then another, until finally he came to a door opening directly on the stairs.

He opened it and found to his surprise that he was in a tiny, low-ceilinged room, furnished with a bed, a table, chair and surprisingly a number of books set in a bookcase in the wall. There was also a long narrow window which let in the sunlight and through which he could look down on to the front of the house.

He crossed to it immediately and realised how skilfully the priest hole had been built. The window must be completely concealed from the outside by a buttress and the eaves of the old roof, but it let in a considerable amount of light and air, and it was also possible to look out not only over the countryside, but also directly on to the courtyard.

Here the Duke could see a large travelling-coach piled with luggage. The servants, who were unloading it all, wore dark green uniforms emblazoned with a silver braid and silver buttons. He was amazed that there were at least a dozen flunkeys. As he watched, he saw another coach approaching and guessed that this carried the maidservants. Georgia's stepmother, whoever she might be, certainly travelled in style. He wondered what sort of entourage would accompany Her Ladyship when she appeared.

But why, if she had all these servants in London, or wherever she had come from, should the house be left in the charge of no one but old Nana and Georgia? It was a question to which he had not the answer. As he turned from peeping through the thin, narrow window he sat down on the bed and began to laugh. Never in his wildest dreams had he expected to find himself in such a predicament or taking part in such an adventure. And all because some over-ambitious wench had climbed into his bed in the hope of forcing him into marriage with her.

'To hell with all women!' the Duke exclaimed as he realised that yet another woman had got him into his present position.

At least, he thought with relief, Georgia was married. He would not have any further difficulties by becoming entangled with her. A real tomboy if ever there was one. And yet in woman's dress he thought she looked frail and somehow pathetic. 'What a ridiculous idea!' he told himself.

Well, this escapade would be something to make him chuckle in the years to come when he thought about it. In the meantime he could only hope that Georgia or Nana would remember that eggs and ham were not a very filling breakfast for a hungry man. However, as there was nothing else for it, he might as well catch up with his sleep.

He took off his coat, noticed it had been stained and rubbed on the shoulders by the kegs, and thought that Pereguine would certainly insist on having a new one from Weston. He took off his cravat and threw it on the chair. He had meant to take off his boots, but it was too much of an effort without a valet to assist him, so he settled himself comfortably on the bed, propped the pillow behind his head and with hardly a pause fell into a deep dreamless slumber.

He was awoken by the slight sound of the door opening. For a moment he wondered where he was. Then, as Georgia came into the room carrying a basket, he remembered everything.

'I had to come myself,' she said almost apologetically. 'Nana said the stairs would bring on her wheezes. Besides, she is in the kitchen fighting with the chef and cursing the scullions for making a mess on her freshly scrubbed flags. Nana hates the servants from London worse than if they were the armies of Napoleon. In fact, she looks on them as an invading force.'

The Duke guessed that Georgia was talking because she was embarrassed. Sitting up on the bed, he reached for his cravat.

'Pardon me if I look somewhat dishevelled. I was tired, so I slept. Have you any conjecture of the time?'

'Yes, indeed, it is after two o'clock in the afternoon. I should have brought you some food before, but Nana was preparing a pigeon pie for you.'

'That's most kind of her,' the Duke said. 'I am certainly hungry enough to eat a flock of them.'

33

Georgia stood the basket down on the chair and lifted from it a pie, a new loaf of bread, butter, cold sliced ham and a small basket of strawberries.

'I picked these fresh from the garden,' she said. 'It was of little use to ask the gardener, he has retired into the greenhouse and locked himself in. He loathes my step-mother.'

The Duke had tied his cravat. He would have put on his coat but Georgia stopped him.

'Eat in your shirt-sleeves,' she said. 'Charles always does.'

'Is Charles your husband?' the Duke asked.

'No, Charles is my brother,' she said. 'He is under the command of Admiral Collingwood.'

'I expect you are hoping he will soon get shore-leave,' the Duke said conversationally. He spoke lightly, almost without thinking, and he was surprised to see Georgia's face cloud over and her eyes darken.

'No,' she said, 'he will not come home.' As if she were afraid the Duke would ask further questions, she went on:

'Perhaps I have been foolish in hiding you here. But you cannot conjecture how difficult it is. The servants would have reported to my stepmother that there was a man here when they arrived. She would have questioned me and it might have come out that you had taken part in the carry. Then she would have been very incensed.'

'So your stepmother knows about your smuggling activities?' the Duke said, cutting open the pie from which there instantly arose a delicious aroma.

'Yes, she knows,' Georgia said.

The Duke was sitting on the only chair and now she sat down on the edge of the narrow bed. She looked tired and worried, her hair falling untidily around her white face. The Duke felt sorry for her.

'Your nurse is a remarkable cook,' he said lightly, to change the subject.

'She said she had promised a pie to a family in the village who is sick,' Georgia answered. 'Otherwise they would have thought it strange that she was baking anything so large just for herself and me.'

She paused a moment and then she added, almost as though she spoke to herself:

'Lies, lies, nothing but lies. Life seems hedged about with little else.'

The Duke helped himself to some more pie and said nothing. After a moment, as if she regretted her outburst, Georgia said tentatively, as if she was a little shy:

'I also brought you some brandy. Nana was certain that that is what you would prefer.'

'I am certainly not prepared to argue with that conjecture,' the Duke smiled.

The brandy was in a decanter and the Duke poured himself some into the glass which Georgia had taken from the basket. He tasted it and recognised it as the very best French cognac, far superior to anything he had drunk for a long time.

'I do not know who your wine merchant may be, but he certainly has most discriminating taste in brandy.'

'Do not mock at me,' Georgia pleaded. 'You know as well as I do where the brandy came from. It was more expensive, so I supposed it was a finer quality than what we usually bring.'

'You must be exceeding strong,' the Duke said. 'I'm not supposing that you pull an oar, but the physical endurance of crossing the Channel twice in twelve hours must be quite considerable.'

'Sometimes it is,' Georgia answered, 'but I am very careful not to go out unless the sea is smooth. Our men are not sailors and they turn seasick at the slightest wave.'

'You would not like to tell me about it?' asked the Duke, and realised as he spoke that he had said the wrong thing.

Georgia jumped to her feet.

'No, no,' she said violently. 'And I cannot conceive why I keep talking to you in this manner. I suppose it's because there is no one here with whom I can discuss anything. If I mention such matters to Nana she gets in a huff; she hates even to contemplate what must be done, and when I am away I think she suffers.'

'I am convinced she does,' the Duke agreed. 'Anyone who was fond of you would feel the same, that is why I cannot understand your husband. . . .'

'I have already told you my husband knows nothing of this.'

'Then your stepmother, why does she allow it?'

'I have got no more to say,' Georgia answered. 'Let me make it quite clear, Mr. Raven, the quicker you are out of this house the better. Maybe I made a mistake in concealing you, but you must leave tonight as soon as it is safe. Do you understand?'

'I am yours to command. Will you thank Nana for the pie and tell her that I appreciated the brandy also, whatever its origin.'

The Duke meant to be provocative and succeeded. Georgia tossed her head and vanished through the door without another word. He heard her footsteps going slowly down the stairs and laughed to himself as he poured himself another glass of brandy. She had spirit, that girl, he would say that for her. He did not envy her husband the task of trying to control her when he came home from the sea. It was obvious that he would have to assert himself if he was to be master in his own house!

A sound from below took the Duke to the window. It was the noise of a horn being blown loudly and insistently. He saw a magnificent carriage drawn by six perfectly matched horses. Their silver harness glittered in the sunshine and the painted panels of the coach were brilliant with colour, as it circled to draw up at the front of the house. There were four out-riders in the same green uniform which had been worn by the other servants who had arrived first.

The Duke craned his head to see the owner of such a spectacular cavalcade dismount, but unfortunately his view was obstructed. He could only see the horses tossing their heads, the lather on their bridles and the two coachmen with their high beaver hats and tiered coats sitting stiffly on the box.

Then, following down the drive, there came two other coaches and a phaeton driven by a gentleman with his hat at a jaunty angle and handling the reins with the ease and confidence of a Corinthian. The Duke almost felt envious. There was obviously to be a party downstairs, but he was to have no part in it.

It would have been inhuman if his curiosity had not almost burst the bonds of control. He wanted to see who these people were, and he realised to his own annoyance that he had not asked the name of Georgia's stepmother.

'Perhaps I know her,' he thought to himself. 'I wonder what would happen if I joined the party,' but he knew he could not betray Georgia in such a manner. No, he must creep out into the darkness as she had requested of him and forget his whole strange fantastic sequence of events.

'Damn it,' he said to himself as he sat down again on the bed. 'It will irritate me for the rest of my life if I never learn the truth of this strange drama.'

3

THE Duke found that the afternoon passed slowly. He stared out of the narrow window, seeing the sunshine on the lake, the foliage gently blowing in the breeze and the ducks circling high against the sky. He longed for action, he wanted to do something positive, although he was not certain what it might be. It was frustrating to wait alone in the tiny room, to have no idea of what was happening in the house below, which he knew must be seething with activity.

He glanced through the books on the bookshelf. Most of them were religious and must, the Duke calculated, have been there for years—perhaps centuries. Looking round he noticed a cupboard in the wall and opened it to find a miscellaneous collection of objects. A pewter basin, a coloured drinking-glass, a tinder box, some sewing materials—the needle rusty from want of use—and at the back a worn and dilapidated rag doll.

The Duke smiled. He had already guessed that Georgia used this room as a hiding place. He had noticed that the blankets on the bed were clean and the sheets and pillow-cases were of fine linen and smelt of lavender. The tablecloth of drawn-thread work, which covered the small oak table, could not have been there for long, and there was surprisingly little dust on the floor and the book-shelves.

Perhaps, he thought, other strangers had been concealed here by Georgia, and then he remembered her agitation and the manner in which the idea of the priest hole had only come to her mind at the last moment. Somehow he was certain that he was the first outsider to use this secret place.

Why did she have to hide, and from what? That was the

question that nagged at his mind. He could imagine her concealing herself here as a child, and listening while her nurse and perhaps her parents called her name, searching for her in the gardens and having no idea where she could have spirited herself away.

But childish pranks and playing truant from lessons were very different from the conviction that a grown woman must hide herself in fear. Or was he imagining things? Why should Georgia Baillie, who was brave enough to risk imprisonment should she be caught smuggling, be afraid of anything save the Coast Guards? And yet there was no doubt in the Duke's mind that she was afraid.

He lay down on the bed because it was more comfortable than on the rush-bottom chair, and tried to make sense out of all he had learnt and observed. But as the afternoon passed slowly and the dusk fell he knew himself utterly puzzled.

He drew his watch from his vest pocket. It was nearly six o'clock! He wondered how many more hours he would have to wait before it was safe for him to creep to the stables, saddle his horse and ride away.

Suddenly he heard a sound, low but distinct, from the stairs. He jumped to his feet eagerly. At last something was happening. He crossed the room and pulled open the door. Again there came the same sound, but this time there was something breathless about it. Before he rounded the stairs he guessed who would be standing on the tiny landing . . . Nana, not Georgia.

'Here you are, sir,' she said to him, holding out a basket, the same one in which Georgia had brought his lunch. 'There was little enough I could procure for you with all those suspicious, nosy servants a-swarming over my kitchen, and grudging me so much as a cup of milk.'

Nana spoke in a whisper, and in a low voice the Duke replied:

'Come up to the room, I wish to converse with you.'

'I daren't, sir; they might be asking for me! 'Tis dangerous enough for me to be a-visiting you as it is.'

'I can understand that,' the Duke said, 'And I am very grateful for the food.'

He glanced down, but it was too dark for him to see what the basket contained.

39

' 'Tis just some boiled gammon,' Nana said, 'and a bite of cheese. I apologise for it, I do indeed, sir. I know how a gentleman should eat. I've not been in service all my life without knowing that.'

'This gentleman's not particular,' the Duke said, with a hint of laughter in his voice.

'I've boiled you some water,' Nana went on. 'I couldn't carry it all up this breakneck stairway so I slipped it in through the panelling while the footman were a-laying the table for dinner. You'll find it at the bottom of the stair.'

'And for that I am most obliged,' the Duke said. 'I am sadly in need of a shave also.'

'I thought of that too, sir,' Nana replied. 'You will find one of Mr. Charles's razors and a clean neck-cloth in the basket.'

'You think of everything,' the Duke said. 'Miss Georgia, or should I say Mistress Baillie, is a very fortunate young woman to have you to look after her.'

'Miss Georgia—I always forgets her married name, it don't seem to come natural like—is all I have left,' Nana answered. 'I love her as though she were my own, and that's as true as I'm standing here.'

'I repeat, she is a very lucky young woman,' the Duke smiled.

'Not that I can do much . . . as things be,' Nana said in a low voice, almost as though she were talking to herself. ' 'Twas different when Sir Hector was alive.'

'Sir Hector . . . who?' the Duke enquired. 'I only know Mistress Baillie's married name.'

'Sir Hector Grazebrook,' Nana explained, 'and a fine gentleman he was, straight and just in all his dealings—the Lord knows what he would have thought now were he not under the soil.'

The Duke sensed, rather than saw, that the old woman made a helpless gesture with her hands. Then in a different voice she said:

'Miss Georgia says she will be a-fetching you, sir, as soon as it is safe. Please be obliging enough to be ready sometime after midnight.'

'I will be ready,' the Duke said, 'although in a way I am reluctant to leave you in such a tangle.'

'A tangle is the right word for it, sir, and whatever Miss Georgia may say, I shall be sorry to see you go. There's no denying you're nice-spoken and gentle-born—despite any trouble you may be in.'

'My trouble is not too hard to overcome,' the Duke assured her.

'It's glad I am to hear it,' Nana answered. 'I only wish I could say the same for Miss Georgia. Oh, sir, it's feared for her I am!'

The Duke heard something like terror in the old woman's voice.

'Persuade her, Nana, not to run foolhardy risks,' he said quietly. 'What she is doing is no task to be undertaken by a woman, especially one delicately bred.'

'Do you suppose I haven't said that over and over again?' Nana asked. 'But you don't understand, sir. There are reasons which I cannot divulge but which impel Miss Georgia to behave in such a manner. All I asks myself is what will be the end of it?'

'What indeed?' the Duke echoed.

Nana sighed; it was almost a groan.

'I prays with all my heart that something, somehow, will save us.'

The Duke would have replied, but she had put her hand on his arm to silence him. Then she bent forward, listening at the concealed door through which she had entered the staircase.

'Someone's about,' she whispered.

The Duke, straining his ears, could hear nothing.

Nana's hand touched the catch and the door opened very slowly. The aperture was small and narrow and she had a little difficulty in squeezing through it. The Duke had a quick glimpse of a long corridor, off which he guessed the servants' rooms opened. Then Nana was through and the door was closed in his face.

He waited until he felt sure that Nana was out of hearing; then very cautiously he tried the catch himself. He could feel it beneath his fingers and for a moment he was not certain how it worked. But quickly he found the knack and the panel moved. Without risking disclosure by opening it wide, he merely eased it forward, closed it again, and felt a sense of relief in realising that he was no longer a prisoner of Mistress Georgia Baillie. He could leave any time he wished.

He picked up the basket of food and took it to the room

above and set it on the table. Besides the cold gammon there was a freshly baked loaf, a large pat of golden butter and a chunk of cheese. Beneath it all there was a set of razors in a neat leather case.

For a moment the Duke thought Nana had forgotten the neck-piece she had mentioned. Then he saw that it was tied neatly to the handle of the basket so that it would not get creased. He laid the food out on the table and then decided to go down the stairs to fetch the jug of water which Nana had left for him on the ground floor.

He was well aware that his footsteps on the oak stairway might be heard, so with some difficulty he divested himself of his riding-boots and in his stockinged-feet started down the narrow stairway. By this time it was pitch dark and he cursed himself for not having asked Nana for a candle, for the tinder box was little use without one. In a short while the last glint of the setting sun would be gone and there would be no hope of shaving.

As he moved cautiously down the stairs, suddenly, so near to him that it made him jump, a woman's voice said:

'Fah! You will do as you are told! There will be no argument about it.'

'But it is impossible! Can you not comprehend that because we crossed last night we cannot cross again?'

The Duke recognised the second voice: it was Georgia's.

'What of it? It is of great import that you bring back a gentleman who will be waiting at the same place as before.'

'I do not like to carry passengers,' Georgia said almost sulkily.

'It does not matter to me, Miss High-and-Mighty, what you like and what you don't like,' a sharp voice replied.

The Duke guessed it must be Georgia's stepmother who was speaking, as she went on:

'This gentleman is to be conveyed to England, and who better than yourself to accommodate him? You have such a knowledge of the illicit traffic of the Channel.'

'Do you believe that I am proud of such knowledge?' Georgia demanded angrily. 'You drive me to it, and with every journey you become more and more avaricious. Isn't this last cargo rich enough for you? The proceeds should last you for at least a month.'

There was almost a pathetic note of optimism in the last words.

'You must be more bird-witted than I thought, if you believe those chicken-pickings will keep me in comfort,' the other woman retorted sarcastically. 'Why, the plucking will hardly supply my house with tapers!'

'You sneer,' Georgia accused her, 'and yet the men on this estate risk their freedom, their lives, every time they leave these shores. Have you any idea what it is like to be hunted, to know that somewhere in the darkness there are guns ready to shoot? There are Revenue officers with fast cutters patrolling the sea, and Customs men waiting on land?'

'You should take a role in the Cheltenham Theatricals, my girl. You will obviously be a success on the boards,' a sneering voice replied. 'Now stop arguing! This gentleman you will collect tomorrow night is of consequence. He is, I assure you, a very much more valuable cargo than brandy or tea.'

'Do you mean he will pay you for bringing him over?' Georgia asked.

Her stepmother gave a light laugh.

'Good Lord! But you are innocent! Of course I am paid! Do you imagine that I would put myself to such exertion if I were not handsomely upholstered?'

'I cannot conceive that you are put to any exertion. It is I and the crew who take the risk. The men obey me only because they served my father.'

'They obey because they are paid to do so! And if they will not do as I command then they will starve, as I have made it unmistakably clear to you a dozen times. They will starve and so will their families. You can come to me whimpering for money, and I will not give them so much as a fourpenny piece. Nothing! Nothing!—do you hear?—unless they bring me more and yet more cargoes. These at the moment, I admit, yield quite a fat harvest!'

'I am glad you are satisfied,' Georgia said sarcastically. 'But in return you pay our men less then any smuggler around the whole coast of England.'

'If they are dissatisfied to whom may they carry their complaints? The Coast Guards? The Military? Or perhaps they would wish to send a petition to His Majesty? That would be the height of absurdity!' "We, the smugglers from the estate of Four Winds, beg your Majesty's intervention that we may receive a higher remuneration for our illegal carrying of contraband." '

'Oh! be quiet!' Georgia's voice was furious. 'You jibe and snigger at these men who were once honest, decent country folk. Smuggling was at first an adventure, a piece of dare-devilry because they had heard of the vast rewards earned by other gangs. Yes, they made the run, but it was something that only happened perhaps once or twice a year, until you learnt of it.'

'And do you remember how I received that information?' the ugly voice asked insidiously. 'Do you remember who told me what had occurred? Do you remember?'

There was silence. Then Georgia in a voice low and defeated said:

'I will tell the men we will cross tomorrow night. What is the name of this gentleman we are to collect?'

'That is better, much better! I thought you would be reasonable. After all, a word from me in certain high places would do so much damage, wouldn't it? Just a suggestion, a suspicion . . .'

'Will you be silent?' Georgia demanded, almost beside herself. 'I have said I will go. I will inform the men this instant, because if I leave it until the morning some of them may be away to market and not return in time. You have not yet told me the name of the person who will be waiting for us.'

'That is none of your business!'

'Is he a Frenchman?'

'Of course. Your French is rather good I remember. You should be able to converse with him, enough at any rate for ordinary politeness.'

'Then why is he coming to this country?' Georgia asked. 'I was afraid after we brought the last man over. I may be a smuggler but I am not a traitor. How can I be certain he is not a spy?'

'You little milksop, you can be certain of nothing,' her stepmother replied. 'And the less you know the better. That tiresome honesty of yours would make you a zany in a witnessbox. Fetch this gentleman, treat him with respect, and once he has set foot on these shores forget he has ever existed—just as has happened before.'

'I do not like it, I have told you I do not like it,' Georgia murmured.

'And I have bid you do as you are told and not argue with me.'

There was a sudden pause. The Duke could visualise the two women facing each other, their eyes meeting across the room. Then the older woman said in a different tone of voice:

'You could be attractive, you know, if you made the best of yourself. Lord Ravenscroft is here tonight. Remember the fancy he took to you last year. He likes females to be young, fresh and dewy-eyed. Put on one of my gowns and come down and entertain him. It might be to your advantage, and mine too, for that matter.'

'You forget,' Georgia objected, 'that I am now a married woman. When I was a girl you dangled me in front of those depraved, nauseous, evil-minded old men. But now I shall no longer be of interest to them. As you say, Lord Ravenscroft likes his women young, untouched and innocent. I am now Mistress Baillie with a wedding-ring on my finger. I am no longer attractive.'

There was a peal of laughter.

'You must be a sap-skull if you think a gold band will make all that difference. Actually it will make it easier: the men are always afraid that an unmarried girl will march them up the aisle. Come downstairs, Georgia; you will find that a ripe peach is sweeter to the tooth than one that is still green.'

'You shock and disgust me.' Georgia spoke slowly and deliberately. 'I wept the day that my father married you and I have wept ever since when I thought of you taking the place of my mother. She was good and pure, but every time I see you in this house I am ashamed, for you are nothing more than ... than ... a st ... strumpet.'

There was a cry of anger and then the sharp sound of a hand slapping on soft cheek.

'How dare you speak to me in such a manner! Get out, you calf-faced chit, before I take a horse-whip to you! Obey my instructions or you know who will be swinging on a gibbet!'

A door was slammed before the last words were spoken and the Duke knew that Georgia must have gone from the room. He realised almost guiltily that he had been eavesdropping, but he had been too fascinated by what he had overheard to move.

Now he crept very carefully down the last flight of stairs. He stubbed his toe in the darkness against a brass can filled with water which stood at the bottom of the steps. Something which had been laid on top of it rattled to the ground and he held his breath at the noise. As he groped round he discovered a cake of soap and two tallow candles which had been wrapped up in a bath-towel.

Hesitating a moment, the Duke put down on the bottom of the stairs the things he had collected and felt in the darkness for the door by which he had originally entered the priest hole. It took him a little time to find the catch, and when he found it he knew it was the same type as the one on the top floor. Presumably there was yet another door by which he could enter the bedchamber of Georgia's stepmother.

His lips twisted in a wry smile at the thought. Then gathering up the things Nana had left for him he carried them to the upper room. He closed the door, lighted the tapers, fetched the basin from the cupboard, and proceeded to wash and shave. The water in the jug was by now nearly cold, but somehow he managed to make himself reasonably presentable. The neck-cloth, old-fashioned to one who preferred a 'waterfall', was white and crisp and after the Duke had tied it in front of a small gilt-framed mirror which hung on one of the walls he looked almost his usual immaculate self.

He sat down at the table to eat the cold collation that Nana had brought him for dinner, but the full impact of what Georgia was being driven to do the following evening took away his appetite.

It was bad enough that the English people should supply Napoleon Bonaparte with gold. The Emperor had boasted on more than one occasion that the golden guineas which crossed the Channel helped him both to dress and feed his army. But the actual smuggling of spies into England was a very different matter.

No one pretended for one moment that there were not spies in the country already. Many of them were French immigrants who had been rescued from the guillotine at the time of the Revolution. They were still loyal to their own country whatever the political changes, and they felt no obligation to England who had given them sanctuary.

But the knowledge that new spies were being brought in surreptitiously must give rise to greater apprehension.

Georgia's stepmother was being paid to bring this man across the Channel. He was therefore of importance, at least to those who sent him. And the mere fact that they were prepared to pay in any large degree showed that as far as England was concerned he must be dangerous.

The Duke put down his knife and fork and drummed his fingers on the table, as he often did when he was thinking. It was an extraordinary dilemma in which he found himself. As one who had held His Majesty's Commission, and as a member of the House of Lords, his obvious duty was to make sure that this Frenchman, and all who had aided his entry into the country, were arrested immediately. On the other hand, could he possibly justify to himself the betrayal to imprisonment or transportation of a young woman who in her own way had treated him with hospitality?

He was still puzzling over what he should do and his supper was still unfinished several hours later. His only course, he decided finally, was to try to persuade Georgia that she must on no account obey her stepmother. And yet he had an uneasy feeling that this would be impossible. Whatever threat the woman held over Georgia's head it was obviously one which could not be disregarded. At least, he thought, he must try to learn what it was.

In a way the Duke felt almost relieved that Georgia was not, as he had first imagined, a hard-bitten, mannish woman, smuggling either for personal greed or just the thrill of it. He thought he was beginning to understand the pattern of events, but there were still great gaps in the puzzle for which he could not find an explanation.

The time seemed to drag very slowly. He ate a few more mouthfuls of cheese and finished the brandy which Georgia had brought him for lunch. He decided that, as it seemed likely to be several hours before Georgia appeared, he would go down the staircase and see if anything else was happening.

He passed the top floor, resisting the impulse to open the door, and descended another flight of stairs. There was no sound now from the bedroom, but before he went further the Duke heard the chatter of voices from a different direction. The staircase curved at this point, and it took him some time to notice a faint light coming from one of the steps. Sitting down, he put his eye against it.

At first he could see nothing. He dusted the tread with his hand and something moved. A second later he had pushed aside a small shutter, not more than two inches square, and found himself gazing down into what was obviously the main salon of the house. The peep-hole through which he was looking was a part of the cornice.

Below him, seated on damask-covered sofas or grouped round two green-baize tables, was the house party. From the noise and shrillness of the women's voices and the thick tones of the men the Duke realised that they had dined and wined well. The footmen were still offering the gentlemen brandy in crystal glasses and most of the ladies held a glass in their hands. They were vulgarly decorative, glittering with jewels, their high-breasted gowns cut exaggeratedly low and ther skirts outrageously transparent.

As the Duke searched for a familiar face, a woman who had had her back to him bent over one of the men seated at the card-table, dropped a light kiss on his forehead and turned to signal to a footman. The Duke bit back an exclamation as it came to his lips.

'Caroline Standish!' he exclaimed beneath his breath. 'By all that's holy, the last person I expected to see here!'

There was no doubting the fact that the woman in question was outstanding. Her directoire gown, designed in a fashion which had originally crossed the Channel from Napoleon's Court, was of silver lace embroidered with rubies. There were ruby-red ribbons—which had most certainly been manufactured in Lyons—to cup her breasts and fall in a cascade over the almost transparent skirt to her satin slippers. There was a necklace of blood-red rubies round her neck glittering and sparkling in the candlelight, and the Duke's face was grim as he remembered how much that necklace had cost him!

He could still hear Caroline's voice whispering against his ear:

'Give it to me, Trydon, my love. I will repay you in a thousand delectable, delightful ways, if only you will purchase it for me.'

Her arms had been very soft round his neck, her lips close to his, her exotic perfume bemusing his brain.

He had been but a callow fool at the time and Caroline had certainly been worthy of the toasts offered to her nightly by the bloods of St. James's. It had been a feather in his cap when she had preferred his protection to that of her more well-breeched suitors.

It had been a brief but very passionate interlude before his regiment had been ordered to Portugal. He had known even in the most ardent moments of their intimacy that Caroline was not faithful to him. But he was foolish enough not only to be infatuated with a woman ten years his senior, but an amoureuse skilled and experienced in the oldest profession in the world.

When the troopship was held up at Southampton because of bad weather he had been posted back to London, only to find Caroline receiving consolation for his departure in the arms of a man he had always disliked—Lord Ravenscroft.

There had been a noisy, embarrassing, vulgar scene when Ravenscroft had ordered him out of Caroline's house, and he had said defiantly that after all it had cost him he had a better right to be there than His Lordship. Then Caroline had shown herself in her true colours. She too had told him to go, and the Duke had realised all too clearly that she wished to be rid of him because she was afraid of losing a new, richer and more influential protector.

The Duke could still painfully recall the shrillness of her voice, the hurried manner in which she had clutched at his arm, her whispered asides, her impatience, and her final withering expletives as she showed him to the door.

He had hated her and Ravenscroft so violently that outside on the pavement his loathing of them had made him feel physically ill. It was only his military training which had kept him from going back and challenging Ravenscroft—a much older man—to a duel, which had prevented him from breaking the windows of the house and proclaiming to the whole world his own stupidity in being duped by a woman so utterly and completely heartless.

'The young are very vulnerable!' the Duke told himself now, but as he wondered how he could have been deceived by Caroline he knew he would always carry the scars of the wounds she had inflicted on him.

Crouching on the steps and looking through the peephole, which had been made in the reign of Elizabeth I for some Jesuit priest terrified for his life, the Duke appraised slowly and dispassionately the woman to whom he had once given a young, ardent and unsophisticated devotion.

Caroline was still beautiful, there was no doubt about that, but riotous living had taken its toll. There were sharp lines at the corners of her mouth; those white, helpless hands seemed more claw-like than ever. But she could still be gay and amusing, and the men listening to what she was saying now were all laughing. She outshone every other woman in the room.

The Duke did not recognise any of them, which was not surprising, for he thought to himself that though Caroline might have become Lady Grazebrook, decent Society and certainly the *bon ton* would have none of her. But there would, of course, always be some who would be ready to accept her hospitality. They would be the high-steppers, not quite on a par with the lady-birds and little bits o' muslin, but in a half-world of their own on the fringe of Society, as it were, not of it.

With the men it was different. The Duke looked them over and saw, just as he expected, that they were the gamblers, dashers and the riff-raff of the St. James's clubs. There were, too, several old men like Ravenscroft who knew Caroline would supply them with just the type of young woman they required. Ravenscroft, for instance, was well known to have a penchant for virgins and his reputation stank through the length and breadth of London.

The guineas were piling up on the green-baize tables. Caroline's guests were sorting themselves out into couples. A man and a woman walked through the open french window and on to the lawn. Another woman beckoned a man to a dimly lit alcove at the far end of the salon.

The Duke yawned. He knew only too well how this sort of party would end. Most of the male guests would be so foxed that they would have to be helped up to bed; a great deal of money would change hands, and the poorest in the company would be plucked. It was inevitable that a certain amount of cheatng would take place when everyone was too drunk to notice.

And Caroline—what would Caroline gain from it? the

Duke wondered. It couldn't be Ravenscroft that she was still interested in, otherwise she would not have asked Georgia to come down and amuse him. There must be someone else.

His eyes searched the assembled company. A man wearing an inconspicuous grey coat with grey satin knee-breeches was standing alone by the fireplace. He had a thin, lined, sardonic face and he was watching Caroline with an expression that the Duke thought was half admiring, half derisive.

Suddenly she went towards him eagerly, her hands fluttered out and her head was thrown back as she looked up into his eyes.

There was a sudden silence in the room as the gamblers were waiting for the turn of a card and the Duke quite clearly heard the man in the grey say:

'Is it arranged?'

'Of course,' Caroline answered. 'Tomorrow night.'

The man raised his hand and patted Caroline's cheek with long, thin, bony fingers. She turned her face and kissed them.

The Duke very quietly closed the little shutter. He had seen enough to feel nauseated. What did it matter to him what Caroline did in this house or anywhere else? But another question was chasing itself round and round in his mind:

'Who is the man in grey?'

4

THE small priest hole at the top of the staircase seemed almost a sanctuary. The Duke closed the door and threw himself down on the bed to think. The flickering tapers on the table cast strange shadows on the low ceiling.

The Duke looked back into the past and forced his mind to recapture scenes that had happened so long ago that he believed he had forgotten them. He saw himself at a party—who was giving it, or where it was he could not recall. But he was talking to several men and one of them said:

'You've heard about Caroline Standish?'

'No,' he replied. 'What has she done?'

'Jumped the bounds,' his informant had answered. 'You've been out of town, Trydon, or you would have heard that the authorities have learnt of the duel which took place in her house last week. Young Lancaster was killed and they say that the fair Caroline was taking bets on who would be the winner. It has been reported to the Prince and he is furious.'

'And what will happen to this foolish Cyprian who allows such carousings in her house?' a woman's voice had asked.

The Duke had started as Lady Valerie Voxon joined the circle. She was looking exquisite, but she always did, and he had hardly listened to the rest of the conversation, even though now it came back to him in fragments.

'Subjects such as these are not for your Ladyship's shell-like ears,' an elderly peer said.

'But I am curious,' Lady Valerie insisted. 'I have seen Mistress Standish driving in the Park and have heard how many of your warm hearts and even warmer pockets have been laid at her feet.'

She had given a little sideways glance with her green

eyes at the Duke as she spoke, and he had been still young enough to flush as he realised that Lady Valerie knew of his connection with Caroline.

He had been finished with Caroline for at least a year before this conversation took place, and he had then been too interested in Lady Valerie Voxon to be really concerned with what happened to a past mistress. He had come to his senses to face the hard fact that Caroline had sucked him dry of every penny he possessed. Because he had been too raw to know how to refuse an attractive woman, he had landed himself in debt up to his ears, and had to petition his uncle in the most humiliating manner to prevent himself being taken to the Fleet.

Someone was answering Lady Valerie's last question.

'Caroline has realised that discretion is the better part of valour. Never at a loss for a solution to the most tangled problem she has repaired to the country with an admirer who I fear may be foolish enough to marry her.'

'Who is that?' came the question.

The Duke, trying to attract Lady Valerie's attention, missed the name but heard the end of the sentence.

'. . . you may have seen him about, a rather distinguished-looking chap, a member of the Beefsteak.'

It seemed incredible that anyone who had known of Caroline's notorious and infamous past should have believed that she would settle down at Four Winds. But perhaps Georgia's father, respectable and gallant where women were concerned, was bewitched into playing Sir Galahad. He had not guessed that those soft, little, white hands appealing to him for protection were really grasping claws, ready to take and take and take.

Apparently Sir Hector had not lived long, perhaps not long enough to recognise the greed which drove Caroline to extort exorbitant sums from her admirers and the craving for notoriety, whatever the cost to her reputation.

'The poor fool,' the Duke murmured, 'to be taken in by Caroline.'

He then remembered with a sense of embarrassment that he had been besotted by Caroline when he had first met her. She had in fact been the first bit-o'-muslin he had set up under his protection in one of the small houses in Chelsea and for whom he had bought a carriage.

He guessed later when he was free of Caroline's spell

53

that he was not her only banker but at the time he had believed himself the sole object of her affections.

'I have certainly paid for my experience,' the Duke thought with a wry smile.

But he hadn't been very much wiser when having rid himself of Caroline, or rather when she had cast him off, he had returned from the Peninsula to be enamoured by another alluring Circe—Lady Valerie Voxon.

He was certainly not alone in his pursuit of the most-acclaimed and the most-talked-of 'Incomparable' in the whole of London. Lady Valerie Voxon was not only beautiful, she was sensational. Dowagers shook their heads over her behaviour and prophesied that her mother must be 'turning in her grave, poor woman!' Her contemporaries bit their lips and hated her.

Valerie had all the bloods of St. James's at her feet, and very pretty feet they were too. The Duke declared himself even though he knew his cause was hopeless. Valerie reached up to pat his cheek with her long slim fingers.

'I like you, Trydon,' she said. 'I might, in other circumstances, have grown to love you. But, my dear, I cannot conceive myself the wife of a penniless soldier.'

'Perhaps my uncle will help us,' the Duke said, knowing it was a forlorn hope.

Valerie shook her head.

'What sort of hope do you anticipate your uncle would provide?' she asked. 'A cheap house in an unfashionable part of London, or a cottage in the country! Can you see me milking the cows! No, Trydon! I want position, I want houses, carriages and horses; to be able to afford balls and routs; to have clothes and jewels and all exotic and delectable things which cost money.'

The Duke was silent. There was nothing he could say. Valerie put her hand on his.

'I am going to marry the Earl of Davenport,' she said softly.

'Darcy!' the Duke ejaculated. 'You can't, he is a decent enough fellow, but not for you, Valerie.'

'His Lordship is a very wealthy man,' Valerie answered, 'and I would not wish to offend him by being here alone with you.'

She put up her hand once again and touched his cheek.

'If only things had been different,' she said with a little sigh.

The Duke could still recall the feeling of emptiness and despair when she was gone, but what could he do? He had no money and no prospects, and there had been no seer to look into the future and tell him that within a year two seemingly healthy men who stood between him and the Dukedom would both be dead.

As it was, he had returned to the Peninsula declaring that 'women were the devil!' and the less one had to do with them the better. He had not altered his opinion when on his return Valerie—radiant and even more beautiful as the Countess of Davenport than she had been before her marriage—made it quite clear that they could take up their acquaintance where it had been left, only on much more ardent terms.

'If only I had known you were to be a Duke, Trydon,' she sighed, as they danced together at the Lady Blessington's Ball.

'Darcy's a good chap,' he replied, knowing that from the other end of the room her husband was watching her with admiration written all over his fat, honest face.

'I am bored, bored, bored!' Valerie complained. 'Except, of course, when I am with you.'

Like a horse sensing danger, the Duke had shied away from the suggestion he saw all too clearly in Valerie's eyes. It was, in fact, Lady Davenport's behaviour which more than anything else had made him accept what had seemed to him the quite preposterous suggestion of his godmother.

'Come to the dance I am giving in the country,' she said, 'and try to choose yourself a suitable wife!'

He knew now that he had no intention of marrying anyone. The Carolines, Valeries, Janitas, and those simpering, well-bred chits who ran after him for his money, were all the same. They wanted something from him, they didn't want him. They wanted his position, his money and perhaps his manhood. They were not interested in Trydon, the person he had lived with all his life, the man who had never expected to be a Duke. He had taken life as it came, light-heartedly in the face of death, seriously when it concerned his honour.

He thought now, as he lay on the narrow bed where

other fugitives had lain over the past centuries, that a man was a fool if he did not know when it was wise to retreat. He had no wish to encounter Caroline again; she was something which belonged to the past. And from what he had overheard behind the secret panel in her bedchamber, age had not improved her.

She had always been a shrew, and a shrew inevitably grew more shrewish as the years went by.

'I must get out of here,' the Duke thought.

He drew out his watch and saw it would soon be midnight. Surely after that hour it would be safe for him to slip out to the stables, saddle his horse and be away across the downs. He had no wish to be entangled further with anyone in this house. He only wished he could remember the name of the man in grey. He had seen him before somewhere and, irritatingly, could not put a name to him.

Anyway, why should one of Caroline's new conquests matter to him or even excite his curiosity. He was sorry for Georgia, sorry indeed for anyone who found themselves in the position of being Caroline's stepdaughter. The best thing she could do was to get her husband back from sea and set him the task of sorting out the whole untidy coil. A pretty pickle for any sailor to return to, but that, after all, was his business!

The Duke suddenly felt stifled. The room was so small, it was as if the walls were crushing in upon him. He wanted to be away, but he knew at the back of his mind it was the past that was affecting him. By seeing Caroline again he was forced to remember her soft blandishments, the manner in which she had coaxed money out of him, but he could still feel the softness of her arms round his neck, her face upturned to his:

'Please, Trydon, please, I must purchase a new gown. I would not have you anything but proud of me.'

'Please, Trydon, a new bracelet to wear with my green gauze.'

And finally there was the mad, crazy folly of the ruby necklace. She had worn it one evening 'to show him' and she had worn nothing else on that white, sweetly curved, sinuous body, which could have almost a mesmeric effect on a young man as inexperienced as Trydon had been then. She had driven him wild with desire of her, but she had not given in to his demands until he had promised to pay for it!

The Duke rose from the bed. If it had been possible he would have walked restlessly about the room to lay the ghosts which haunted him. But there was not the space, and he was forced to sit on the hard chair beside the table containing the dirty plates left over from his supper.

Because he was incensed with himself and his memories, and because he was bored and wished to be free, he found his temper rising. He had no intention of being involved in this unsavoury mess any longer. It was certainly no place for the Duke of Westacre, and he wondered why he had been so foolhardy in the first place as to commit himself to helping a gang of amateur smugglers.

The tapers were burning low, but there was still enough light to illuminate the Duke's resolute and somewhat grim expression when at one o'clock in the morning Georgia came tiptoeing up the stairs.

She came into the room and shut the door behind her.

'I anticipated you would be here earlier,' the Duke said in a disagreeable tone.

'My apologies,' she answered, 'but certain things demanded my attention.'

'Is it safe for me to leave now?' the Duke inquired. 'For I may inform you, Mistress Baillie, that I have every intention of departing whatever the consequence.'

'Yes, it is safe enough,' she said. 'The coachman will be asleep, and I told Ned some hours ago to have your horse saddled and waiting for you down by the creek.'

The Duke gave a sigh of relief.

'Then let us be away.'

He would have risen from the chair but Georgia put out her hand as if to stop him.

'One minute, Mr. Raven. Before you leave I have something to ask of you.'

'What is it?' the Duke asked wearily.

' 'Tis a favour.'

The Duke raised his eyebrows.

'A favour?' he inquired. 'Then, before you ask it, may I reply that I am in no mood for favours. To be frank I wish to be rid of this house and all it contains as speedily as possible.'

'I certainly cannot blame you for that,' Georgia answered. 'But at the same time will you hear what I ask? I would not voice it if I were not desperate.'

The Duke had a foreboding of trouble. He looked across the room at Georgia, who was standing with her back against the door. Her face was very pale and she looked drawn and tired, as though she had driven herself beyond her strength. Her hair flopped untidily over her forehead, and he saw now that the dress she was wearing was stained at the hem, as though she had been walking through the mud.

'Well, what is it?' His voice was sharp because he dared not think to himself that she looked pathetic, and he was trying not to recall the sound that Caroline's hand had made when she slapped Georgia's face.

'I am an oarsman short.' The words seemed to be jerked from between her lips.

'Indeed, it is no concern of mine.'

As if the very defiance in his words changed her mood from one of supplication to an answering challenge, she said:

'Suppose I make it your concern, Mr. Raven! Suppose I tell you that unless you help me I will not let you go from here! That unless you do as I say I will denounce you! Not as a smuggler—that might involve other people—but as a sneak-thief, a man who was hiding here for what pickings he could get from the ladies of the party who all possess valuable jewels.'

As Georgia almost spat the words at him, the Duke was so surprised and taken aback for a moment that he could only stare at her. Then he put back his head and laughed.

'Go ahead,' he said, 'denounce me! Fetch up those drunken fops from downstairs if they are capable of standing by this time—which I very much doubt—tell them to capture me and drag me before the magistrates. They will certainly find it difficult to manage the stairs and I can knock them off one by one as they reach this hidey-hole. But do not forget, my dear, that your secret sanctuary would be no longer secret. They would all know of it, including your stepmother.'

Almost before he had finished speaking the Duke realised that he had broken the Queensberry Rules and punched below the belt. Georgia put her hands up to her face.

'I did not mean it,' she whispered. 'Forget what I said. I had not meant to do anything but plead with you for help.'

'With an illicit journey across the Channel?' the Duke asked. 'I deeply regret I must be ungallant, but the answer is "no".'

'I was afraid it might be,' she said. 'And that means we shall either have to proceed with one man short, which will slow us up and make the journey all the more dangerous, or else we shall have to invite a stranger from another village and that would be madness! The only thing that has kept us safe so far has been that nobody outside the estate has any idea of what is occurring.'

'Those are your problems,' the Duke said briskly, 'and if you will take my advice you will leave this house immediately! You must have relatives or friends; go and stay with them.'

'You do not understand,' Georgia replied quietly. 'But, as you have said, 'tis not your problem. I will escort you to your horse.'

'Thank you,' the Duke answered, and picked up his hat.

'We must go very quietly,' Georgia said. 'Even though I doubt if any of them are capable of hearing any noise, however strident—one never knows.'

She did not wait for his reply but blew out the candles and started tiptoeing downstairs. The Duke followed her. It was dark and they could only grope the way with their hands on the wall. They were guided downwards by the noise and laughter coming from the salon.

As the Duke had anticipated, the company were obviously very drunk by this time. There were shrieks from the women, as though they were being chased, or were making a voluble but insincere protest against aggressively masculine behaviour. There were guttural noises from the gentlemen and a verse of a lewd song, which the Duke recognised, was being sung by a man who would certainly have been incapable of standing to render it.

The Duke had expected Georgia to let him out into the hall, and he was wondering whether there might be a sleepy servant there waiting up to extinguish tapers after the gentry had proceeded to bed. But instead, she opened a door on the opposite side of the staircase and he followed her down a narrow passage.

There was a sound of a key being turned in the lock, a bolt being drawn back, and suddenly he felt the night air on his face and stepping out realised he was in the garden.

Georgia closed the door behind her. The Duke found that they had to clamber through a clump of flowering shrubs before they reached the gravel path which led round the house. There was a faint moon but not enough light to see clearly, and as he stumbled he felt Georgia's hand take his.

'Let me lead you,' she said in a whisper, 'I know the way so well.'

They avoided the lawn and keeping in the shadow of the trees they came to a small gate opening on to a paddock which lay at the back of the stables.

'I hope you escape from your difficulties,' he said conversationally, almost as though they had met at some social reception.

'Our only safety lies in speed,' Georgia replied, her mind still concerned with the missing oarsman.

'What has happened to the fellow?' Duke asked.

'He has left for market. 'Tis over twelve miles away and his wife says he plans to stay the night. There is nothing I can do; it would be foolery to send after him. He would have to give his friends some explanation of why he was wanted. Such men are not good at lying. They are country folk, men who have looked after the soil all their lives, and who weren't bred to combat danger and treachery and engage in foolhardy adventuring.'

'They get paid for it,' the Duke snapped, almost unpleasantly.

'A pittance,' Georgia answered. 'They get no share of the profits, such as other gangs receive.'

'Then why in heaven's name do they do it?' the Duke asked.

'Because otherwise they would starve,' Georgia replied. 'Do you realise how hard it is to get work in this part of the world? Besides, they have lived here ever since they were children and their parents occupied the same cottage before them. They are our men, they are our responsibility, or rather mine as Charles is away at sea.'

'You must have some provision to run a house like Four Winds,' the Duke said.

'My father left everything he possessed to my stepmother for her lifetime,' Georgia answered. 'She is not interested in the house or the estate. She comes here when she has friends who wish to spend a night or so in the country. They come, they gamble and they leave, usually without having been outside the front door.'

The Duke could understand the truth of this. Caroline would find Four Winds a convenient place for assignations, a place where she could arrange parties to amuse old men like Ravenscroft, or where she could infatuate some new admirer who could not be brought up to scratch in the bustle and the turmoil of social London. The countryside itself was something to which she was completely alien. The Duke could not quench a sudden pang of pity for Caroline's unfledged stepchild who had become hopelessly entangled in the web of a very astute and evil spider.

He stopped suddenly in the darkness, and as he did so the moon came out from behind a cloud and he could see Georgia's face quite clearly.

'You cannot go on like this you know,' he said. 'Sooner or later you will be caught. Smugglers always are! Then the men that you care for so much will be hanged or sent for transportation. God knows what will happen to you.'

'Yes, we will be caught,' Georgia agreed, 'probably tomorrow night. It is as dangerous to be a man short as if you yourself sent a message to the Coast Guards.'

There was a moment's silence; then she said in a voice that trembled:

'I beg of you, Mr. Raven, to help us.'

'I cannot,' the Duke said. 'I cannot explain why.'

'You are in trouble yourself, so surely you have a kindred feeling for me,' Georgia pleaded. 'I am in trouble, desperate trouble! I would not ask you this if it were just a question of monetary gain. Then I would expect you to spit on us and walk away. But . . . some . . . someone's life depends on this.'

'I think you should confide in me,' the Duke suggested.

'I cannot,' Georgia replied. 'It is not my secret. I cannot tell anyone. I only know that, unless I do what I have been told to do, the consequences are so frightening that I would rather die here and now, than see them happen.'

The Duke put out his hands and laid them on her shoulders.

'You foolish little goose,' he said kindly, 'you cannot carry this burden by yourself. What is this threat that your stepmother holds over you? Whatever it is, you must not listen to her. She is a bad woman! I know all about her, Georgia. When I saw her tonight I recognised her.'

He felt Georgia's body stir beneath his hand.

'Yes, she is bad,' she whispered, 'bad and evil. But I cannot escape from her, I must do what she says.'

'You must not,' the Duke almost shouted. 'You must defy her, tell her that you are no longer afraid of anything she may do.'

'But I am afraid,' Georgia answered. 'You do not understand! She will make me obey her desires, whatever you may say.'

'Even to bringing this tool of Bonaparte into the country? A man who is undoubtedly a spy?' the Duke asked.

Georgia started, then shook herself free of him.

'So you heard that?'

'I could not help it,' the Duke answered. 'Did you not realise that every word that is said in your stepmother's bedroom can be listened to by anyone who is on the staircase?'

'I had forgotten!" Georgia exclaimed. 'I remembered that one could look into the salon, but the bedroom has been empty for a long time. It was my mother's, and my stepmother insisted on using it on this visit only because the other guestrooms were occupied.'

'It may seem reprehensible, but I heard all she said to you,' the Duke said. He knew that Georgia was embarrassed by the way she turned her head aside, and he guessed she was blushing.

'I heard her strike you,' he continued more gently. 'How can you endure such humiliation?'

'There is nothing I can do,' she replied in a low voice.

'It is a crack-brained plan to cross the Channel again tomorrow night,' the Duke said. 'And, even more serious, it is wrong and reprehensible to bring this French spy into the country. We are at war, Georgia. Men like your brother are fighting the might and terror of Napoleon. Do you not understand that spies and traitors undermine our strength, and that our soldiers and our sailors lose their lives because of them.'

Georgia gave a little cry and put her hands over her ears.

'Do not say it,' she begged. 'I have lain awake night after night puzzling as to how I con refuse to do her bidding. But there is no loop-hole: I have to obey.'

There was a sudden silence. Then in a voice of utter helplessness she added:

'I am afraid, yes, I will admit that I am a coward where tomorrow night is concerned. I have a premonition, I do not know why . . .'

The Duke stood irresolute. Every instinct of common sense told him to walk on to where he knew his horse was waiting, and yet everything that was chivalrous and protective in him kept him standing where he was. It seemed that the silence between them would never be broken, until Georgia said:

'You must go. Ned will be wondering why you are so long in coming.'

The Duke seemed to rouse himself almost as though he had been in a stupor. They walked slowly across the rough grass which gradually gave way to stones and shingle. They were nearing the creek and there, in a little hollow out of sight from the house, the Duke could see his horse. He stopped again and turned towards Georgia.

'There must be a solution to this,' he said angrily.

'That is what I thought,' she replied. Now her voice was no longer broken but firm and impersonal.

'I suppose I could reason with your stepmother,' the Duke said reluctantly.

'And what good would that do?' Georgia asked. 'Even if you knew her in the past she would not thank you to interfere with her plans. Besides, I suspect that they are not always her commands that we carry out.'

'Then whose?' the Duke demanded, but as he asked the question he felt that he knew the answer: the man in grey, with his sneering, supercilious face; the man in grey, who had seemed to dominate the rest of that raffish, drunken party.

'I do not know his name,' Georgia answered. 'But I

think from some of the things my stepmother has said that he is a Frenchman.'

'A Frenchman!' The Duke's exclamation rang out like a pistol-shot. 'Georgia, can you not see what this means? These must indeed be spies that you are bringing into the country.'

'I know, I know,' Georgia answered, 'but there is nothing I can do about it. I have told you I receive my orders and I carry them out.'

'But why?' the Duke asked. 'You are a woman, and this is no woman's job.'

'That is part of the story I cannot tell you,' Georgia answered. 'Sufficient to say that so far we have escaped capture, and that someone is safe.'

'Someone you love' the Duke asked gently. 'Then it must be either your brother or your husband.'

'You are not to question me on this,' Georgia retorted hotly. 'You have no right! Leave at once!'

She would have walked ahead of him down the hill towards the horse, but the Duke put out his hand and caught her by the arm.

'I will get to the bottom of this,' he said. 'Your stepmother has some hold over you, and it concerns your brother.'

'Let me go,' Georgia said furiously. 'I know nothing about you and I do not trust you. You even came here pretending to be someone that you are not.'

'I would have been a dead man by now if I had not prevaricated,' the Duke answered. 'Not that I think your pigman, or whoever was holding the musket, was likely to prove a crack-shot.'

'It was not the pigman,' said Georgia childishly. 'It was old Sam, the forester. He can shoot a rabbit through the head at forty yards, so you would not have had a chance.'

'Do not distrust me because I preserved my skin,' the Duke begged. 'Listen to me, Georgia, let me help you.'

She had been struggling against him, but now she was still.

'You can help me by pulling an oar in that boat tomorrow night,' she answered.

'And if I do,' the Duke said, 'will you tell me your secret? Will you trust me to help you?'

'If you come with me tomorrow night I might trust you,'

64

Georgia answered, 'for then you will have proved yourself. But you would be wise to go now as you intended. Your horse is there, you can ride away and forget us. Oh, I know I have pleaded with you to stay, but I have a feeling that it was wrong of me to do so. This is not your coil. It is mine and I must get myself out of it as best I can.'

'You are a woman,' the Duke answered. 'Women were not meant for this sort of thing.'

'I wish I could believe that,' Georgia answered. 'But I have to forget I was a woman and make the men forget it too. They take orders from me because I am my father's child: 'tis the old Squire speaking, not a frail little creature in petticoats.'

'You are a strange girl,' the Duke said.

For a moment she looked up at him, and in the moonlight he could see her eyes searching his face as though she reassured herself.

'Do you mean what you say, you will really accompany us tomorrow night?'

The Duke threw away his last vestige of restraining common sense.

'I will come,' he said, 'but God help me! For I think I'm a clod-pate and my brain must be to let.'

She laughed a little gurgle of laughter which surprised him.

'You sound almost desperate,' she said, 'and yet I feel relieved, light and carefree. The premonition I had of danger is gone. I somehow believe that because you will be there we shall do what we have to do and return in safety.'

'Bringing a spy to the shores of England?' the Duke said quietly.

'Bringing another cargo,' she corrected. 'It is not my responsibility, I merely take orders.'

'It is all our responsibility,' the Duke said. 'And now when you return to the house I wish you to do something for me.'

'What is it?' she asked.

'I want you to discover the name of a man who is wearing grey—a grey coat and grey breeches. He is tall, dark and somewhat sinister in appearance.'

'I never concern myself with any of my stepmother's guests,' Georgia said in a tone of distaste. 'I loathe them, can you understand that? I loathe Society and all that it means. In the past I met these men; now when they come to my home I hide.'

'I can understand that,' the Duke said gently.

As if she had not heard him, Georgia went on:

'I hide until they have gone. That man, Lord Ravenscroft, with his thick lips and soft hands . . . and those others . . . when they first came . . .' She gave a little shudder and then continued in a voice which was so low he could hardly hear what she said: 'I hate them! If I have to meet them again I would rather die!'

'Forget it,' the Duke said sharply. 'Do not let what has happened poison you.'

She turned her face up to his.

'Is that what it does?' Georgia asked, wonderingly.

'It poisons your mind and your heart and your soul,' he said. 'Whatever you have been through, and I can guess what it was, forget it. They cannot touch you now, you are married and your husband should be here to protect you.'

'Yes, I know,' Georgia said hurriedly, 'but there is a war and he is at sea. He cannot be here, and I—I must protect myself.'

'You have your secret hiding place,' the Duke said with a little smile.

'Yes, I have that,' she answered.

'I will not press you,' he said, 'but somehow I feel that it is of import that we should know that gentleman's name. Ask Nana if she can discover it from one of the servants.'

'I will ask her,' Georgia said doubtfully, 'but we have to be careful. Lord Ravenscroft does not know I am in the house, and if he did he might ask to see me.'

The Duke realised that some terrible experience lay behind the horror in her voice and consolingly he put out his hand and laid it on hers.

'Shall we go back to the house?' he asked. 'We have to make plans for tomorrow and, as you said before, Ned needs his sleep.'

'You really are coming with us?'

Her voice was breathless as if she could hardly yet believe that it was indeed the truth.

'I will pull an oar,' the Duke promised, and wondered if there was any madness in his family. Never in the whole of his life had he undertaken quite such a crazy enterprise!

66

5

NANA was almost asleep when Georgia opened the bedroom door softly and slipped into the room.

'Is that you, dearie?' Nana asked, raising herself on the pillows.

'Who else?' Georgia answered.

'Has the gentleman gone?'

Georgia crossed the room to the bedside to stand looking down at the old woman with her apple-red cheeks, and soft wrinkled face.

'No, Nana,' she answered, 'he is staying.'

Nana sat up.

'Staying? You mean Mr. Raven will cross with you tomorrow night?'

'I persuaded him,' Georgia explained. 'Oh, Nana, I feel it was a foolhardy action! He is not one of us; we are not even convinced that we can trust him! But what else was I to do? There is no chance of Enoch returning home from market until long after we set course for France—if indeed he does not stay until Sunday morning.'

'Mr. Raven will not betray you,' Nana said quietly. 'I am sure of it—as sure as I'm lying here.'

'But he is indeed mysterious!' Georgia replied. 'Well clothed, a gentleman, and yet a fugitive. He is in hiding, he told me so.'

'I wonder what the reason can be?' Nana said reflectively. 'Debts are what sends a gentleman into the shadows: yet there is something different about this Mr. Raven. If you asked me, I would say he was of noble birth and I should know having lived all my life in the service of gentlemen.'

'There has not been anything very gentlemanly about the way we have been living these last few years,' Georgia retorted. 'Perhaps you have forgotten how a real gentleman should look. Those who have stayed here would not have jogged your memory.'

'That is true, dearie,' Nana agreed, 'but do not be thinking about them—you know how it upsets you.'

'It is impossible not to think of them,' Georgia replied with a sudden break in her voice. She sat down on the edge of Nana's bed.

'I can never see them come to this house,' she went on in a low voice, almost as though she was speaking to herself, 'without remembering what happened the first time my stepmother brought a party down from London . . .'

'Forget it, Miss Georgia,' Nana begged her.

But Georgia continued as if she had not heard.

'I can see Her Ladyship now,' she murmured, 'elegant in a new muslin and a wrap trimmed with swansdown. "Georgia," she said to me, in that hard voice which always seems to make me quake at the knees: "You look like a milkmaid. Forget your yokel ways for this evening, at any rate, and dine with us. I have a friend who is anxious to make your acquaintance." '

'Forget it! Forget it!' Nana pleaded. She knew the story by heart, as she had heard it far too many times.

But Georgia's eyes in the light of the candle stared, without seeing it, at the picture of the Crucifixion which stood over Nana's bed, and in her mind she was re-living the events of that terrifying night.

She had gone down to dinner excitedly. It had been quiet and lonely at Four Winds since her father had died. So there was an unexpected thrill in putting on the expensive gown her stepmother had given her, and arranging her hair in what she believed was the latest fashion. The joy of dressing up, which no woman can resist, brought a light to her eyes and a flush to her cheeks.

She knew as she looked in the mirror that she need not be ashamed of her appearance.

'You're in looks tonight, Miss Georgia,' Nana enthused. 'I only wish your poor father could have seen you.'

'I believe that Papa would have liked me to dine downstairs,' Georgia replied, thinking of the past year in which she had worn black and felt that the empty loneliness of the house was sometimes overpoweringly depressing. But now her stepmother had arrived from London with servants and a vast amount of tapers to light the chandeliers.

There were chefs bustling in the kitchens to prepare what seemed to her inexperienced eyes a gargantuan meal. Flowers had been brought in from the gardens and greenhouses to decorate the salon and fill the big Chinese bowls in the hall. The covers were off the furniture and there were fires in every room.

The gown her stepmother had given her was more luxurious than anything she had ever owned before. As she entered the salon, the eyes of everyone present had seemed to turn to her, but she had not been afraid. It was only later she had known fear, known it because of the raw passion in Lord Ravenscroft's voice; known it because of the dark, smouldering expression in his bloodshot eyes; known it as his thin hands went out to touch her.

She tried to avoid him but failed. Everyone else at the party appeared to be gaming or paired off together. She seemed to be isolated with him. She tried to think of an excuse for retiring, but she did not wish to annoy her stepmother, who had made sure that she was acutely aware of His Lordship's importance.

He invited her to show him a picture in the ante-room. In her inexperience she agreed. The moment they were alone he seized her in his arms and drew her close to him. 'No! No! Let me g . . . go, my Lord!' Georgia cried hastily.

'You are very sweet!' he said in the thick, deep voice which made her think of an animal. He held her so close that she could hardly breathe and she could feel his hot, wine-sodden breath on her cheek.

'I must go b . . . back . . . people will think . . . I . . . let me go!'

'People will think the truth, that you are entrancing and I desire you.'

Panic-stricken she struggled, twisting and turning, trying to beat him off with her fists. But he was too strong for her. She felt his thick lips burning against her cheeks and knew that his kisses were brutal and disgusting. She tried to scream, but he found her mouth!

'You excite me,' he cried triumphantly, 'a little bird I must capture. Flutter as you will, but you will be mine!'

He kissed her again, and though she felt she must faint with the horror and degradation of it she fought herself free. She escaped, but because she was confused she ran through the salon and out through the door into the hall.

It was then the full horror of that evening occurred. The other male guests, inflamed by drink and Lord Ravenscroft's hunting-cry 'Gone away!' chased her through the house.

Overcome by Lord Ravenscroft's kisses, Georgia had not the sense to seek Nana in the servants' quarters. Instead she ran up the stairs in full view of them all. Someone picked up a hunting-horn which usually lay on the hall table, and the noise and cries as they followed her made her as fearful as any young deer fleeing before a pack of baying hounds.

As she climbed higher up the stairs, still they came in pursuit. Breathless and shaken she realised all too well that they fully intended to drag her downstairs again into the arms of Lord Ravenscroft. Then she remembered the secret entrance to the priest hole. She reached it just before the first of the hunters sighted her on the top landing. She slipped through it and collapsed panting and almost unconscious on the tiny twisting stairs.

She could hear the party seeking her. She listened to them opening all the doors in the passage and slamming them again, while the cries of 'Tally-ho!' 'Gone away' and the blowing of the horn continued for a long time.

Later she dragged herself up into the tiny room at the top of the staircase and lay on the bed, trembling as if with an ague, until the dawn came. With daylight her courage had returned and with it the resolution that, whatever threats or inducements her stepmother offered, she would not meet Lord Ravenscroft again.

Lady Grazebrook had not been pleased.

'You country turnip,' she sneered, 'does it not enter your cork brain that Lord Ravenscroft could be of vast assistance to you unless you wish to stay in this isolated, cow-dunged hole all your life.'

'I want nothing else,' Georgia replied. 'I am content here and never again—never, do you hear?—never again will I join your friends at dinner or any other meal. If they come to the house—and that I cannot prevent—they must not see me.'

'Do not be so nonsensical,' Lady Grazebrook began, only to be checked by the expression on Georgia's face.

'I would rather kill myself,' she said slowly, 'than have that man touch me again.'

For once Caroline Grazebrook had the grace to look embarrassed.

'Perhaps His Lordship was over-rough,' she conceded. 'He is used to women being flattered by his attention. You have to grow up, Georgia, and learn how to handle men. Let me speak to Lord Ravenscroft. If he had not been foxed he would not have rushed his fences.'

'I refuse to see him again, speak to him or come into his presence,' Georgia declared. 'If you force me to meet Lord Ravenscroft or any other men you bring into the house then I shall run away.'

'Fustian! Where would you go?' Lady Grazebrook asked scornfully, but she knew that she had driven Georgia too far and from then on she had not insisted on her making an appearance at her parties.

But Georgia had a further frightening experience. The following evening she went to bed early, not to sleep but to go over and over in her mind what had happened the night before. Suddenly, at one o'clock in the morning, there was a faint sound outside her bedchamber. She had not blown out her candle; indeed, after what had happened, she was afraid even of the darkness. Sitting up in bed she watched with mesmerised eyes the handle on her door turn very slowly. Fortunately she had locked herself in, something that she was not in the habit of doing. Perhaps some sub-conscious instinct of self-protection had made her turn the key that night.

Someone was outside, she could hear him breathing.

'Who is it?' she asked, trembling.

In reply there was a whisper low and utterly repulsive:

'Let me in, little Georgia, I wish to talk with you.'

She had known who it was, and the same panic of fear that had made her run the night before swept over her in a flood tide. She sprang out of bed and started with all her strength to push the furniture in front of the door. First the chest of drawers, then the chairs, the wash-hand stand and anything else she was capable of moving. It seemed she had an almost superhuman strength, for when she had finished her whole body ached with the effort. She stood still listening, and then through the darkness came his voice, hateful, arrogant and confident.

'I will wait, little Georgia, I will wait.'

And he laughed before he went away.

She had been ill with terror the following day and for a long time after the party had returned to London. It was Nana who had found the solution, insisting that whenever Her Ladyship and her friends descended on Four Winds, Georgia should sleep in the tiny room which opened off her own bedroom.

It was littte more than a wardrobe, but in it Georgia felt safe. In fact, there were only two places where she knew she would not be found, either in the room that opened out of Nana's or in the priest hole.

'Forget it, dearie,' Nana said again now, as Georgia finished her story, recalling the horror and confusion of those shattering experiences.

'I cannot,' Georgia replied. 'Whenever Lord Ravenscroft is here in this house, Nana, I remember his lips on mine. He is evil and even the rooms seem polluted after he has been in them.'

'It's all over,' Nana repeated.

'Yet I feel somehow that I shall never be safe while he is still alive,' Georgia objected. 'And I feel, too, although my stepmother does not say so, that he still asks for me. She suggested tonight that I should put on one of her gowns to entertain her guests. Who would wish to be entertained by me except him?'

'I think you may be exaggerating what must have been but a trifling incident in His Lordship's life,' Nana suggested. 'You may be sure that there are many women of all sorts ready to please a nobleman. He will have forgotten you.'

Nana did not really believe her own words, but she wished to reassure Georgia.

'If only I could credit that was the truth,' Georgia sighed.

'Anyway, they will be gone tomorrow,' Nana told her.

'Tomorrow?' Georgia's face suddenly lit up. 'But why so soon?'

'From what Her Ladyship's coachman was saying, the party is only staying here between two visits. They rested at Lord Ravenscroft's house the night before, which was why they arrived so early. 'Tis not more than twenty-five miles away. And tomorrow they leave to stay with another friend of Her Ladyship. I am not certain of his name.'

'That reminds me,' Georgia said. 'Mr. Raven is anxious to know the name of the gentleman who is wearing grey. I gather that he is my stepmother's new beau.'

'In grey?' Nana reflected. 'I think I saw him going down the passage before dinner. A thin, dark gentleman, with a lined face.'

'That must be him,' Georgia said. 'Do you know his name?'

'I'll try to discover what it is tomorrow,' Nana promised. 'The valets will know. There is one who is not as bad as the rest, quite a pleasant-spoken young man.'

'That is indeed a change,' Georgia smiled, 'and let's hope they do not leave the house in such a disgraceful state as they did last time.'

'It took me over a week to get the place clean and decent again,' Nana sighed. 'If it hadn't been for Mrs. Ives, who came in and gave me a hand, I'd have taken twice as long.'

'We cannot afford help, you know that,' Georgia reminded her.

'Mrs. Ives doesn't charge, dearie,' Nana replied. 'She has a few vegetables out of the garden from time to time, and when I make chicken soup I take a basinful down for her youngest lad. He'll always be a weakling, I'm afraid.'

'I cannot conceive what the village would do without you, dearest,' Georgia said, and bent forward to kiss her Nana's cheek.

'And don't you lie awake all night,' Nana admonished her in the scolding voice that nannies have used to their charges since time immemorial.

'I will try to sleep,' Georgia promised. 'I have not forgotten what lies ahead tomorrow.'

'Her Ladyship has no right to ask it of you,' Nana declared. 'It's too soon and too dangerous. Oh, will there ever be an end to this terrible trafficking? I think sometimes, Miss Georgia, I'll not live to see you return in safety. When you are away I feel as though I cannot breathe.'

'There is nothing we can do about it,' Georgia replied.

'And I know, and so do you, that Her Ladyship is beginning to demand more and more cargoes. 'Tis we who must provide the money to pay for all those supercilious servants and expensive horse-flesh. Can't you explain to Her Ladyship how dangerous it is? She must know that if you are caught there'll be no more kegs and bales, no more baccy and ribbons for the pack-horses to carry. Without you her pocket will soon have holes in it, for the Squire, poor man, couldn't have left her enough for extravagant spending.'

'I do not think my stepmother reasons things out,' Georgia said with a little sigh. 'I think what she wants she is determined to have, and her desire for gold is insatiable.'

'Has she given you payment for the men?' Nana asked. 'They won't set forth without it—not a second time.'

'Yes, I forced a purse from her before dinner,' Georgia answered. 'Fortunately she had won at cards, and I made her give me another guinea for each man because they were carrying a passenger. They are not empty-headed, they know as well as I do that these Frenchmen are tools of Bonaparte.'

'What did Mr. Raven think of that?' Nana asked unexpectedly.

'He was shocked,' Georgia said. 'Of course, it is crazed for me to take a stranger into my confidence, but what could I do? We cannot set out with an oarsman short. Our only safeguard is to be able to move quicker than the Revenue officers.'

'Your only safeguard, dearie, is the fact that no one would suspect you,' Nana corrected her. 'Four Winds has always been beyond reproach; for your father—God rest his soul—was respected throughout the countryside.'

'Poor Papa!' Georgia sighed. 'I wonder what he would say if he knew. Oh! I hope he does not know.'

'Go to bed, dearie,' Nana admonished her. ' 'Tis no use getting fanciful at this time of the night. Go to your room, and I'll get out and lock the door.'

'I will lock it,' Georgia replied. She turned the key and also shot home the bolt which had been newly attached to the door.

'Now I feel safe,' she said. 'But until that man has left the house I am always afraid.'

' 'Tis a pity Mr. Raven can't deal with the likes of His Lordship,' Nana said. 'A fine, outstanding young man he is! I will take him one of Mr. Charles's shirts tomorrow, so that while you are away I can wash the one he is wearing now.'

'Do not worry your head about Mr. Raven!' Georgia exclaimed. 'If he were not in trouble himself he would not be here. And I dare say that if things are as you surmise he will be glad of the guineas.'

'I best give him Mr. Charles's fishing-jersey,' Nana went on, as if she had not heard Georgia's interruption. 'He can't go a-rowing in that swell coat he's a-wearing now. You know, Miss Georgia, I'm glad he will be with you; I've a feeling that if there is trouble you could depend on Mr. Raven.'

'I depend on no one,' Georgia snapped. 'You know what I think of men, especially those you call the gentry. The only thing I depend on is my pistol. I do not trust Mr. Raven any more than I trust other creatures of his breeding.'

Despite her brave words she felt as if she defamed the gentleman unnecessarily. He had been obliging in consenting to pull an oar, and although she pretended to herself that he was doing it for the guineas, she knew he had been determined to ride away. Why then had he changed his mind?

'He can leave as soon as we get back,' she told herself defiantly, then felt a little tremor of fear: supposing they never came back, supposing they were caught?

No one would have known the following evening, from the tone of Georgia's voice or from the proud manner in which she carried her head, that she was anything but utterly confident as she led the Duke from the hiding place in the priest hole through the house and down the cellar steps.

He had spent a boring day resting on the bed and attempting to read some of the ancient books in the bookcase. He had not gone down the stairs to listen at the secret doors or peep through the concealed shutter into the salon. He felt disgusted with the party and had no desire to look on Caroline again.

His brief glimpse of her the night before had told him that, though she was still beautiful, her face had coarsened, and her expression was harder. Even if he had not overheard her conversation with Georgia he felt he would have known that her presence in this house and the company that she kept would be out of line with all decency. He was old and experienced enough now to see Caroline for what she was—a greedy, grasping doxy.

Since he had come into his inheritance, he had treated Caroline and her sort with a kind of amused tolerance. Knowing they considered him a desirable plum for the picking, he was not likely to become entangled again. Caroline had taught him a sharp lesson and he would never repeat such a mistake. But it jarred on him to think of her here with this unsophisticated girl and it aroused in him an active distaste to know that she had press-ganged a dozen decent countrymen into defying the law.

The Duke was honest enough to wonder to himself how much his feelings of anger against Caroline were influenced by the fact that he had no desire to take part in the adventure which lay ahead of him. He had given his word to Georgia, therefore could not go back on it, but he did not pretend to himself that he was looking forward to rowing the twenty-two miles which lay between them and France.

Apart from anything else, he wondered if he would be up to it. He had not rowed since he was at Oxford, but he was glad that he was at the moment extremely fit, having recently undertaken the task of schooling some young horse-flesh over the sticks and backing them against Pereguine's more experienced mounts.

'An unpleasant mess your stepmother's party appears to have left behind,' he remarked conversationally to Georgia as he walked beside her through the deserted house, seeing through the open doors tumbled beds and basins full of dirty water. The floors were dirty and the dining-room table still laden with silver dishes and unwashed plates.

'They always leave it like this,' Georgia answered.

The Duke did not pursue the subject. He watched with interest the well-oiled cellar door slide silently forward and picked his way carefully down the worn stone steps as Georgia held a lantern to illuminate the darkness.

'The kegs and barrels are still here,' the Duke remarked casually.

'I suspect they will be collected later tonight,' Georgia answered.

'Who fetches them?' he inquired.

'I have no idea, except that his name is Philip,' she replied. 'They are taken from the cellar through another door which opens into the stable-yard. No one in the house sees them go.'

She spoke easily, and then stopped, her wide eyes raised to his and watching his face.

'Why are you interested?' she inquired. 'Oh God, if this should be a trap! You know too much!'

'You are nervous,' he assured her, 'or you wouldn't imagine such foolishness. I have told you I will do nothing to harm you; that I promise.'

'Yet you ask questions,' she said in a voice which trembled.

'Only because I'm inquisitive,' the Duke said, 'and you would be the same in my place. Can you not imagine how you would feel if you went for a ride across the downs and landed up in a situation like this. What would you think? Wouldn't you want to know what was going on? Wouldn't you be curious as to what the people concerned were like? Besides, I am really interested in smugglers, I always have been, since I was a boy.'

'You would not be interested if you knew as much about them as I do,' Georgia said bitterly. 'I have no choice but to believe you. But do not probe too deeply. Tomorrow when you leave you have sworn to forget everything you have seen or heard.'

'Aye, aye, mistress, I'm taking my orders!' the Duke said with a grin. 'You should have been a boy. You issue commands like a sergeant-major.'

Georgia gave a little laugh.

'Have you not wondered why I am christened Georgia?' she inquired. 'I was to have been George, after His Majesty, and my parents grew so used to thinking of me as George before I was born that their only concession to my sex was to add an "a" to my name."

The Duke threw back his head and laughed. The sound echoed eerily down the long passage which they were now descending towards the rickety steps.

'Hush" Georgia said quickly, 'the men will think it strange. When we reach the lower cave let me go ahead and explain why I have been forced to invite you to join them. They will not like it.'

But whatever objections there were to the Duke's

presence, Georgia obviously overcame them. When he joined the crew a little while later he was accepted without question, even though he thought the looks they gave him were cold and suspicious.

It was just on the edge of dark. By the time they had the boat launched in the water and were all aboard the last glow of the sun had vanished over the horizon and the first evening star was twinkling above.

The Duke took his place beside a burly man who he learnt was the local blacksmith. He grasped his oar firmly, straightened his back and hoped that he would not disgrace himself. To his surprise the boat seemed light and moved smoothly with a good balance over the water.

He glanced towards Georgia sitting in the stern with her hand on the tiller and thought with a grin that no one would think of describing her as a lady of quality. She was wearing the high sea-boots and the ancient full-skirted coat that she had worn the first time he saw her. A black kerchief covered her fair hair. She had certainly made no effort, because he was present, to make herself look less of what Nana would call a 'rapscallion'.

'Steady, men,' Georgia said authoritatively, 'take your timing from Fred. Now, let us see if we can make the crossing in record time.'

As they settled down to the serious task of rowing, the Duke felt with a sense of relief that it was not so exhausting as he had anticipated. At the same time he was using new muscles and he knew that long before they were home he would feel as if his back were breaking.

The sea was almost dead calm and soon they were in mid-channel, keeping up an excellent speed. They rowed in silence except for an occasional word of command from Georgia. One of the men began to whistle almost without realising what he was doing, and was hushed into silence.

'Pray do not waste your breath, Cobber,' Georgia admonished him. 'Besides, we never know who might hear.'

The hours passed without incident. Once the Duke noticed a green light far to the west. If it was a ship it soon passed out of sight and they rowed on. Three and a half hours later Georgia said quietly:

'Land ahead.'

She seemed to know her way and as they beached in a small cove the two men in the bows jumped ashore, steadied the boat and dragged it up the sand. Then all the men clambered out, splashing in the shallow water. The Duke, following them, wondered a little ruefully what Pereguine would say to the salt water on his best Hessians.

The men stayed by the boat, but Georgia walked away into the darkness.

'What happens now?' the Duke asked.

'Her always makes us wait,' a man replied. 'If there be danger and her cannot cum back, us has orders t' put out t' sea without her.'

'That sounds exceedingly unchivalrous to me,' the Duke said drily.

'Us does as we's told,' the man replied surlily.

'I don't hold with grown men using females as a shield,' the Duke said scathingly, and, disregarding the muttered protests behind him, he walked after Georgia.

It was not a dark night. He soon saw her ahead of him and in a few strides caught up with her. She turned angrily as he reached her side.

'What are you doing?' she demanded. 'My orders are for the men to stay with the boat.'

'There are enough of them to put out to sea without my assistance should the situation prove dangerous,' he answered.

'I will not have you questioning my commands,' she said sharply. 'I know full well what I am about.'

'I hope you do,' the Duke replied, 'because I'm coming with you and have no desire to run into some well-contrived ambush.'

'There will be no ambushes here" Georgia retorted. 'Go back and wait for me.'

'I have no intention of doing anything of the sort,' the Duke replied, 'so do not let us waste time in enemy country. Where is the passenger?'

As if she knew that anything she might say to him would be ineffective, Georgia walked on in what was obviously an angry silence. A few steps and they were underneath the cliffs. They rounded some rocks and there hidden conveniently from the shore was a cave.

Georgia stopped and gave a long, low whistle. Almost immediately a fisherman shading a lantern in his hand appeared at the mouth of the cave.

'You are early, madame,' he said in a patois which was

79

rather difficult to understand. 'Otherwise we would have been waiting by the sea.'

'We made better time than usual,' Georgia replied in excellent French. 'Is everything ready?'

'Everything, madame. There is no cargo as you know, only monsieur, who is very nervous.'

'Tell him we must leave at once,' Georgia instructed him.

The man vanished into the cave and a moment later reappeared. There was now another man with him, wrapped in a long travelling-cloak, his hat pulled low over his eyes.

'*Bon soir, monsieur,*' Georgia said.

Although it was dark and the lantern did not give much light, the Duke could see the surprise on the Frenchman's face when he heard a woman's voice.

'*Une femme?*' he asked of the fisherman.

There was a quick exchange of words, and Georgia said to the Duke in an aside which could not be overheard:

'Passengers are never told that I am a woman or they would be too frightened to embark.'

Then the Frenchman turned and raised Georgia's hand to his lips.

'*Enchanté, madame,*' he said in a tone which suggested that his feelings were very different from his words.

'Come quickly,' Georgia said crisply, 'we cannot wait here.'

The fisherman with the lantern helped the passenger over the shingle and down on to the sand.

When they came to the boat Georgia said to the Duke:

'You had best carry him aboard, he will not be wearing boots.'

With a smile the Duke obeyed her. The Frenchman seemed about to protest but had obviously no wish to get his feet wet. The Duke set him down in the stern, the oarsmen pushed the boat into deeper water, and the Duke heaved himself aboard, just in time to prevent the waves topping his Hessians.

The crew settled down to the same rhythmic stroke as they had employed coming out. It might have been because they were tired that the Duke fancied they were not moving so swiftly as they had on the outward passage. But it was fast enough and the sea was smooth. Although the night wind was chill, none of them felt cold except, perhaps, the passenger huddled in his cape who seemed to shiver now and then. But that, the Duke thought, might easily have been due to fear.

It was now that the Duke began to feel the strain of employing muscles that he had not used for over eight years. He knew too that his hands were beginning to blister from the oar. He felt ashamed at his own weakness and was almost relieved that his burly companion, the blacksmith, was breathing heavily.

'Only another twenty minutes,' Georgia cried, 'and we shall be home!'

Her voice roused the Frenchman, who sat up and attempted to look round him.

'Just a little while longer, *monsieur*,' Georgia said in French to console him.

He grunted and the Duke had a sudden desire to chuck him overboard. 'Blasted spies,' he thought to himself, 'creeping like serpents into England.'

It was said that Bonaparte's knowledge of British troop movements and British ships was all due to these slimy creatures, worming their way into people's confidences and even buying information from those weaklings who were always prepared to turn traitor in any community when there was a question of payment.

His anger swept away his tiredness and he applied himself to rowing more diligently. He was in fact wondering if there was any way he could denounce this man to the authorities without involving Georgia and her gang.

It was then that out of the darkness came a sudden shout.

'Boat ahoy! Heave to, in the name of His Majesty King George!'

'Revenue officers!' Georgia hardly breathed the words, but they all heard them. 'Quick, move quicker!'

There was no need for her to admonish them. It was as though the whole crew suddenly came to life, the oars flashed, they were rowing for dear life.

'Heave to,' shouted the voice out of the darkness. There was a pause, and then: 'Obey, or we fire!'

'Faster! Faster! Keep your heads down!'

The boat seemed to be flashing over the water at an almost unheard of speed. There was a sudden loud report and the Duke felt a bullet whiz uncomfortably near his left ear.

'Heads down!' he said in a voice which the men he had commanded in Portugal knew only too well. 'Georgia, get down in the boat immediately.'

She obeyed him! Now there were more shots, mercifully whizzing over their heads, but none the less uncomfortably near.

'Hurry! Hurry!' Georgia's words were not a command, they were a plea. 'Hurry! Oh dear God let us escape . . . let us reach home!'

Suddenly the Frenchman got to his feet

'C'est dangereux! J'ai peur!' he screamed the words aloud, standing up and waving his arms as though he thought he might jump out of the boat in his terror.

'Sit down, you fool!' the Duke cried, but it was too late. There was another shot, a scream, and the Frenchman crumpled up, falling against Georgia, who had been trying to pull him down beside her.

'Row! row!' the Duke cried, 'take your timing from me, one two . . . one two . . .'

They obeyed him and seemed almost to lift the boat out of the water with the effort. There were more shots, this time to the left. The Duke looked up. They had run into a low mist under the cliffs. The cutter must be off course. But he would not let the oarsmen relax. 'One two . . . one two . . .' They were pulling the boat faster and ever faster.

Georgia was back at the tiller, the Frenchman lying in a crumpled heap at the bottom of the boat.

'Steady,' she said quietly. Then her voice trembled "We . . . We're . . . the . . . there.'

She swung the tiller over, and the men brought the boat into the little creek, jumped over the side and dragged it to safety. The Duke shipped his oar and as the boat came to a standstill on the shingle Georgia spoke:

'Go home!' she cried. 'Go home and forget what you have seen tonight.'

It seemed to the Duke that they were gone almost before she had finished speaking.

'W . . . We had best g . . . get him into the c . . . cave,' Georgia said in a trembling voice.

'I will manage,' the Duke answered. 'Get a lantern.'

Georgia climbed out of the boat and the Duke picked up

the Frenchman in his arms. He knew as he carried the man over the rough shingle and into the cave that he was still breathing. In fact, his breath was coming in small gasps. The Duke carried him slowly along the back-breaking part of the cave to where it opened up. Georgia was waiting, the lantern in her hand.

He set the wounded man down on the floor and saw at once that the bullet had passed through his chest. The blood had soaked into the Frenchman's cape and was spreading rapidly over the pale coat he wore beneath it.

'Is he b . . . bad?' Georgia asked breathlessly.

Before the Duke could reply the man spoke slowly in a thick voice.

'T . . . tell J . . . Jules,' he said in French, his voice hardly audible. 'Tell . . . J . . . Jules to k . . . kill the Prince, im . . . immediately, the Em . . . peror's orders.'

The blood suddenly flowed into his mouth and spilled over his chin. He gave one convulsive movement with his hands and was still.

The Duke had seen many men die, and he knew that the French spy was dead.

6

FOR a moment neither the Duke nor Georgia moved, standing there and staring down at the Frenchman. Then in a voice hardly above a whisper Georgia stammered:

'Is . . . he . . . is he d . . . dead?'

'He is dead,' the Duke said slowly.

Georgia gave a low exclamation and put her hands over her eyes. Slowly the Duke bent down and searched the pockets of the dead man. First he pulled out a large purse filled with English guineas.

The Duke looked at it grimly, then threw it on the ground at Georgia's feet.

'Divide this amongst the men,' he said, 'they have earned it.'

'No! No!' Georgia protested.

He glanced up at her and by the light of the lantern he could see the terror in her eyes.

'Give it them,' he insisted. 'This is the last cargo they will carry.'

Making no further protest, Georgia shuddered and turned her face away as the Duke put his hand in the breast pocket of the man's coat, now sodden with blood. There was only one thing there, a visiting card, which the Duke held out to the light of the lantern.

'*Comte Pierre Lamonté*,' he read aloud. 'Now I wonder if this is the dead man's own card, or is it the name of someone with whom he wished to make contact?'

Georgia's head was still turned away; she could not look at the bloodstained face and staring eyes.

'Was that the name of the passenger that you carried on the previous journey?' the Duke asked.

Georgia shook her head.

'I never learnt his name.'

'All we know is that Jules—whoever he may be—is to kill the Prince,' the Duke said, almost to himself.

'You are . . . c . . . certain that is what the Frenchman said?' Georgia asked.

'You heard him, you know that is what he said,' the Duke replied sharply.

'But it is impossible that there could be such a plot against the Prince of Wales.'

'Nothing is impossible!' the Duke retorted. 'But this is not the time for argument or for conjecture. I have business to do. You had best wait for me up the staircase. I shall not be long.'

As he spoke the Duke lifted the dead man up in his arms. With a shudder Georgia turned away.

Ignoring the heavy purse lying on the ground at her feet, she climbed the staircase to the cave above. There she sat down on the ground and buried her face in her cold hands.

She tried not to think of what had happened. But her mind was in a turmoil and she could only remember the terror of the bullets whizzing past them in the darkness, the Frenchman's cry of unbridled fear, and his face as he died, with the blood pouring from his mouth.

Meanwhile the Duke carried the dead man out of the cave. Already the darkness was lifting and there was a faint glow on the horizon. He filled the pockets of the Frenchman's cape with stones, wrapped it closely round him and carried him to the very edge of the creek. As he had anticipated, the tide had turned and the waves splashing against the rocks had a deep and strong undercurrent.

As the spray splashed over him the Duke flung the body into the sea. He had one glimpse of it turning over and over, and then it was no more to be seen. He waited a few minutes to be certain that the waves would not cast up the corpse near the creek. But their splash and spray carried nothing save a few pieces of driftwood and the body of a dead seagull.

He went back into the cave, and climbing the staircase found Georgia sitting on the floor.

'You left this behind,' he said, showing her the full purse which he carried in his hand.

'I would rather we did not touch his money,' she protested, feeling disgusted at the idea of handling anything which belonged to the dead man.

'It is not his money,' the Duke corrected, 'but English guineas which have crossed the Channel to finance Napoleon and have now returned to where they belong. Think of it that way.'

'I will try,' she murmured faintly.

The Duke glanced at her sharply.

'I thought you had too much spirit for the vapours,' he said, and the tone of his voice whipped the colour back into her cheeks. Her little chin went up proudly.

'I shall not embarrass you with the vapours or with hysterics,' she said angrily, as she rose to her feet. 'But I have never seen a d . . . dead man before.'

'Then you are lucky he was a stranger,' the Duke replied almost roughly. 'If it had been any of the men in the boat you would have had their wives and their families to comfort.'

He saw that his matter-of-fact attitude had swept away her weakness. She walked ahead of him leaving him to carry the lantern, and in a few seconds they entered the cellar.

It was empty. All the contraband which had lain on the stone floor had vanished. There was nothing there but some old barrels which had once held home-brewed ale.

'They have gone!' the Duke exclaimed absently.

'They never stay long,' Georgia replied.

On the steps of the cellar there was a small bag. She picked it up and the Duke inquired:

'Is that your payment?'

'It is for the men,' she answered.

Without asking her permission the Duke took the bag from her and opened it. He lifted the lantern so that he could look inside.

'Hardly generous,' he remarked.

'The men grumble,' Georgia answered, 'but what can they do? If they refuse to go they starve, for my stepmother will not pay them for the work they do on the estate.'

The Duke's lips tightened, but he merely said:

'On this occasion at least they will be in funds.'

With the Frenchman's purse and the bag of coins in one hand and the lantern in the other he stood to let Georgia open the door into the house. Before she turned the key which they had left on the inside of the cellar she listened.

Then, opening the door as noiselessly as possible, she listened again before she pushed it fully open.

The house was very still. The Duke guessed that it was about five o'clock in the morning, for now the dawn was lightening the windows. In silence he followed Georgia into the small room where she had taken him the first time he had entered the house. He set the lantern and the gold down on the table, and stood watching Georgia as she pulled the black kerchief from her hair. She transformed herself, he thought, with just one gesture from a mannish woman into a woman dressed as a man.

Georgia put the kerchief down on the table and said with a sigh:

'I will get you something to eat, you must be hungry.'

'It is of more import that we discuss what we are to do,' the Duke said.

'What can we do?' she asked.

'You heard the Frenchman's words,' the Duke replied.

'Perhaps he was delirious, and, anyway, how could we ever find this Jules, whoever he might be?'

'There is only one person who can find him,' the Duke replied.

'Who is that?" she asked innocently.

'You,' he answered. 'You saw him, you brought him to these shores.'

Georgia looked at the Duke with an expression of panic creeping over her face as she realised the full implication of what he was saying.

'But how can I find him?' she protested.

'This is what we have to decide,' the Duke answered. 'Listen, Georgia, this man is not only a spy but he has actually been ordered to assassinate the Prince of Wales.'

'How can we be sure of that?' Georgia asked. 'And if he did kill him, what would it signify?'

'Bonaparte would like to create chaos in England,' the Duke answered. 'It is no secret that the King is mad; there has been talk for some time of making the Prince of Wales the Regent. Should the heir to the throne and the virtual ruler of the country be assassinated, the repercussions amongst the armed forces might be far-reaching and perhaps disastrous. But, anyway, it would be a trump card in Bonaparte's favour.'

'But Jules will wait for this Frenchman—the one who is dead—to bring him instructions to proceed.'

'That is a reasonable argument,' the Duke agreed with a sudden smile, 'except for one thing . . .'

'What is that?' Georgia inquired.

'The dead man said *immédiatement*—at once. To my mind that means that Jules so far has been told to assassinate the Prince but has not been given any particular time in which to do it. Now Bonaparte, with his usual impetuosity, requires action.'

'But even if that is so, what can we do about it?' Georgia asked. 'This man Jules crossed the Channel nearly three weeks ago; he will be in London, and London is a large place.'

'But we know where he will be in London', the Duke answered. 'He will be as near as possible to the Prince.'

'I suppose so,' Georgia agreed hesitatingly.

Her eyes met the Duke's and he saw the appeal in them. He knew that she pleaded with him wordlessly but desperately.

'It is no use, Georgia,' he said quietly, 'we have to find the assassin and you are the only person who knows his visage.'

'But I cannot journey to London,' Georgia protested, 'and even if I do, what chance have I to see the people who are near the Prince, or indeed anyone who moves in such grand Society? It is you who must warn the Prince; you must tell those who surround him to be on their guard.'

'Against whom?' the Duke interposed. 'I have not seen the man, how shall I describe him?'

'He was thin and dark,' Georgia said quickly. 'He was, I imagine, about middle-aged. His face was lined . . .' Her voice faltered and came to a standstill.

'That might describe quite a number of men,' the Duke answered, 'but if you saw him again you would recognise him, would you not?'

'Yes, yes I suppose so,' Georgia answered. 'When the boat was beached he was anxious not to get his feet wet, so he took my arm and I held the lantern so that he could see where to step from stone to stone. When we reached safety he thanked me and quite without thinking I held the light so that it shone on his face. He then walked quickly away up the creek. I suppose someone was waiting for him.'

'You must identify him.' The Duke's voice was firm.

'I have no conveyance to take me to London and if I make the journey there are a million chances to one that I shall not catch a glimpse of this man.'

'The odds are better than that,' the Duke assured her. 'We will leave as soon as you are ready. Go and change, and I will tell Ned to saddle the horses.'

There was a moment's silence, and then the Duke felt two small hands gripping his arm. Georgia's face was upturned to his.

'Please, please do not make me do this,' she begged him. 'Nothing will come of this wild goose chase, and if my stepmother hears of it she will be exceeding angry with me.'

'We will deal with your stepmother later,' the Duke said. 'The first thing we have to do is to save the life of the Prince of Wales. Everything else is of little consequence. Now, do as I tell you: change, but before you do we wake Nana and ask her to prepare us something to eat. She would not have us faint by the wayside.'

Georgia turned away from him. He knew that she was hating him, resentful that he was bullying her. But he knew there was nothing else they could do but pursue the spy. He drew out the card that he had found in the Frenchman's breast pocket and read the name again.

Comte Pierre Lamonté.

He turned the card over. There were a few words on the back written in French in a spindly hand. The Duke translated them aloud:

'This is the man!'

He put the card back in his pocket, walked briskly to the stables and woke Ned from where he slept in the loft. He told him to saddle his own horse and another for Georgia. Then he walked back to the house.

He entered by the kitchen door. There was already a smell of sizzling ham coming from the stove.

'Has Georgia told you that we are leaving for London, Nana?' he asked.

She wheeled round on him, her face puckered with worry.

'If you harm one hair on that child's head . . .' she began angrily.

The Duke looked at her and somehow the words died on her lips.

89

'No harm will come to Georgia,' he said quietly. 'She has told you what happened last night?'

The old woman nodded.

'We have to save the Prince.'

'I knew that evil and wickedness would come out of these terrible ways!' Nana exclaimed. 'It was Her Ladyship that drove her to it, and there was naught she could do, poor child, but obey. Nothing but worry and trouble has there been in this house ever since the Squire brought that woman home as his wife.'

'I am sure that is true,' the Duke said, 'but if it is possible Georgia must put right the harm that has been done.'

'She will not know her way about London,' Nana objected, 'and she has not the garments for moving amongst Society folk.'

'That will all be attended to,' the Duke replied. 'As soon as Georgia has identified this man I will bring her safely back to you.'

'And if Her Ladyship should hear of it?' Nana asked and her voice trembled.

'I doubt if Her Ladyship will return within the next few days,' the Duke replied. 'If she does you must say Georgia is ill. But on no account inform her where we have gone.'

'I shall give away no secrets,' Nana promised. 'There have been too many around this place. But remember, sir, Miss Georgia, for all she has had to break the law and do things that no respectable well-born girl should do, is as innocent and guileless as a babe in arms.'

'Have no worry,' the Duke said, 'I will take care of her.'

'And how do I know I can trust you?' Nana asked defiantly.

'I think you are convinced in your heart that I am trustworthy,' the Duke replied quietly.

The old woman's eyes searched his face until, as if she was satisfied with what she saw, she turned to the stove.

'You will find a can of hot water, a clean shirt and necktie behind the secret panel,' she replied. 'You could have used a bedroom, sir, now that the house is empty, but I knew your own coat was up the stairs.'

'Thank you, Nana,' the Duke said, and hurried away to wash, shave and prepare himself for the journey.

By the time he returned to the kitchen he found

Georgia, dressed in an ancient green-velvet riding-habit, being coaxed by Nana to eat a proper breakfast.

'Best do as you are told,' the Duke said, as he saw her reluctance. 'This will be no journey for a weak woman to undertake, and I will not have you falling off the saddle for want of food.'

'You will not find me falling from my saddle,' Georgia said proudly. There was a flash in her eyes and the Duke knew that she was hating him.

As they set off a quarter of an hour later, the first labourers were moving into the fields. It was a crisp, sunny day, and as they cantered down the drive, the Duke could not help thinking how beautiful Four Winds looked. He glanced at Georgia and saw that she was pale. He guessed that the effort of leaving home and all that was familiar was more of an ordeal than she was prepared to admit.

They avoided the village, which she told him was called Little Chadbury, and soon they were out in the open countryside heading north over soft green fields.

There was no doubt that Georgia rode well, and though her horse could not compare with the Duke's spirited stallion, they moved at a good pace for the first few hours of the day.

The Duke had decided to avoid the main roads and the popular coaching inns where they might meet travelers who would recognise him. Instead he found a small country inn where they lunched satisfyingly off a cut of cold ham and a big wedge of cheese.

They sat outside the inn in the sunshine, and after they had finished eating from the rough wood table the Duke said:

'Are you prepared to tell me what hold your stepmother has over you?'

Georgia had recovered her spirits and had been chatting quite gaily. Now she felt silent and he saw her shiver.

'I cannot speak of it,' she said, 'for it is not my secret.'

'All the same,' the Duke answered, 'I think you must confide in me. Because, after what has occurred, I have no intention of allowing you to carry another cargo.'

'You are talking foolishly,' Georgia retorted. 'What I do in the future is not your concern.'

'After what has happened I am afraid it does concern

me,' the Duke answered. 'Besides, do you not realise that, although it was the Frenchman who was killed, it might easily have been you or one of the men from your estate?'

'We have been lucky in the past,' Georgia said doggedly.

'No one's good luck lasts for ever,' the Duke answered. 'Moreover, do you think that your stepmother is going to be satisfied with what she is receiving now? She will always be wanting more.'

Georgia clasped her hands together.

'That's true enough,' she admitted. 'The runs have been getting more frequent, but I cannot refuse to obey her.'

'Why not?' the Duke inquired.

'That is something I cannot tell you,' Georgia replied.

'Suppose I inform on you,' the Duke said slowly.

'But you would not,' Georgia protested, 'you could not do anything so mean, so underhand. Besides, you are implicated, so you would also be arrested.'

The Duke laughed.

'You are quite a little tiger cat when aroused! You are right: I would not inform on you. But I am going to speak to your stepmother and tell her this must stop.'

'You speak to Her Ladyship!' Georgia cried incredulously. 'Do you really credit that she would pay the least attention? Besides, whatever you say it would not prevent her making me obey her wishes.'

'Why, what hold has she over you?' the Duke's question was like a pistol-shot.

'I cannot tell you,' Georgia replied almost piteously. 'I have given my word to Charles . . .'

The name slipped out.

'Then let me guess,' the Duke said. 'Charles is himself implicated in this. Your stepmother has some knowledge which she could use to his detriment. Could it be Charles who in the first place was found smuggling contraband across the Channel?'

Georgia stared at him, the blood draining away from her face.

'Someone has told you,' she said, 'for I never led you to think . . .'

'No one told me,' the Duke said quietly. 'It was obvious, wasn't it, that Charles is the person that you are trying to protect, for he would be dismissed his ship if it was known he had taken part in some lawless and reprehensible action.'

'It was only a boyish prank,' Georgia explained. 'He never thought of it as being wrong. The men on the estate were dissatisfied, and all up and down the coast farm labourers and their like were trying their hands at smuggling and were making more money in an evening than they could earn by a year of honest work. Charles was home on leave while his ship was being refitted at Portsmouth. He thought that it would be a hum to see what they could smuggle; so he and the men from the estate crossed the Channel.'

'In complete safety!' the Duke said. 'Gambler's luck!'

'They brought back a cargo,' Georgia continued, 'that Charles managed to sell to a friend for one hundred pounds. A hundred pounds, think of it!'

'A lot of golden guineas,' the Duke smiled.

'To Charles and the men it was a fortune,' Georgia answered. 'My father had just died. We found that he was deeply in debt because my stepmother had pledged his credit up to the hilt.'

'I was certain of that,' the Duke said, as if to himself.

Georgia ignored him and continued:

'The money from that cargo made us seem rich. Charles decided to try again, so as to leave me enough money to maintain the estate while he was away.'

Georgia paused and the Duke saw her eyes had darkened at the memory.

'What happened?' he asked gently.

'They got back without any trouble. My stepmother was at home, and when Charles came from the cellar, having helped carry the cargo there for safety, she was waiting for him.'

'How did she find out?' the Duke asked.

'I have never known,' Georgia replied, 'except that I fancy that she had a tenderness for Charles. He is so good-looking.'

'Caroline would have a tenderness for any young and attractive man,' he thought savagely. 'Go on,' he said aloud.

'She . . . she pretended to think it was a tremendous joke,' Georgia said. 'She suggested to Charles that they should sample some of the brandy that he had brought from France, and they sat drinking together. When Charles was drunk, so drunk that he did not know what he was . . . d . . . doing, she made him sign a . . . con . . . confession.'

There was a little silence and Georgia turned her face aside so that the Duke should not see her tears.

'He knew not what he was doing,' she whispered, and her voice broke. 'He thought she liked him and was being k . . . kind and . . . understanding.'

The Duke put out his hand and laid it over Georgia's. For a moment her fingers quivered beneath his. Then she turned her face, streaked with tears, towards him and said:

'Now you know the truth. Now you understand why I must do as my stepmother says. If I refuse, if I default, she will take Charles's confession to the Admiralty. He would be ruined and disgraced.'

'I admit it's a damnable situation,' the Duke said. 'But I still feel, Georgia, that something can be done. Do not despair.'

'I have lain awake night after night praying for a solution,' Georgia said. 'But you do not know my stepmother: she is not only greedy, she is spiteful. I think, though I have never dared say it before, that she hates Charles because he did not find her attractive. I think she would be glad to do him an injury. I am convinced that it is only the gold that our men make for her that has kept her from denouncing him.'

The Duke knew that Georgia's suppositions were not far-fetched. It would only have been the money which prevented Caroline from venting vengeance on a young man who had refused her advances. He could understand so well that anyone as decent and clean-living as Charles would have felt repelled at the idea of an intrigue with his own stepmother. Such scruples would never trouble Caroline, and if she had not found the money useful there was no doubt she would have denounced him ages ago.

'You are certainly in a toil,' the Duke said, and then he smiled. 'But do not despair. The night is always darkest, they say, before the dawn. We will jump our fences one by one. Perhaps we shall get into the straight far sooner than you anticipate.'

She smiled a little watery smile at him, knowing that he was trying to cheer her up but feeling despairingly that nothing could lighten the burden of depression that she had carried for so long.

She thought as she faced him, across the rough oak table, how handsome he looked in his elegantly cut coat and freshly crimped cravat. She was well aware that her own habit was faded, threadbare, and sadly out of fashion. She pulled her hat a little more firmly over her forehead and thought defiantly, 'Who cares? When this is over he will disappear, and I shall return to Four Winds.'

'We had best move on,' the Duke said.

The horses having been rubbed down and watered, they set off again avoiding the well-travelled roads. It was nearly four o'clock in the afternoon before they stopped for the last time. The empty countryside was now giving way to prosperous-looking hamlets and even the side roads carried coaches, carriages and what seemed to Georgia an inordinate amount of elegant phaetons, travelling at a spanking rate.

They found another small and unobtrusive country inn, and while the Duke ate cold roast beef Georgia toyed with some lamb cutlets. Quite suddenly she stopped pretending to eat and pleaded:

'I cannot go any further. Please let me return home. I know this journey to London will be useless. I shall fail you and you will be incensed with me for being so stupid. The more I think of the man I brought from France, the less it seems possible to recall his face.'

'You are merely nervous,' the Duke assured her. 'When you see him you will be quite certain who he is—I promise you that.'

'But I have no wish to go to London,' Georgia said in a low voice. 'Oh, I know how foolish you must think me to be talking like this, but I have told you before how I hate anything to do with Society and the so-called gentlemen.'

'But they are not all like the riff-raff that your step-mother includes in her circle,' the Duke said. 'I have friends that you will like, and I—I am not distasteful to you in any way, or am I?'

'You do indeed seem different,' Georgia admitted, 'but what do I know about you? We are alone. No well-brought-up young woman would travel alone with a man; you know that as well as I do.'

'This is different,' the Duke pointed out. 'We are not an ordinary couple, or, as you put it, a well-brought-up young woman and a gentleman travelling together for pleasure. We are instruments of war! That is how you must think of yourself, Georgia, a weapon with which to fight Bonaparte.'

He saw her chin go up.

'I am sorry,' she said, 'for being so feather-brained. Forgive me.'

'That is easy,' he replied, 'and I prefer you when you are not so aggressive. I promise you, Georgia, that the first time I saw you I was terrified of you. "An Amazon!" I said to myself, and until now I have seen no reason to reverse that impression.'

She laughed.

'I wish I could think of myself as an Amazon.'

'Do you know what else I thought?' the Duke asked.

'No, what was it?'

'I felt sorry for your husband,' the Duke said. 'And, by the way, he might not be so easily convinced that you were a weapon of war at this particular moment.'

He was amused to see her blush.

'I have no wish to discuss my husband,' she said stiffly.

'Nor have I,' the Duke answered. 'But one satisfaction is that, so long as her husband does not object, a married woman can do far more outrageous things than a young girl.'

'What sort of outrageous things?' Georgia inquired.

'Travelling alone across country with another man, for one,' the Duke teased, 'and because you are married there is nothing to prevent you listening to compliments and even having a little flirt, should it please you.'

'That is Society stuff, and I have no desire for it,' Georgia flared up.

The Duke laughed.

'Now you are being an Amazon again, and I am utterly at a loss.'

'You are being quite nonsensical,' she said, rising to her feet. 'Come, let us ride to London.'

It was growing dusk when the Duke pulled up the horses in Half Moon Street.

'Will you wait here,' he asked, 'while I speak with a friend of mine?'

'You will not be long?' Georgia begged, in a curiously childlike voice.

He realised that the busy streets, the grand horses, the well-dressed passers-by and the curious glances she had received from some of the men, were beginning to unnerve her.

The Duke called a boy who was loitering against the railings and told him to hold his horse.

'Look after this lady,' he said, giving the boy a coin which made his eyes pop out of his head. 'And if anyone annoys her, come and fetch me. I shall be in the house opposite.'

He did not wait for an answer, but strolling across the street he hammered on an elegant silver knocker. The door was opened almost immediately by a manservant.

'Is Captain Carrington in?' the Duke inquired.

'He is upstairs, sir,' the man replied.

The Duke ran up the stairs and burst into the sitting-room to find Pereguine lazing on a sofa, with a glass of brandy in his hand.

'By Jove, Trydon, I didn't expect you!' he exclaimed as the Duke entered. Then he added in tones of horror:

'What the devil have you done to my coat?'

'I will buy you another,' the Duke replied absently. 'Listen, Pereguine. I need your help.'

'I should think you do indeed!' Pereguine ejaculated, 'and my boots! Really, Trydon, you look a real out-and outer. What can you have been doing with yourself?'

'It's a long story,' the Duke began.

'And before you begin,' Pereguine interrupted, 'I want to tell you what a hell of a time I've had. There was a real confubble when it was found that you were absent. Your godmama was not at all satisfied with my explanation, and as for that Dalguish girl, she walked about looking as though someone had sat on her by mistake.'

'Yes, yes,' the Duke said impatiently. 'You must tell me all about it another time. Listen, Pereguine, I have a woman outside . . .'

'A woman!' Pereguine exclaimed 'But I thought you had given up females for good.'

'She is not a female,' the Duke replied. 'Well, not exactly. As a matter of fact she is a smuggler.'

'A smuggler? Are you out of your senses?'

'For heaven's sake stop interrupting,' the Duke demanded, 'and let me tell you the whole story. And while I am trying to talk, be obliging enough to give me a glass of brandy, for my throat's like a rattle-trap.'

'All I can say is that I'm not lending you my gear again,' Pereguine grumbled as he poured out the brandy. 'Jason will have a stroke when he sees those boots.'

'Stop talking about clothes,' the Duke said. 'This is important business, Pereguine, this is something that concerns England.'

He was glad to see that his words had an effect and Pereguine was suddenly serious as the Duke sat down and began to recount his tale. When he was finished, making it clear that Georgia had no idea of his identity, Pereguine was wide-eyed.

'Never have I heard such a story!' he exclaimed. 'If I didn't know you to be a sober chap, Trydon, I would think you had been on a bosky brawl for these past forty-eight hours.'

'It's all true, every word of it,' the Duke said. 'Now, what are we going to do about Georgia? For one thing, she has got to be decently dressed if we are to take her to Carlton House, and that, you must admit, is the place where we are most likely to find this assassin.'

'Is she presentable?' Pereguine asked.

'She could look passable if she was properly gowned,' the Duke answered. 'You must see, Pereguine, our only chance of catching this man out is first to find out who he is and then have him watched.'

'And this woman, this smuggler, is the only person who knows what he looks like,' Pereguine said slowly.

'You are getting quite quick on the uptake,' the Duke retorted sarcastically.

'Very well then,' Pereguine went on, 'there is only one person we can take her to.'

'Who is that?' the Duke asked.

'My grandmother,' Pereguine replied.

The Duke looked at him incredulously.

'Your grandmother? You mean the Dowager?'

'If ever there was an old girl who was up to snuff it is my grandmother,' Pereguine said. 'She was a pretty high-stepper in her day! Caused innumerable scandals and is the only woman who has ever driven a six-in-hand round

Hyde Park. What is more, I suspicion, she would enjoy a plot like this to the utmost.'

'If you really think it is the best thing to do . . .' the Duke began, as the door opened and Georgia walked in.

'I am embarrassed by waiting outside,' she said a little plaintively. 'People are staring at me. So I thought I would come and find you.'

'I was just coming out,' the Duke replied. 'Let me introduce my friend Captain Pereguine Carrington—Mistress Baillie.'

As he spoke he was amused to see that Pereguine was staring at Georgia in some surprise.

'Is this the smuggler?' he asked in an aside to the Duke. 'I thought you said she was a hefty Amazon.'

'An Amazon, but not hefty,' the Duke corrected. 'Georgia, I have told Pereguine our story, and he has agreed to help us.'

'I am glad of that,' Georgia answered, 'because I'm tired. And despite what I said about not falling from the saddle, I think if I have to go much further that is exactly what I shall do.'

'Oh, come and sit down!' Pereguine invited her. 'You oughtn't to be here, you know that. Not in a gentleman's rooms, it's not done, you know.'

'Not done by whom?' Georgia asked with a hint of laughter in her voice. 'By well-bred ladies, or by smugglers and Amazons?'

'By females,' Pereguine replied seriously.

Georgia gave a tired little laugh.

'This female is undoubtedly an exception,' she retorted.

7

GEORGIA sank down on a sofa and accepted gratefully a glass of wine which Pereguine brought her. She felt that in some way the two men were embarrassed by her position, and because the knowledge made her shy she asked nervously:

'Have I done something wrong? Would you prefer that I had remained outside with the horses?'

Pereguine glanced at the Duke, who said quietly:

'It is of no consequence, except that it is considered unconventional for a lady to enter a gentleman's rooms.'

'But I am married,' Georgia said defensively.

The Duke smiled.

'I'm afraid that would not make your action any more acceptable to those who fabricate the rules about such matters.'

Georgia flushed.

'Perhaps it would be best if I left at once,' she said, making as if she would rise from the sofa.

'No! No!' the Duke said hastily. 'The harm is done, if harm there be, and we have much to discuss. My friend Captain Carrington has solved one of our problems by suggesting that he should take you to stay with his grandmother—the Dowager Lady Carrington.'

Both men saw the dismay on Georgia's face before she stammered:

'N . . . no . . . no, I could not impose myself on a stranger.'

'Unfortunately there is no alternative if we are to put our plan into operation,' the Duke insisted. 'It will not be for long, only until we find the Frenchman you carried across the Channel. But if you are not under patronage of

100

one of the Beau Monde, then it will not be possible for us to obtain an invitation for you to Carlton House.'

'I understand,' Georgia said in a low voice.

She bent her head and her dusty velvet riding-hat hid the troubled expression on her face.

'Will you allow me,' Pereguine said, breaking the somewhat uncomfortable silence, 'to leave you for a few moments. I have to write a note of apology to my hostess with whom I should be dining within an hour. I will send my man with it, and then we can repair to my grand-mother's.'

He went from the room and the Duke followed him. They left the door ajar and Georgia heard the Duke say:

'First ask your man to convey the horses to my stables and tell them to despatch a coach here immediately.'

The fact that he owned stables sounded affluent, and Georgia thought with a sense of relief that, though he might be in trouble, it could not be connected with finance. She was glad of this because, being so conscious herself of the difficulties where a lack of money was con-cerned, she had been afraid that she was involving Mr. Raven in an expenditure he could ill-afford. He had paid for the food they had eaten on their way to London, and at the posting-house she had heard him insist on the top grooms attending to the horses, and had seen the guineas from his purse change hands.

She had been awkwardly aware that she could not pay for herself. It had been foolish and indeed irresponsible that she had left Four Winds without any money. In the flurry of departure she had forgotten that once outside the village of Little Chadbury she must pay her way in coin, rather than in credit. During the last few miles of her jour-ney she had been wondering how she could confess her penury to her companion, but somehow she could not find the words.

Sitting now in Pereguine Carrington's elegantly fur-nished room, with his sporting prints mingling with what were obviously ancestors in their gilt frames, with valuable polished furniture and rich damask hangings, she felt sud-denly afraid. This was a world of which she had no knowledge. The thought of having to stay with a noblewoman, who she was convinced would despise her, made Georgia long, with an almost passionate desire, to run away. She wanted to find refuge at Four Winds. There things might be difficult, there might be the problem of smuggling, of risking her own life and the lives of the men who served her, but at least she was amongst people she knew and understood. London was unknown and therefore terrifying.

As the Duke came back into the room, without thinking she sprang to her feet and walked towards him.

'Please take me back,' she pleaded in a low voice. 'I cannot stay. I shall do you no good. Indeed, I shall but shame you. Please, Mr. Raven, take me home.'

'Why?' he asked quietly, in his low deep voice. 'What has upset you?'

Instinctively her hand went out to touch his arm and she raised her face to his.

'I am afraid,' she whispered.

He saw the fear in her eyes and the trembling of her lips. For a moment he looked at her incredulously; then, because he had seen men look the same way when they were about to go into battle, he knew instinctively what to do.

'You afraid? I cannot credit such a thing!' he said sharply. 'Remember how I saw you last night, commanding a crew of tough men, facing without flinching the bullets that flew around our heads, and you did not even appear squeamish! Most women would have had the vapours and been in hysterics. And if I remember rightly it was you who told the men to go home; who was ready to assist me carry a dying man into the caves. It was you who waited calmly while I deposited him in the sea. And yet, now, you are afraid!'

He saw some of the panic recede from her face, but she still trembled.

'I still wish to return to the country,' she said in a calmer tone of voice. 'I shall be useless to you, you must be aware of that.'

'And I shall be useless without you,' the Duke replied. 'How can I identify a man I have never seen?'

'How can we be certain that he is in London?' Georgia said faintly

'You know he is here,' the Duke said 'You know what task he has to do, and you know that you and I have to prevent it. Courage, Georgia! It is a quality you have not lacked until now.'

There was silence and then she said:

'If I have been brave in the past it was because I was fighting not for myself but for someone else.'

'Good God!' the Duke ejaculated. 'Who do you think you are fighting for now? You are fighting for your brother and the country which he is serving. You are fighting for every man, woman and child in this island. Can you not understand what it would mean if we were overrun by Bonaparte? Have you no idea of the suffering, the privation and the hunger which is endured in the European countries now under the dictator's heel? I have seen the peasants who have been driven from their homes by the enemy, cluttering the roadsides, hungry, thirsty, possessing nothing except what they carry on their backs.'

The Duke paused as Georgia sank down on the sofa again and put her head in her hands.

'The death of the Prince,' he went on, 'would undermine morale and cause political and national disturbance, which might prove fatal to this country. If ever you needed to be brave and resolute, Georgia, it is now.'

She took her hands from her face, and he saw that while she was very pale there were no tears in her eyes.

'I am sorry,' she said humbly, 'forgive me. I was thinking only for myself.'

'That is better,' he said approvingly. 'And you will find that Pereguine's grandmother is not nearly so formidable as a fog at sea or a Revenue cutter.'

A faint smile twisted Georgia's lips.

'I am sorry,' she repeated, 'it is just that I have such a hatred of Society. If this lady is old, she will be different, will she not?'

It was a plea and the Duke understood.

'Very different from your stepmother's guests,' he said. 'And I promise you something else: you will not be alone. Pereguine and I will do everything in our power to protect you from the type of person you fear.'

He saw a sudden flash in Georgia's eyes and knew this was the reassurance she really needed.

'It's Ravenscroft who is at the back of this,' he thought. 'God damn him! One day I will get even with that cur!'

Pereguine came hurrying into the room.

'Everything is arranged,' he said to the Duke. 'The carriage should be here in a few moments, and we do not have to go far; my grandmother has a house in Grosvenor Square.'

'That is indeed convenient,' the Duke said. He walked to the window. 'The carriage is below. Come, Georgia.'

He helped her rise from the sofa, and was conscious that her fingers were cold. He could not help thinking it extraordinary that she should be so afraid; and then, remembering the conversation he had overheard with Caroline Grazebrook he understood.

Pereguine went ahead. The Duke still held Georgia's hand. They were alone, and suddenly he remembered what he should have told her.

'Listen, Georgia,' he said, 'there is something I must impart to you . . .'

But before he could say more Pereguine reappeared in the doorway.

'We had best make haste,' he urged. 'My grandmother will not be best pleased if we arrive in the middle of dinner. She dislikes above all things to be disturbed at a meal.'

'Then we must not delay,' the Duke said.

He had been about to tell Georgia the truth about his identity. He cursed himself for having left it so long, but he had not wished to disturb what trust she had in him. He had a feeling that once she knew that he was a Duke it would create a new barrier between them, and one that might make their task even more difficult than it was already.

All the same, on the short journey to Grosvenor Square, as he sat beside Georgia on the soft padded seat, with Pereguine opposite, he found himself rehearsing in his mind how he could explain to her the reason for his subterfuge. She might be curious as to why he had pretended he was in trouble, and if he were to say it was no pretence, she might learn the truth that he had been running away from women and marriage.

'To hell with them!' he muttered beneath his breath.

Georgia was peering through the carriage window.

'How tall the houses are!' she exclaimed, 'and there are so many people about. Look, there is a performing bear, and a man with a monkey in a red coat! My mother used to tell me about such things when I was a child, but I never thought to see them.'

'There are far too many beggars in the street,' the Duke remarked.

Pereguine laughed.

'You sound as pompous as an alderman,' he said accusingly. 'You must not permit him to be so stiff-necked, Mistress Baillie.'

Georgia looked at the Duke with curious eyes.

'Is he stiff-necked,' she asked. 'I have never thought that he was. I do not care for people who laugh too much.'

The Duke knew that she was thinking of Caroline's guests and said hastily:

'That's a set-down for you, Pereguine! You must be more circumspect in the future.'

'Do you know what I think, Mistress Baillie?' Pereguine asked.

'No, what?' Georgia inquired.

'I think that, from the little my friend Trydon has been able to tell me, you have been taking life far too seriously. You are young and pretty: you must learn to be gay.'

'Me pretty?' Georgia asked, picking woman-like on the word which referred to her appearance. She sounded incredulous.

'Yes, pretty!' Pereguine said firmly. 'Wait until you are all dolled up in your fal-de-lals. My grandmother will know exactly where to purchase such embellishments and then you will surprise us all!'

Georgia bent forward in her seat.

'Are you persuaded of this?' she asked. 'I know I have no appearance garbed as I am now, but if you are really convinced that I shall not embarrass you and Mr. Raven, then I shall not be so apprehensive. Or are you just funning?'

'I promise you,' Pereguine replied, 'lick my finger and cross my heart, as the children say, that I am speaking the truth. Dolled up, you will be well up to snuff and a deal more.'

'Oh, I wish I believed you,' Georgia said.

Pereguine reached out and took her hand.

'Would you like to bet on it?' he asked.

Georgia looked confused and he continued:

'I'll wager my gold signet-ring for one of your

gloves—which had best be on your hands before you meet my grandmama—that when Trydon and I take you to Carlton House all the gentlemen in the room will be asking your name.'

'You are nonsensical!' Georgia protested with a little gurgle of laughter. 'But if I could credit a quarter of what you say, then, indeed, I would feel less timid!'

'Believe it all,' Pereguine answered, and bending his head he kissed her hand.

The Duke watched them with a puzzled expression on his face. It was unlike Pereguine to take so much trouble over any female. But he was well aware that his friend was giving Georgia confidence in herself, sweeping away her apprehensions.

It was hard to take her fears seriously. He wondered how many women of his acquaintance could endure physically all that Georgia had been through in the last twenty-four hours and not collapse. Yet when they arrived at the Dowager Lady Carrington's house in Grosvenor Square, Georgia stepped lithely out of the coach and entered the big marble hall with her head held high.

'I had best have a word with my grandmother alone,' Pereguine said hastily. He waved the major-domo aside and opened a door leading off the hall.

'You and Georgia can wait here,' he said to the Duke.

He ushered them into a white-panelled sitting-room, with great vases of hot-house flowers scenting the air. Although it was summer, a fire was burning in the grate. Pereguine smiled reassuringly at Georgia and shut the door.

'It is very grand,' Georgia said in an awed voice, looking round her. Then before the Duke could answer she added:

'Suppose Her Ladyship will not permit me to stay?'

'In that case we shall have to think of someone else to chaperon you,' the Duke replied.

'You are all so sure of yourselves, are you not?' Georgia said accusingly. 'I like your friend Captain Carrington, but I feel his life has been a singularly comfortable existence. He has never had to worry or to take risks. Everything has gone smoothly for him.'

'When we were fighting on the Peninsula,' the Duke answered quietly, 'some of our men, a troop of them, ran into an ambush. When it was dark, Pereguine and two of his sergeants went out alone on foot. They carried twelve men who were wounded, but still alive, to safety. They did it right under the noses of the French. Only because it was a dark night and pouring with rain were they not observed!'

There was a pregnant silence. Then Georgia said humbly:

'I am sorry! I always seem to be saying that, but I did not understand. I thought that people who were gay and laughed a lot must be utterly carefree or even licentious.'

'May I say something without offence?' the Duke asked.

'Of course,' she replied.

'The men and women you have met with your stepmother are not members of what is understood by Society. The men might have titles, but by decent people they are considered to be bounders and are despised, and the women would not be accepted. I am being brutally frank, but I hope you will forgive me.'

'It is what I thought myself,' Georgia answered, 'but I suppose I was too stupid to put it into words.'

'Not at all!' the Duke contradicted. 'You were too well bred to understand the half-world in which such creatures thrive.'

'My mother was so different,' Georgia said softly, 'but she seldom went to London. She and my father were very happy in the country and they were not interested in balls, receptions or dinner parties. They just wanted to be together. I think . . . I think that was why my father was so lonely after she died, and why . . . he married again.'

'He obviously had no understanding of the type of woman he chose,' the Duke said harshly.

'You can have no conception of what my stepmother is like,' Georgia said miserably.

The Duke did not enlighten her. Instead, he realised that this was the moment when he must tell Georgia the truth about himself, but once again he had left it too late. Even as he started to speak the door opened and Pereguine came in.

'My grandmama is enraptured,' he proclaimed. 'There is nothing she enjoys more than an intrigue! She is prepared, Mistress Baillie, to welcome you with open arms, while the idea of providing you with new gowns has taken twenty years off her life. She is as excited as a débutante planning for her first ball!'

'Oh, I am so relieved!' Georgia breathed. 'I was afraid Her Ladyship would cast me out.'

'She is already hoping that you will not be too swift in finding the Frenchman you seek,' Pereguine said reassuringly.

The Duke frowned.

'You have begged your grandmother to be discreet?' he asked.

'You don't know the Dowager,' Pereguine replied. 'You could trust her with the secrets of the whole War Office and she would not divulge them to a soul. She is not a loquacious tittle-tattler, like half the old ladies you see powwowing at Almack's!'

'I apologise,' the Duke said with a little bow.

'Come and find out for yourself,' Pereguine said to Georgia.

He held open the door for her to precede him through it, and then turned back to the Duke.

'Have you told her who you are?' he asked in a low voice.

The Duke shook his head.

'I told Grandmama that you were incognito,' he said, 'but a slip of the tongue is so easy. If you take my advice you will leave Mistress Baillie with me. I'll effect the introductions, then meet you at your house.'

'Very well,' the Duke said.

He felt almost disappointed that he would not be present at the meeting of the two women, but he remembered that he was urgently in need of a bath and a change of clothes.

'Good night, Georgia,' he said, holding out his hand.

'You are leaving me?' she asked, her eyes instantly apprehensive.

'You need sleep,' he answered. 'I shall call tomorrow morning and we can then make our plans.'

He felt her fingers clinging to his as he raised her hand conventionally to his lips.

'Poor child!' he thought compassionately as he stepped into his coach.

An hour later, when he had bathed and changed, there was still no sign of Pereguine. Then as the Duke sipped a glass of wine an idea came to him. He remembered something which had lain in the back of his mind for so long, that he had, until this moment, forgotten it.

When he was first infatuated with Caroline he had wakened one night in her bed, shaped like a silver shell, to realise that she was not beside him. There was no light in the room, save a gentle glow which came from a dying fire. For a moment, half between sleep and wakefulness, he had wondered vaguely where she could be. Then through half-closed eyes he saw her coming through a door which led to the adjoining room in which he had undressed.

She seemed almost like a ghost in her diaphanous nightgown, moving with bare feet silently over the carpet. Then he saw that she carried something in her hand. For a moment he would not admit even to himself that he knew what it was, but the truth was inescapable.

He had won heavily at the tables that evening. Caroline had sat beside him, and he had given her half his winnings. She had played too, but very cautiously, and they had both left laden with gold. Caroline had put the guineas he had given her into a drawer in her dressing-table. She had made some laughing remark about it as she had done so. He had left his coins in the other room beside his discarded clothes.

He had not troubled to count what he had won, and he knew as he watched Caroline cross the room that in the morning he would not have missed what she had taken. At the same time, considering what he had already given her, he felt both irritated and repulsed by her greed.

She stood for a moment in the light of the fire looking down at the money. Her body was silhouetted against the light and, despite his anger, because she was so beautiful he felt himself stir with desire. She had swiftly opened the wardrobe door and taken down from the top shelf a round cardboard hat-box, such as the milliners use when they deliver their customers' hats and bonnets.

He had heard a faint clink as Caroline placed the money inside. She closed the hat-box and returned it to the top shelf of the wardrobe. Softly Caroline fastened the wardrobe door and turned towards the bed. For a moment he had thought to upbraid her, to tell her what he had seen, but as she crossed the firelight he knew it was of little import. There was something more urgent to be said and done. He reached out his arms and drew her down beside him . . .

He had, in fact, never referred to the incident, but he thought now that if in the past Caroline had used a hat-box as a hiding place for her valuables it was unlikely that she would have changed her habit in the passing years.

The Duke had been feeling tired and his muscles were still aching from the journey across the Channel, but now he suddenly felt vigorous and energetic. He set down his glass and jumped to his feet. He told his butler to ask Captain Carrington to not wait for him when he arrived.

'I do not know when I will be back, Hargraves. Tell Chef that I will dine when I return.'

'Your coach is not at the door, your Grace,' the butler replied. 'Shall I send for it?'

'I have not far to go,' the Duke replied. 'I will walk.'

'But your Grace . . . !' the butler would have expostulated, only to find that his master was already halfway down the street.

The Duke casually without being really interested had asked Georgia where her stepmother lived. Georgia had replied that her father had bought Caroline a house in Charles Street. It was, in fact, only a few minutes' walk from the Duke's house in Berkeley Square. Reaching the front door, he saw the curtains were pulled and no light in the hall: obviously Caroline had not yet returned to London.

'Which,' the Duke said to himself, 'is exactly what I had hoped.'

He turned into the mews which lay at the back of Charles Street. There were few people about. In the stables the grooms were rubbing down their horses and paying no attention to any passers-by.

The Duke had made more difficult climbs, but not perhaps such adventurous ones as getting up to the first-floor window by a drain-pipe which ended in a water-butt. He had seen that the window was open, and it took him only a few seconds to lift it and get his legs inside.

He found himself in the narrow part of an L-shaped drawing-room. The room was in darkness. After listening for a few moments to discover if there was anyone about, the Duke lit a candle from a tinder-box he found after groping around on what was obviously a writing-desk. The light of the candle revealed a very elegantly appointed room. The curtains and the covers were in Caroline's favourite strawberry pink. There were china knick-knacks everywhere—the Duke remembered that her taste had always made him shudder.

Carrying the candle, the Duke opened the door on to the stairway. He knew how these houses were planned. There would be a dining-room and a small morning-room at ground level, with Caroline's bedroom situated on the floor above where he was. The servants would be safely down below in the dark, damp basement.

He climbed the staircase. Caroline's bed he noted was no longer a silver shell but draped with pale chiffon curtains hanging from a corona of gold angels. Having lighted three candles on the dressing-table, he inspected the cupboards. There were four doors and he opened three before he found a cupboard which had a shelf on which reposed several hat-boxes.

He lifted two and decided they were too light to be interesting, but the third was heavy. He took it down and found just as he had anticipated: it was Caroline's hiding place, her personal safe in which she kept her secrets as a squirrel keeps his hoard of nuts.

There were jewel-cases, some loose money, and two piles of papers and letters. The Duke put down the hat-box and taking the first pile undid the ribbon with which they were tied. He opened a piece of paper reposing on the top. He read it, and his expression was grim as he read the next, and yet the next.

Caroline, he discovered, was making a considerable income from blackmail, and a peculiarly unpleasant type of blackmail at that! The Duke knew just the type of young man whom she would discover doing something illegal or at least indiscreet. Caroline would make it plain that if she revealed what she knew it would mean the destruction of his career or his good name. Her victims were all very young men, like Charles Grazebook. Caroline was a very experienced and seductive Circe and there was no escape for her willing slaves.

The Duke put the first pile of letters into the breast pocket of his coat and turned to the other pile which was smaller. Charles Grazebrook's confession was the first piece of paper he opened. There were others, but the Duke

111

did not trouble to read them. He added them to the first pile in his breast pocket. Then he picked up the hat-box. As he did so he realised that there had been a considerable amount of noise going on below for some time. There had been voices, doors shutting and opening, but because he had been so intent on what he was doing he had paid no heed.

Now, as he placed the hat-box back on to the shelf, he heard someone coming up the stairs. There was no mistaking that sharp voice, which could be so beguiling when it desired.

'Get the tapers lighted! Bring up a bottle of wine from the cellar. Tell Cook that I will require dinner for eight in an hour's time, and be quick about it. If you can't do the job for which you are employed, I will find someone who can.'

The Duke just had time to close the wardrobe door, jump across the room and throw himself down on the bed. As Caroline flung open the door, he was lying back with his head on the pillows smiling at her.

'Who the devil . . .' Caroline gave a little scream. 'Who are you . . . ? What . . . ?' she began, and then her voice changed. 'Trydon . . . Trydon, you have come back to me.'

8

GEORGIA stood in Madame Bertin's salon in Bond Street. She had been standing for over three hours, trying on ball-gowns, carriage-dresses, morning half-dresses and pelisses: having muslins, gauzes, thread-lace and satin polonaise draped around her, pinned here and there, and then waiting for the verdict from the Dowager.

Lady Carrington sat in state in a high-backed chair, her lorgnettes to her eyes, and a small black boy seated at her feet. Despite her age, the Dowager was dressed in the height of fashion, and from her neck cascaded row upon row of magnificent oriental pearls. Every time she moved her arm there was a jingle of diamond bracelets and a flash of the many rings she wore on her long, bony fingers.

She was formidable, frightening and quite incredibly fascinating. Georgia had entered her presence quaking at the knees, and yet by the time they had retired to bed she knew that in Pereguine's grandmother she had both a friend and an ally.

'Hideous!' the Dowager exclaimed now. 'Take it away, Madame Bertin. Can you not see that that pastel shade throws into prominence the child's sun-touched skin. Why a young lady of quality should be roaming about in the sun without a parasol to protect her complexion I cannot conceive!'

Lady Carrington looked at Georgia as she spoke, and there was a twinkle in her eye and an almost roguish twist to her lips. Georgia knew that the Dowager was teasing, knowing full well why her protégée's skin was darker than fashion decreed.

'You are wise, m'lady,' Madame Bertin agreed. 'Mademoiselle's beautiful eyes are not enhanced by the pastel, but bright colours for her are *ravissante. Mais pour une jeune fille* such vivid colours are not *comme il faut.*'

'Mademoiselle is not a *jeune fille*,' Lady Carrington replied sharply. 'Have you not noticed her wedding-ring?'

'Indeed, m'lady, I did perceive that Madame was wearing a ring on her left hand,' Madame Bertin replied. 'But I thought to myself that it could not be a token of anything so serious as *le mariage*. Madame appears so young, so unsophisticated, so innocent! I could not credit that she was already wed. *Je m'excuse*, I am at fault, my felicitations, madame.'

'Thank you,' Georgia answered a little uncomfortably.

'Now I understand,' Madame Bertin went on, 'why your Ladyship has chosen the apple-blossom sarsnet, the eau-de-nil gauze, the batiste with the emerald-green ribbons. For a married lady they are in perfect taste, and how proud Monsieur will be to have such an attractive wife.'

When they had first entered the shop Georgia had imagined that they were going to purchase just two dresses, one evening-gown for her to wear at Carlton House and a muslin for the day, to replace the shabby velvet riding-habit in which she had journeyed to London. But to her surprise the Dowager had seemed scandalised at such cheese-paring.

'You will need at least a dozen gowns,' she said positively and began ordering without even consulting Georgia.

Terrified of what debt she might be incurring, Georgia had hurried to the formidable old lady's side and whispered:

'But, ma'am, who will pay for these things? I assure you that I have no money, and I could not permit Mr. Raven . . .'

'I should think not indeed,' the Dowager interrupted, 'that would be inconceivable! No, dear, this is my contribution towards the adventure!'

'But, ma'am, you do not know me, I cannot allow . . .' Georgia said, only to be shushed into silence with a wave of an imperious hand.

'You must allow me to enjoy myself,' the Dowager said. ' 'Tis a long time since I had someone young and pretty to consider. I had a figure like yours when I was your age, but alas the fashions did not allow me to show it.'

After that Georgia made no protest: but she felt, as every new gown was approved and chosen, that she was incurring an agonising debt, which she would never be able to repay.

The small black boy, dressed in a brilliant emerald-green coat with gold buttons and a turban to match, watched impassively. Occasionally he had to jump to his feet to pick up the Dowager's ivory-handled stick which had fallen to the floor. Once he fell asleep and was prodded awake by the sharp point of his mistress's shoe. The old lady wore a directoire gown of purple satin, and her high-peaked bonnet was trimmed with a whole flurry of ostrich feathers of the same hue. To Georgia she made a fantastic picture.

Finally, when Georgia felt she was about to collapse with exhaustion, finding that fitting clothes in the hot and stuffy little shop was far more tiring than crossing the Channel, the Dowager declared that they had enough.

'All these must be finished today,' she said.

'*Hélas!* It is impossible, m'lady!' Madame Bertin exclaimed. 'Two, perhaps three, will be delivered at Grosvenor Square by dinner-time. The rest—tomorrow morning. My girls must work all night.'

'Very well,' the Dowager conceded, 'but I know you would not wish the latest and most sensational beauty to burst upon London not to be decently robed in your distinctive creations.'

Georgia stared at her in perplexity. She had not thought Madame Bertin's extravagant compliments worth listening to. She might come from the country, but she was not addle-brained and she recognised the flattery with which the dressmaker boosted her sales. But for the Dowager to say she was a beauty took her by surprise.

As if she sensed what Georgia was feeling, Lady Carrington smiled.

'Now you must wear the white muslin with the turquoise-blue ribbons,' she said. 'Robe her, Madame Bertin, and order the shopkeeper next door to bring lotions, powders and lip-salve. The child's face looks naked, and that is something I never could abide.'

A dozen hands seemed to Georgia to be helping her into her new garments. She felt embarrassed, for the delicate muslin was almost transparent. She thought apprehensively that she must be too thin, for, when she and Nana were alone at Four Winds, the meals were scanty and consisted only of things procurable off the estate.

She hoped that Mr. Raven would not be shocked by her ultra-fashionable attire. She had a sudden desire to see admiration in his eyes, rather than the expression with which he habitually regarded her. She had a feeling, though she could not put it into words, that she amused him, and that he looked on her as a rather tiresome rampageous boy.

Thinking of Mr. Raven she found herself wondering how, in the circumstances, he had such rich and influential friends. He was in trouble, he had told her so; and yet here he was returning to London, arranging for his friend Pereguine to introduce her to his grandmother, and making plans for them all to be invited to Carlton House. How could he do it and yet be a fugitive, riding alone over the downs?

Georgia's thoughts were so intent on Trydon Raven that she hardly noticed what was being done to her face or that finally a high-brimmed bonnet had been placed on her head, its ribbons tied under her tiny chin.

'*Viola!*' Madame Bertin exclaimed. '*C'est merveilleux, n'est-ce pas?* A picture, m'lady, a picture which only an artist such as I myself could have created!'

'You have done well,' Lady Carrington said approvingly. 'Turn round, child, and let me look at you.'

But Georgia was transfixed, staring at her own reflection in the mirror. As the assistants who had been robing her moved away, she had a full view of their handiwork. For a moment she could hardly believe that she saw herself.

The white muslin, of an almost cobweb fineness, clung to her figure revealing every soft curve of it, but showing too the sweetness of her immaturity. Turquoise ribbons, which could only have come from France, cupped her small breasts, falling in a cascade to the hem of her gown. The little cut-away coatee which covered her shoulders and the upper part of her arms was of turquoise taffeta, and the same colour was echoed in the ribbons of her high-peaked bonnet and in the shell-like feathers which peeped over the brim. The bonnet made her face look very small, but her eyes seemed enormous, her lips very red. A touch of cucumber lotion and hand-pressed powder on her skin had taken away the colour burnt into it by the sun and the chill breezes of the sea. Only her hands still betrayed her, and Madame Bertin, as if she sensed her thoughts, brought her a pair of long turquoise-blue gloves, which matched the rest of her ensemble.

'Is this really me?' Georgia asked half to herself.

'Madame will know who it is when the gentlemen's glasses are raised to toast her,' Madame Bertin smiled.

'I hope they will do nothing of the sort,' the Dowager snapped. 'A lady's name should never be mentioned by gentlemen, as well you know.'

The Frenchwoman's eyes twinkled.

'I have often been told that your Ladyship was the toast of St. James's, and that you were known over the whole breadth and length of London as "The Incomparable of Incomparables".'

'Stuff and nonsense!' Lady Carrington retorted, but nevertheless she smiled. 'I was a madcap! Let us hope that Mistress Baillie is more circumspect in her behaviour than I was.'

'You must have had a wonderful time!' Georgia interposed.

'We were certainly very gay,' the old lady conceded. 'And we were more frank and outspoken in my day. Now there is too much mealy-mouthed, hypocritical prosing over the iniquities of the younger generation. Too many frusty old Dowagers, of whom I hope I shall never be one, making rules which merely restrict the young from enjoying themselves. Almack's is becoming nothing more than a ladies' chatterie, and a dead bore it is too.'

The Dowager paused suddenly, as if interrupting herself in one of her favourite discourses. 'Nevertheless, child, you will find it entertaining. We will go there tonight—that is, if my grandson will be so obliging as to escort us. We will ask him, for I have commanded him to partake of luncheon with us and he should be waiting.'

She turned towards the door, her little black boy running ahead to pull it open for her.

'And what would m'Lady wish done with the riding-habit in which Mistress Baillie arrived?' Madame Bertin inquired.

'Burn it!' Lady Carrington ordered before Georgia could speak. 'Burn it, and burn the past with it. It is always wise to start life afresh when one is in a new environment.'

Georgia longed to countermand the order but she didn't

dare. What, she wondered, was going to happen when she returned home to Four Winds? She would have no riding-habit and would be unable to afford another. For a moment she contemplated protesting, but already the Dowager was out in the street. The footmen had jumped down from the back of the coach and were helping their mistress through the painted door with its resplendent coat of arms.

There was nothing Georgia could do but follow. All the same, she paused long enough to put out her hand and say to Madame Bertin:

'Thank you, I can never thank you enough.'

'*Mais,* Madame, it is always a privilege to dress *une femme si élégante,*' Madame Bertin replied.

Georgia hurried into the carriage, and the horse, restless from having been kept waiting, started off at a brisk trot towards Berkeley Square.

'I know not what to say,' Georgia began softly.

'Say nothing, child,' the Dowager replied, 'I have enjoyed this morning more than I have enjoyed anything for a long time. If you only knew how depressing one's own contemporaries can be you will understand that I welcome the opportunity to be with young people. Tonight we will go to Almack's, tomorrow to Carlton House.'

'Are . . . are you sure?' Georgia stammered.

'Sure of what?' the Dowager inquired.

'That I . . . I shall be allowed in,' Georgia explained.

'You can go anywhere and everywhere under my patronage,' Lady Carrington said proudly. 'I may be old, but I am still of consequence in the *beau monde,* and I shall be proud of you.'

She patted Georgia's hand as she spoke.

' 'Tis a pity nevertheless,' she went on, 'that you are already wed. It would have amused me to do a little matchmaking. Unfortunately I was not blessed with a granddaughter.'

'Yes, I am already married,' Georgia said quickly, 'and to tell the truth, ma'am, I have no interest in Society gentlemen. In fact, I hate them!'

The Dowager looked at her in surprise.

'And what has happened?' she asked, 'to make you feel like that.'

Georgia flushed.

'It is nothing I can explain, ma'am, just that I know these gentlemen for what they are—loathsome, evil and lustful.'

'Strong words!' the Dowager remarked. 'And would you apply such description to my grandson Pereguine, and to his friend Trydon?'

Georgia looked embarrassed.

'No, ma'am . . . indeed I am afraid I have been exceedingly rude. I was not speaking of Captain Carrington, who has been extremely kind to me, or indeed of Mr. Raven, who has been understanding and gentle beyond belief. B . . . but . . . of other people.'

'And who in particular?' the Dowager asked probingly.

Georgia turned her head away.

'I would rather not speak of it,' she said, and her voice trembled.

Lady Carrington was wise enough not to pursue the subject. On their arrival at Berkeley Square the red carpet was laid across the pavement and they walked into the hall.

'Is Captain Carrington here?' Lady Carrington inquired of the butler.

'Yes, m'lady, he is in the library.'

Lady Carrington turned to Georgia with an air of conspiracy.

'Listen, child,' she said, 'I wish to see my grandson's face when you appear. I shall know then if I have been successful in turning you into a butterfly. Wait a few minutes, and then come into the library.'

She gave a chuckle and walked away down the marble hall.

Georgia could see that the transformation of herself was amusing from the Dowager's point of view, but from her own she was not so certain. She stared into the gilt mirror which hung over an elaborately carved marble-top table. She would have been lying to herself if she had denied that she looked pretty. Her blue eyes were wide, the lashes framing them were dark and silky. But she knew by the coldness of her fingers and the sudden trembling of her lips that she was apprehensive, not because of what Captain Carrington might think of her, but because she had seen two high beaver hats in the hall and knew that he was not in the library alone.

Suppose that the second gentleman waiting there was

disappointed? Suppose that after all the trouble the Dowager had taken this morning Mr. Raven decided in the end that he would not escort her to Carlton House?

Then Georgia told herself that there was nothing personal about Trydon's interest in her appearance. She was useful to him because she, and she alone, could identify the Frenchman she had brought across the Channel from France. It did not matter what she looked like. As long as she was tidy and presentable, he would drag her there if it suited his purpose. And once her task was done, he would be ready for her to return like an unwanted parcel to Four Winds.

The excitement that she had felt was dimmed, but pride came to her rescue. Instead of moving towards the library apprehensively she went there defiantly. Only as the doors were opened for her by two flunkeys did she feel her heart beat a little faster.

They were all three of them standing at the far end of the room by the mantelpiece and as she entered six eyes stared at her. Her first impression was that Mr. Raven was looking different. And then she knew it was because for the first time since she had known him he was dressed in the height of fashion. His dark green coat with pale satin lapels seemed to accentuate the breadth of his shoulders; his skin-tight pantaloons, the elegant waistcoat and gold fob made him seem someone very different from the man with whom she had ridden only the day before.

She had a sense of unreality, of having stepped into a world to which she was entirely alien. The Dowager, with her jewels and feathers, the gentlemen, with their polished Hessians and high, snowy cravats, seemed to belong to some fairy-tale she had imagined in her loneliness. Then Pereguine broke the silence.

'Good Lord!' he ejaculated, 'it can't be, but it is! Grandmama, you are a genius!'

Georgia could only laugh. As she walked towards them she realised that Mr. Raven had not spoken, but in his eyes there was something she had hoped to see. She put out her hand first to Pereguine, and because she was embarrassed she did not at once turn to his friend. She knew instinctively, as women know, that his eyes were on her face. She knew, without even having to look at him, that after that first glance he had perceived the elegance of her dress and perhaps the perfection of the figure beneath it. She was glad because she was a woman that her sun-touched hands were covered by the turquoise-blue gloves.

'Well, Trydon, what do you think?' the Dowager asked.

The Duke was still looking at Georgia and did not answer. Georgia, a little piqued by his silence, said impulsively:

'Yes, please tell us what you think. Are you still ashamed of me?'

'I have never been that,' he answered, 'but I am a little overwhelmed. I brought to London a very charming, unspoilt and unsophisticated country girl. I see now a sophisticated lady of fashion. I am not absolutely certain that I like the exchange.'

'Shame on you, Trydon, for a spoil-sport,' the Dowager cried. 'The child was hoping that you would pay her a pretty compliment, and why not? Madame Bertin—and who should be a better judge?—says that she will be the toast of London before the night is out.'

'I hope not,' the Duke replied.

Lady Carrington chuckled.

'That is exactly what I said myself! So vulgar! But at the same time Mâdame was not just paying a compliment: the child looks entrancing and well you know it.'

'The breath is squeezed out of my throat!' Pereguine exclaimed. 'I had expected Grandmama to perform wonders—she always does when I ask it of her—but I had not expected a miracle. Mistress Baillie—your servant.'

He made Georgia a low bow, and laughingly she dropped him a curtsey in return.

'Thank you for those kind words,' she said, 'I needed them. For I assure you that under all the fripperies I am as nervous as any ignorant milkmaid. And that is indeed what my stepmother always calls me.'

'Your stepmother?' the Dowager queried.

'It is a long story,' the Duke said quickly. 'May we relate it another time?'

'But of course,' the Dowager replied. 'Let us now proceed to the dining-room, for I declare shopping has made me quite hungry.'

She led the way across the room and Pereguine hurried to open the door for her. Georgia turned to the Duke.

'You are not pleased?' she asked, and her voice was anxious.

'Of course I am pleased,' he assured her, 'pleased for you and pleased that Her Ladyship has been so successful. But I'm rather afraid that the fine feathers will make you fly away.'

There was something in his voice which made Georgia drop her eyes. Then with a little glance at him from under her eyelashes she said:

'I assure you that for the moment I have no desire to fly anywhere, except perhaps to Almack's.'

'That is not exactly what I meant,' the Duke answered.

'No?' She glanced up at him again. 'Then, shall I promise you that I will not fly away, not until you permit me to do so?'

'That is what I had hoped you would say,' the Duke replied.

'But of course,' Georgia reminded him in a low voice, 'we may find the Frenchman tonight. And that would be the end, would it not?'

'Would it?' the Duke asked. 'I think you are the only person who can answer that question.'

Georgia had the feeling that their words were charged with so much more meaning than what they actually said. She did not know why talking in such a manner made her feel suddenly excited and brought a flush to her cheeks.

'Perhaps' she said, speaking in almost a whisper as now they reached the hall, 'perhaps life will seem sad and even empty when this adventure is over.'

As she spoke she thought to herself: 'I'm flirting! I'm flirting in the way he wants, and I can do it because I know that I look right. Because . . . oh, because I feel so different!'

The Duke had spent a busy morning going through the letters he had stolen from Caroline's hat-box. He had read them, put each one in an envelope and addressed it to its rightful owner. He had the feeling that he was bringing happiness and a relief from anxiety to a great number of foolish young men.

Finally there were only two letters left. One, Georgia's brother Charles had written in a scrawling, drunken hand, the other the Duke had first read and thrown aside. Now he picked it up and read it again.

March 28th. 1809.
White's Club, St. James's.

My dear Lady Grazebrook, An auspicious date for the Reception, about which we conversed yesterday evening, will be April the 3rd. I have instructed Philip to arrange the carriages. I remain, your most admiring servant, Ravenscroft.

The Duke first thought it was a note referring to some social event which Caroline and Lord Ravenscroft were arranging between them. Then a name jumped out at him from the letter: 'Philip'.

He remembered where he first heard that name, how he had identified himself with it, and perhaps thus saved his life. Georgia had told him that it was Philip who arranged for the tubman and the pack-horses which took the smuggled cargoes from Four Winds to London. In this letter Philip was referred to as arranging the carriages. Could this mean something very different from what appeared on the surface?

For the first time the Duke considered that Ravenscroft might in some way be implicated in Caroline's trafficking in contraband. He had been so convinced in his own mind that the man in grey was the person involved that it had never occurred to him that anyone else might be assisting Caroline by making the very intricate arrangements for the sale of brandy, tea and other smuggled cargoes.

He was still perusing the note when Pereguine had come into the room.

'Good morning, Trydon,' he said. 'Are you rested?'

'Not exactly,' the Duke replied with a smile.

He told Pereguine how he had climbed into Caroline's house, how he had discovered Charles's confession amongst other letters and how Caroline had surprised him.

'I just had time to fling myself on the bed,' he said, 'and pretend I was waiting for her.'

'Good God!' Pereguine ejaculated. 'Was she astonished to see you?'

'She was delighted,' the Duke replied. 'Ever since I came into my title she has been angling to get me back into her clutches. I have had innumerable invitations from her and many hints from neutral friends that the prodigal's return would be received with open arms.'

'Well, she certainly must have thought it was a most unconventional method of return,' Pereguine remarked. 'Did she question you?'

'Not too closely,' the Duke answered. He thought with distaste of Caroline's lips seeking his; of her exotic perfume which brought back all too vividly memories of the past; of her voice, shrill and sharpened with age, reiterating over and over again how delighted she was to see him.

He had been wondering, uncomfortably, how he could escape, when, to his relief, a voice from downstairs called Caroline's name.

'Caroline! You are taking a hell of a time!' a man shouted. 'Where the devil is the key to the cellar?'

'Ravenscroft!' the Duke exclaimed.

Caroline nodded.

'I will send him away,' she whispered.

'No, don't do that,' the Duke said quickly.

'Then wait for me here,' Caroline suggested. 'I will bring you up a bottle of wine. He will not stay long; we have had a long day and he is tired. Besides, he is not interested in me. Not any more.'

'Then why is he here?' the Duke asked.

'Because I am useful to him,' Caroline replied, 'and we are old friends.'

'Caroline!' The voice from downstairs was imperious.

'Go,' the Duke commanded her. 'You cannot afford to offend old friends.'

'But you will wait for me here?' Caroline begged. 'I will not be long, I swear it.'

She moved towards him and would have flung her arms round him again, but the Duke, rising to his feet, took her chin in his hand and turned her face upwards so that he could look into her eyes.

'Why are you interested in me, Caroline?' he asked. 'You gave me the go-by very effectively. Do you remember?'

Her eyes fell beneath his.

'It was cruel and unkind,' she admitted, 'but I could not

help it. Ravenscroft had . . . has some hold over me. And it was always you that mattered more than anyone else. You must believe me, Trydon. The others were rich and useful. But you—you were a man.'

The Duke knew that for once she spoke the truth and would have been sorry for her if he hadn't remembered the sound of Caroline's hand slapping Georgia's face.

'Caroline!' The cry from downstairs was now thunderous.

'Go,' he said.

She rested her head for a moment against his shoulder, then hurried from the room, crying:

'I'm coming, I'm coming.'

The Duke gave her just time to reach the ground floor, then he slipped down the stairs as silently as a shadow, feeling his way in the darkness of the drawing-room. The window was still open as he had left it. He climbed outside and slid down the drain-pipe into the Mews. The fat wad of letters in his breast pocket gave him a peculiar sense of satisfaction.

Now, as the Duke finished his tale, Pereguine picked up the envelopes from the floor and stacked them tidily on the writing-table.

'She has always sucked them dry,' he said reflectively. 'My cousin blew a hole in his attic after she had cast him off, having extorted the last pennyworth of credit he could pledge on her behalf. The duns were after him and he knew that he couldn't face the Fleet. If ever there was a murderess, that's Caroline.'

'You didn't tell me,' the Duke said.

'I wasn't particularly proud of it, old fellow. I think a man is a bit soft to let a woman bleed him to that extent.'

The Duke thought uncomfortably that he had been a trifle soft himself.

'What do you think of this?' he asked, wishing to change the subject. He passed Pereguine the letter from Lord Ravenscroft.

Pereguine read it through.

'I don't see anything very peculiar about it,' he said. 'Caroline is always giving receptions of some sort. Most of them turn out to be more like orgies.'

'Philip is the name of the man who arranges the smuggling operations at Four Winds,' the Duke said slowly.

Pereguine whistled. 'You surmise then . . . ?'

'I'm only wondering,' the Duke replied.

'I have heard rumours,' Pereguine told him, 'that there is some swell behind a number of the smuggling gangs. We have always known they couldn't finance the runs themselves. It is whispered that someone is doing it on a big scale. I wonder if it could be Ravenscroft?'

'I wonder,' said the Duke slowly, and he rose from the writing-desk and walked over to the window.

'The whole thing is a damned unpleasant business,' he said with his back to the room. 'Everywhere we turn there seems to be more mystery, more things unexplained. And I tell you one thing, I don't like to think of that girl being mixed up in it.'

'Georgia?' Pereguine asked.

'Georgia,' the Duke confirmed. 'She is only a child and not up to scratch when it comes to dealing with sharks of this kind. I have a feeling that we ought not to have let her take part in it. She ought to be protected. She's too good for a racket of this sort.'

Behind his friend's back Pereguine raised his eyebrows, but he said nothing.

However, at luncheon in Grosvenor Square, he had the feeling that Georgia was more capable than the Duke thought of dealing with the difficulties and the dangers.

When the servants had left the room the Dowager said:

'Now, gentlemen, what are your plans? I thought we might go to Almack's tonight.'

'Oh, Grandmama! Must we?' Pereguine asked. 'I'm bored to death with all those gossipy, autocratic hostesses. The last time I went there Lady Jersey had the affront to ask me to stand up for a country dance with some hideous wench whom I had never seen before.'

'We are trying to make you remember your social obligations,' the Dowager said.

'Well, I am against going to Almack's,' Pereguine insisted.

'On the contrary, I think it is a good idea,' the Duke said. 'If this man Jules is moving in Society, as we suspect he may be, then he is quite likely to be at Almack's. And, any rate, I might see another gentleman to whom I wish to put a name.' He was thinking of the man in grey.

'We don't care who you want to see,' Lady Carrington

remarked sharply. 'Georgia wants to show off her new gowns, and I wish to show off Georgia. We will go to Almack's and see if the child is a sensation.'

'Oh, please do not have such high hopes of me!' Georgia pleaded. 'I do not know the dances, I have no idea how to behave in such distinguished company. I shall disgrace you. Perhaps it would be best if I disguised myself as a beggar and stood outside the door watching the guests enter.'

Both gentlemen threw back their heads and laughed.

'Looking like you do now,' Pereguine said, 'you would have half the gentleman guests inviting you to enter with them.'

'That is something you would not have said to me yesterday,' Georgia teased him.

The Dowager looked at her with a little twinkle in her eye.

'Clothes make people appear different,' she said. 'But inside they remain unchanged. You are still the same girl that came here last night, looking tired and frightened, and incredibly dusty.'

'Am I really?' Georgia inquired, and she looked at the Duke as she spoke.

'I see no difference,' he said, looking steadily into her eyes.

Just for a moment something seemed to quiver between them, something which made Georgia catch her breath and which kept the Duke very still. Then, harshly, in a voice which was almost unexpectedly loud, he said:

'I wonder what your husband will think of the difference in you when he returns from the sea?'

9

LUNCHEON was a gay meal and for the first time for many years Georgia felt happy and amused with people of her own age. She forgot that she disliked the world that the Duke and his friends lived in, and she found herself giggling at Pereguine's witty remarks and the way in which he and the Duke bandied words across the table.

The Dowager chuckled too, and encouraged them. Despite her age, it was easy to see why she had been such a success in her youth and noted for her wit and gaiety. They were all laughing at something Pereguine had said when the door opened and a powdered footman approached the Dowager with a note on a silver salver.

'From Carlton House, m'lady.'

The Dowager picked up the envelope with its huge seal.

'This will be your invitation to His Royal Highness's reception tomorrow night, Georgia,' she said.

She opened the letter, lifted her lorgnettes to her eyes and gave an exclamation:

'This is better still!'

'What is, Grandmama?' Pereguine inquired.

'The Prince has asked us to dine with him this evening,' the Dowager explained. 'I have informed him that we intended visiting Almack's, thinking that perhaps His Royal Highness might be interested to drop in later in the evening as he so often does.'

'Grandmama, you are as wily as a serpent!' Pereguine exclaimed. 'You know full well you tried to entice Prinny and he has swallowed the bait.'

'I am doing my best,' the Dowager asserted sternly but with a twinkle in her eye, 'to present Georgia to the *bon-ton*. What could be more advantageous to any young female than to be patronised on her first night in London by the Prince of Wales?'

'Well, dinner at Carlton House, a dead bore though it may be, will certainly put Georgia on a high horse,' Pereguine admitted.

'I will not be bored,' Georgia protested, feeling that Pereguine was being unnecessarily critical of his grandmother's plans.

'Of course you will not,' the Dowager agreed. 'The Prince can be very charming when he is in the right mood, and he is certainly always at his very best and most gracious where I am concerned.'

'I wonder why?' Pereguine asked.

His grandmother looked at him and smiled.

'I dangled the Prince on my knee when he was a child. But, perhaps more important, I was charming to Mrs. Fitzherbert when he was first infatuated with her. They often met here in this house on occasions when I was most regrettably absent.'

Pereguine threw back his head and laughed:

'Grandmama, you are incorrigible! You can't resist intrigue of any sort, and you will be in your element tonight, showing off Georgia like a performing bear to His Royal Highness and telling the whole of London tomorrow how much he admired her.'

'He will admire her,' the Dowager said firmly, 'and without my insistence, you can be sure of that.'

Georgia flushed, for she could not get used to receiving compliments. She had never imagined in her wildest dreams that anyone would admire her, least of all the heir to the throne of England.

She sat at the table, her eyes shining, and realised a little self-consciously that the Duke was watching her.

'Excited?' he asked.

'It is all so overwhelming,' she replied. 'I keep pinching myself to make sure that I am not asleep!'

'If you have all finished luncheon,' the Dowager said, 'I must go and pen a letter of acceptance to His Royal Highness. I told him who was included in my party this evening and that you, Trydon, were escorting us.'

'I shall be delighted to do that,' the Duke replied with a bow.

The Dowager looked at him, seemed about to say something, then checked the words on her lips. She turned towards the door merely saying to Georgia:

'I must send a carriage round to Madame Bertin's immediately. I told her we did not require your best gown until tomorrow; now you must wear it tonight. And you would do well to get a little rest before the hairdresser arrives. Whatever happens, we must not be late, for the Prince dines unaccountably early.'

She had reached the door when the Duke's voice arrested her.

'Will you permit me to have a few words with Georgia alone, ma'am?' he inquired. 'I have something of import to make known to her.'

'But of course, Trydon,' the old lady replied, 'but do not keep her too long. I want her to be in good looks tonight, and she is already fatigued with all the flapdoodle at the dressmaker's this morning.'

'I will not keep her long,' the Duke promised, and turning to Georgia, 'Let us go into the library,' he suggested.

'Yes, of course,' she answered, wondering nervously what he wished to say to her. Could something have gone wrong? she wondered. Perhaps the body of the shot Frenchman had been discovered, and the Revenue officers or the Coast Guards had been asking questions.

As the Duke shut the door of the library behind him she turned towards him a pale and worried little face. She had taken off her bonnet and the sun shining through the long french windows, which opened on to a small ornamental garden, illuminated her golden hair, so that it framed her face like a halo. Anxiety about what he was about to tell her made her eyes seem unnaturally large. Her red lips quivered a little as she asked:

'What is amiss?'

The Duke stood looking at her for a moment, his eyes speculative. Then, almost with a start, as if his thoughts were elsewhere, he said:

'I have something to give you—a present.'

'A present for me?' Georgia's voice was instinctively eager. Then she added quickly:

'Indeed you must give me nothing. I am deeply perturbed because Her Ladyship insists on paying for my gowns. I know that I could not have them otherwise, but I must not accept so much of value, from strangers.'

'I am not a stranger,' the Duke protested, 'and actually my present has no intrinsic value.'

'What can it be?' Georgia asked.

In reply the Duke drew a piece of paper from the inside pocket of his coat and handed it to her.

Taking it from him wonderingly she saw in her brother's scrawling hand his confession of guilt. For a moment she stared at it incredulously. Then she gave a little cry:

'It is . . . Charles's note . . . that . . . that he wrote to my stepmother,' she stammered, 'and . . . and . . . you have it. But how? . . . How can you . . . have got it back?'

'I shouldn't ask too many questions,' the Duke advised. 'Only be content that it is now in your possession. Charles is a free man.'

'Free? Oh, Trydon, Trydon, what can I say?' Georgia asked.

She glanced down at the letter again as if she could hardly believe it was real. Then, blindly, without thinking what she was doing, she moved towards the Duke and flung her arms around him.

'Thank you . . . thank you . . . !' she cried. 'Oh, how can I . . . ever . . . thank you?'

Her voice broke as she clung to him, hiding her face against his shoulder, and he knew that the tears were running down her cheeks. His arms went round her and he held her close.

'Don't cry, Georgia,' he said. 'There is nothing to cry about, it is all over. She can't hurt you any longer.'

'It cannot be true . . . it cannot,' Georgia sobbed. 'If only you knew how . . . frightened I have been . . . How I have lain awake . . . night after night . . . worrying about Charles. Terrified . . . of what I must do . . . do for his . . . sake. And now . . . now . . .'

She was unable to stop her tears and the Duke felt her slim body trembling in his arms. He knew it was a pent-up misery and terror of so many months, and realised a little of what she must have suffered.

'It's all right, Georgia,' he said soothingly. 'The nightmare is over; you and Charles are both free.'

She raised her face to his, the tears standing like dew drops on the end of her long eyelashes, and her cheeks were wet.

'Thank you,' she said, hardly above a whisper. 'Thank you . . . thank you.'

The Duke took out his fine lace-edged kerchief and

gently wiped the tears from her cheeks. She did not seem to realise that she was still resting in his arms with her head against his shoulder.

'I still cannot believe it is true,' she murmured.

The Duke bent his head.

'Forget everything,' he said, 'it's all in the past,' and his lips touched her cheek.

He felt her quiver and then she was free of him, moving across the room with her back towards him, mopping at her eyes with his kerchief. She stood looking down at the piece of paper in her hand until almost violently she asked:

'Could we . . . could we burn this?'

'Of course,' the Duke assured her.

He picked up a tinder-box from the writing-table, lighted one of the tapers and put out his hand towards Georgia. She handed him the letter and watched as he held the point of it in the candle flame. It burnt to the very last inch. Then the Duke threw the charred remains into the fireplace and they crumbled into ashes on the marble hearth.

'We are free!' Georgia cried with a sudden note of joy in her voice. 'Free—and I am so deeply grateful.'

'As I have already said,' the Duke answered, 'forget it ever happened!'

'But my stepmother, what did she say? How did you persuade her?'

'Your stepmother, as far as I know, does not realise that the confession has gone,' the Duke answered.

'You mean . . . ?' Georgia said, her eyes wide.

'I am afraid,' the Duke replied, 'that you are responsible for turning me into a criminal. First you teach me to be a smuggler, and now a thief!'

'You stole it!' Georgia ejaculated. 'How brave of you! Are you certain she will not discover the theft and . . . and denounce you?'

'I think Her Ladyship will have some difficulty in explaining how such a document was in her possession.'

'Yes, of course, I had not thought of that,' Georgia agreed.

'I imagine therefore she will not talk freely of her loss, and certainly not to you. Yet you need no longer obey her commands.'

Georgia gave a little shiver.

'I am still afraid of her,' she confessed.

'I think that is only habit,' the Duke answered, 'you have been under her thumb for so long. But now there is nothing she can do to harm you, save spend your father's money.'

'I imagine she has done that already,' Georgia answered. 'Oh, if only Charles were here he would know what to do. Now he need no longer stay at sea because he dare not come home.'

'We must somehow try to get a message to Charles,' the Duke said with a smile.

'Could you really? Could you?' Georgia asked. 'But how, how can you have such influence, and . . . and how can you come with us tonight? I thought you were in hiding.'

The Duke put his arm on the mantelshelf and looked down into the unlit fire.

'I have something to confess to you, Georgia,' he said.

'You are in further trouble?' she inquired.

'No,' he answered, 'not unless you are angry with me. And that, I admit, would trouble me very deeply.'

'Why should I be angry with you?' Georgia asked. 'Is it something that you have done?'

'You might put it like that,' the Duke replied.

'After your kindness to me and . . . to Charles,' Georgia answered, 'I could never be angry with you, whatever you have done, or however bad it might be. Surely you understand that we are your friends for life, we could never desert you, whatever trouble you might be in.'

The Duke put out his hand and took hers.

'Thank you, Georgia,' he said, and bent his head and kissed her fingers.

He felt them tremble beneath his lips before he looked up in her eyes. For a moment they were both very still. . . . Then the blood came slowly into Georgia's pale face, her eyes dropped before his, and the Duke released her hand.

'What I have to tell you,' he said, 'will come as a surprise, for I am not exactly who you think I am.'

'Not Trydon Raven?' she asked. 'Then you have given me a false name?'

'It is in fact my name,' the Duke said, 'but I have another one by which I am more generally known.'

'What is it?' Georgia asked.

'I am the Duke of Westacre,' he answered.

133

She gave a little start and he saw by the look in her eyes that this was the last thing she had been expecting.

'The Duke of Westacre,' she repeated slowly. 'Then, then you are not in trouble? You were but making mock of me.'

'No, indeed!' the Duke asserted. 'I was, as it happened, a fugitive from the house where I had been staying. I left in the middle of the night for reasons that I would rather not relate. I was not deceiving you, Georgia.'

'I had thought perhaps you were in trouble with the duns or maybe the Bow Street Runners,' Georgia said. 'I had not imagined that you could be important, as you were riding alone in the middle of the night.'

'I had my reasons,' the Duke said, 'and I assure you they were not imaginary or exaggerated.'

'You really were running away?' she insisted.

'I was indeed,' the Duke answered, 'from a trap, as it happens. A well-laid trap, which would have been exceedingly unpleasant had I fallen into it.'

She was silent for a moment, and then she said in a very small voice:

'A trap of that sort could only have been laid by a woman.'

'You are too perceptive,' the Duke said. 'Don't ask questions, Georgia. You do not like me to question you.'

'I did not lie to you,' Georgia said. 'I told you the truth.'

'That is true,' the Duke said, 'and in actual fact I didn't lie to you. I told you that I was in trouble, which was true, and I told you that my name was Trydon Raven. It is still one of my names, I have only inherited a lot more.'

'A Duke!' Georgia said quietly. 'I can guess why you were running away and what sort of trap it was. You are, I suspect, what the Dowager would call a great desirable *parti* from a matrimonial point of view.'

'As I have said already, you are too perceptive,' the Duke answered.

'But it was why you were running away, was it not,' she insisted, 'from a woman?'

'From all women,' the Duke replied. 'I had told Pereguine I was sick of the lot of them, and that I would have nothing more to do with the entire sex. But you see how far such a resolution got me—to carrying smuggled brandy-kegs under the command of a female.'

134

He was laughing, but Georgia said quite gravely:

'I am sorry.'

'But I'm not,' he answered. 'I was furious at the time, and even more annoyed when you shut me up in the priest hole. But now things are very different: I have managed to be of service to you; I have broken your stepmother's spell, and we have still another task to do, you and I, for the good of our country.'

'Yes, of course, we must not forget that,' Georgia said.

She did not look at him and he felt that her tone was cold and that somehow she had withdrawn from him. He put out his hand and caught hers as she would have turned away.

'Listen, Georgia,' he urged, 'I am still the same man that you trusted, still the same man with whom you laughed and talked, and in whom you confided on our journey here to London. Titles and great positions are wrong and frightening only if one abuses the responsibilities which go with them. I know that you have met the wrong type of noblemen in the past. Let me prove to you that they are not all beasts, but can be normal, decent men, of whom you need never be afraid.'

Before he had finished speaking Georgia's eyes were on his face. He felt as though she searched for something in which she could believe, in which she could put her trust.

'You are right,' she said slowly, 'it is nonsensical of me, but whenever I think of someone with a title I remember . . . I remember Lord Ravenscroft.'

'He is another of the things you must forget, with the past,' the Duke said.

'I will try,' Georgia said a little dubiously.

'And will you try to think of me not as a Duke, but as Trydon—just a man like your brother Charles, a man who wants you to be happy?'

A sudden smile illuminated her face.

'You are so kind,' she said, 'and I am being foolish. I will indeed try to forget you are a Duke and remember only what you have done for Charles and for me.'

Once again the Duke raised her hand to his lips.

'Thank you,' he said, 'and now I am going to leave you as I have to talk to Pereguine about tonight. For there is every chance, the Dowager having put the idea into his head, that the Prince will accompany us to Almack's.'

'And if we do go there?' Georgia asked.

'Then we might see the Frenchman for whom we are seeking,' the Duke said. 'We shall have to evolve some sign by which you will let me and Pereguine know if it is the man you carried across the Channel. To point to him or in any way to let him know he is recognised might put him on his guard. In which case he might disappear and that would be disastrous.'

'Yes of course, I understand,' Georgia said. 'You tell me what I must do, and I must be quite sure that it is indeed him. But I am convinced that I would recognise him again were I to see him. He had a strange face.'

'Do not worry about it,' the Duke said, 'I would like you to enjoy this evening without any dramatics. If we find the spy as we suspect in the social world, it is more probable that he will be among the hundreds of guests at Carlton House tomorrow night.'

'I only hope I shall not disappoint you,' Georgia said.

'You could never do that,' the Duke replied quietly.

He turned and walked from the room without looking back, and she stood for a long time staring at the door after he had passed through it.

She thought that she could still feel his lips on her hand and on her cheek. She gave herself a little shake and walked towards the garden. He was a Duke, and yet, although she had been shocked at the knowledge, she knew that it made very little difference. He was still Trydon Raven, the man whom she had trusted almost despite herself, and who had rewarded her by taking away the shadow of evil which had rested on her shoulders for so long that she could hardly now believe that she was free.

Nana had been right, he was of noble blood; and she had been right too in saying that one could trust him in an emergency. She wondered how he had actually obtained the letter from her stepmother, how he had known where to look for it, and how he had been able to extract it without her knowledge.

They were all questions to which she felt she would never know the answer. There was a reserve about the Duke and she knew that, because he was the type of man he was, there were certain subjects on which he would never converse with her.

How long she stood looking into the sunlit garden with its stone fountain and statue of a fawn she had no idea. But suddenly the door opened behind her and a footman announced:

'Lady Grazebrook.'

Georgia wheeled round, and instinctively her hand went to her breast to quell the sudden pounding of her heart. Caroline stood there dressed in the height of fashion, with an almost freakish high-crowned bonnet trimmed with scarlet feathers and a wrap over her gown of scarlet satin.

'So it is true,' she said sharply, her voice echoing across the room. 'I could not credit my eyes when I saw you leave that shop in Bond Street before luncheon today. Madame Bertin assured me that a Mistress Baillie was staying with the Dowager Lady Carrington, and I came here to convince myself that it was the truth.'

Georgia's lips were dry, but she managed to answer in a creditably firm voice:

'Yes, I am here, as your Ladyship sees.'

'But why? How did you manage it? What does it mean? Who invited you?' The words were spat out, and now Caroline advanced further into the room looking around her.

'Such elegance! I have always known that the Dowager was a wealthy woman, but how did you come to know her? And, indeed, how did you get here? It was only two days ago that I left you at Four Winds.'

'I was invited to stay with Her Ladyship,' Georgia replied.

'Stay with her?' Caroline ejaculated, 'and she's decked you out in all this finery? For what reason? She cannot be interested in you as a *partie* for her nephew; for you are married, and indeed who would consider you for any marriage who was not a birdwit?'

'Lady Carrington has been most kind,' Georgia said primly. 'I cannot imagine how it matters to you one way or the other, for you have never previously concerned yourself with my welfare.'

'As far as I was concerned, you were living in the country,' Caroline replied. 'I am not going to have you coming up to London, moving in circles which do not consider me good enough for them. You will return immediately! Immediately, do you hear me? And leave behind those gowns that Her Ladyship has seen fit to bedeck you in. It's not for you to be getting ideas above your station.'

'And what exactly is my station?' Georgia demanded. 'Conveyer of contraband from across the Channel? Is that to be my only position in life?'

'Don't you dare speak to me in that tone of voice!' Caroline shouted. 'Something has changed you. There is something wrong! I do not know what it is. 'Tis incredible enough that you should be here. Who brought you? For I do not believe you travelled alone.'

'It is no business of yours,' Georgia answered. 'You have made it very clear since my father died that you were not interested in me. You have used Four Winds merely to suit your own purpose, and not particularly savoury ones at that. You have hit me, bullied me, overborne me in a manner that was beyond all decency. All that is finished, I shall no longer obey you and you cannot harm me.'

'Cannot harm you!' Caroline almost shrieked. 'Have you forgotten what I hold? Has it gone out of your maggot brain that if I placed Charles's confession in the hands of the Admiralty they would have him dragged from his ship ignominiously in chains?'

'I suspect that their Lordships at the Admiralty would not listen to you,' Georgia said.

She had regained her composure and now her voice was steady. She was not only aware that the knowledge that her stepmother had no further hold over her was giving her courage; it was also the fact that, for the first time in her life, she could speak to her stepmother on equal terms, knowing that she was not looking down-trodden, drab and countrified.

She caught a quick glimpse of herself in the mirror and knew that in a comparison between two women she was younger, more elegant and, indeed, though she hardly dare express it to herself, more beautiful.

'Something has happened,' Caroline muttered again. 'You are different. Why are you no longer afraid? Is Charles dead?'

Georgia shook her head.

'No indeed! I believe my brother to be in the best of health,' she answered. 'And now I think it best for your Ladyship to leave. You have not been invited here, and I

138

should not like to overstep the hospitality I have been accorded by inviting strangers to the house.'

'Strangers!' Caroline spluttered, 'I'm no stranger, I'm your stepmother. If you wish to be presented to Society, then it is my place to do it.'

'And who would pay?' Georgia asked. 'I cannot imagine you dipping into your purse on my behalf, and I believe to be launched into Society means incurring a quite considerable amount of expense.'

'Who then is paying for you?' Caroline demanded.

'The Dowager Lady Carrington has been more than kind,' Georgia said.

'It's a plot, it's a plot to humiliate me!' Caroline stormed. 'Oh, you may think yourself very important at the moment, you may give yourself airs and graces, dressed as you are and flaunting yourself in a house like this. But just you wait, wait till I take the confession of that precious brother of yours, and show it to those who can punish him—and you.'

'And what about your part in the trafficking?' Georgia asked coolly. 'It would not be hard to find out where the pack-horses had gone when they left Four Winds loaded with kegs of brandy. Once the investigation starts, someone will be ready to bear witness to what they have seen and heard. I should be careful before you involve yourself—and, of course, your friends—for it will not be hard to prove that I had no knowledge of what happened to the goods once they had been unloaded in the cellar.'

Georgia had the satisfaction of seeing Caroline turn pale, partly with fear, partly with anger.

'I will destroy you for this,' she threatened, speaking in a low but vehement tone. 'I will destroy you if it's the last thing I do in my life. There is something I don't understand about the whole affair, but I shall find out—you can be certain I shall find out.'

She turned away and pulled the door open violently. Georgia could hear her walking away down the marble hall. Now that Caroline had left, she realised that she was trembling all over. The encounter had forced her to appear a good deal braver than she really felt. Now she felt faint!

She picked up a small gold vinaigrette which stood on a side table and lifted it to her nose; but almost before she smelt it, she put it down again.

'There is no reason for me to be frightened,' she told herself aloud, 'there is nothing she can do, nothing!'

Georgia had a sudden desire to run to Trydon to tell him what had happened, and to seek his reassurance that she was indeed free and that Charles was in no danger. She had been courageous while her stepmother was present, but now she knew she was still desperately afraid.

She found herself remembering how strong the Duke's arms had been around her; she recalled the fragrance of his coat as she laid her face against it. Looking down she saw on one of the chairs his kerchief that he had lent her to dry her tears. Almost automatically she picked it up; it was of very soft lawn and in one corner she saw a monogram, surmounted by the Ducal crown with its strawberry leaves. She stared at it for a long time, gave a little sob, and running from the room went upstairs to her bedchamber.

Four hours later Georgia came down the wide carpeted staircase and knew as she descended that Pereguine and the Duke watching her from the hall had exactly the expression in their eyes that she had wanted to see. Her dress of embroidered gauze glittered with every step she took. Her silver wrap, trimmed with periwinkle-blue Maribou, was exactly the colour of her eyes and opened to reveal a magnificent diamond necklace that the Dowager had clasped round her neck when she had gone to her bedchamber.

'As you are a married woman, child,' she said, 'you can wear diamonds; otherwise it would be a small original string of pearls. There is some advantage, you see, in marriage!'

Georgia had laughed.

'Even a small string of pearls would have seemed wonderful to me,' she said. 'But this . . . this is too grand.'

'Nothing is too grand,' the Dowager said, 'and if you did not look so absurdly young I would have lent you a tiara. But that would have overpowered you. The flowers that André has fixed in your hair are far more becoming and match the star ear-rings I am going to give you for your ears.'

'Your Ladyship is so kind to me!' Georgia exclaimed. 'How can I show my gratitude?'

'By being a success tonight,' the Dowager answered.

'You know that they have always said that everything I touch turns to gold. They are right! I haven't time for dross in my life, and especially not in people. You are gold, my child, pure gold! I knew it as soon as I saw you.'

'Thank you,' Georgia whispered.

" 'Tis sad indeed that you are married,' the Dowager went on, 'for I would have liked to find a suitable husband for you. Trydon, for instance. It is time he was wed. His godmother was speaking to me about it only last week.'

'Indeed I am surprised His Grace is not married,' Georgia said.

The Dowager laughed.

'Too many expensive ladybirds and attractive married women.'

'Married women?' Georgia asked. She felt as though a sudden icy hand had been laid on her heart, but she could not imagine why.

'Yes indeed,' the Dowager chuckled, adding in an aside to her maid: 'No! no! girl, don't be a fool! That bow is much too much to the left. Now let me see, where was I?—married women! Lady Valerie Voxon it was at one time, but now she is the Countess of Davenport and casting eyes at him and anything else that has the appearance of a man.'

'Was she . . . is she very beautiful?' Georgia asked in a low voice.

'A high-stepper, a high-stepper indeed!' the Dowager replied. 'But Valerie has not the animation that I had when I was a girl! That is what is wrong with the young people today; they may be beautiful but they have no animation. A man gets tired of seeing the same pretty face the other side of the table. He wants a girl with some guts—like you, my dear. Your husband is a lucky man, he will not be bored with you. Do you love him very much?'

The question took Georgia by surprise.

'Yes . . . yes, of course,' she stammered.

'Well, as I was saying, 'tis a pity that I cannot pair you off,' the Dowager answered. 'But never mind, enjoy yourself, one is a long time old.'

The Dowager's voice dropped suddenly and she stared at her reflection in the mirror.

'So many lines, so many wrinkles,' she said, 'if only one could put back the clock, if only for an hour or so. I would like you to have seen me in my heyday. My beaux used to say that when I entered a room the sun came out. How the other women hated me! I was always the belle of every ball I attended.'

'I am sure you were,' Georgia smiled. Then, because she could not help herself, she asked:

'Do you think th . . . that the Duke is . . . is still in love with Lady Davenport?'

'In love . . . who said he was in love?' the Dowager snapped. 'Infatuated perhaps. There was another woman he used to go about with, can't remember her name. Some rather common creature, though beautiful enough. A man, like a child, has got to cut his teeth on a hard bone, but it's not love. When it is, well, then, the social world is well lost, happiness has no history.'

There was a throb in the old lady's voice, and Georgia said softly:

'You fell in love, ma'am?'

'Many times,' the Dowager answered, 'but only once when it mattered. We went to the country, my husband and I, and we had twenty-three wonderful years together, until he was killed in a hunting accident. My son was killed two years later in a duel, a senseless, idiotic piece of chivalry which cost him his life. Pereguine is all I have left. And I hope that he one day will find the right woman, someone with whom he too will find the world well lost.'

'I hope he will too,' Georgia said a little wistfully.

'And you?' the old lady asked. 'Have you found it?'

Before Georgia could reply they were interrupted by a knock at the door.

'Who is it?' the Dowager said to her maid. 'Can one never have a moment's peace in this house?'

The maid went to the door.

' 'Tis only to say the gentleman have arrived and are waiting downstairs, m'lady.'

The Dowager turned excitedly to Georgia.

'Go down, child, I want them to see you. Walk gracefully, hold your head high. That dress needs carrying: I had thought it would make you look sophisticated, but you still look unfledged, like a little bird that has fallen out of its nest. No less attractive for all that.'

Georgia felt shy as she reached the top of the stairs. Suppose the Dowager has been mistaken. Suppose that

Pereguine and, of course, the Duke did not admire her as much as she hoped they would do.

'My God!' Pereguine exclaimed. 'Are you really the same girl who came to my room looking like something out of the *Beggar's Opera*?'

'I am exactly the same person,' Georgia answered. 'I hope you are not ashamed of me.'

Her eyes were on Pereguine's face; she somehow could not, after that first glance from the top of the stairs, force herself to look at the Duke.

'You're a stunner!' Pereguine asserted. 'You will knock them through the hoops. If ever there was an incomparable, it's you, Georgia, and I say that with my hand on my heart. Do you not agree, Trydon?'

Now Georgia was forced to look up at the Duke. He was standing there, his face very grave. His eyes looked down into hers and somehow said all the things his tongue left unsaid.

'You will not shame us,' he said quietly. Then, almost as if he forced himself to a change of mood, he added sharply:

'Come into the morning-room, I wish to speak to you both.'

They obeyed him and crossed the hall, where a footman opened the door.

'Listen,' the Duke said when they were alone, 'there is just a chance that we may catch a glimpse of the fellow at Almack's. If you see him, Georgia, you must turn either to me or to Pereguine, whichever is nearest, and say: "It is very hot in here, do you think you could ask the gentleman in the blue, red or pink coat", whichever it is, "to oblige me by fetching a bottle of smelling-salts." '

'I think that is rather cumbrous, old chap!' Pereguine ejaculated.

'And what do you suggest?' the Duke asked, almost angrily. 'Georgia obviously can't point to the chap.'

'No indeed,' Pereguine agreed. 'Well, I suppose it's the best we can do, unless, of course, we are some distance from him.'

'The one thing we mustn't do is to put the fellow on his guard,' the Duke said.

'You are right there,' Pereguine said. 'Anyhow, do the best you can, Georgia.'

'I will try,' she said simply.

'And don't forget all about it!' Pereguine said with a laugh. 'You are going to be the focus of all eyes this evening. I can see that all the gentlemen will be after you, paying compliments, kissing your hand and making sheep's eyes. That sort of thing is like champagne, it can go to your head.'

'I will not forget,' Georgia promised with a little laugh.

She looked up at the Duke.

'You have not told me if you like my gown.'

She tried to speak lightly, almost flirtatiously, but somehow she only sounded pathetic. For a moment their eyes met. Then the Duke looked away and walking to the door opened it.

'I expect my plaudits will be added to the chorus,' he said stiffly.

Unaccountably Georgia felt as if the tapers in the hall were snuffed out.

10

THE Dowager's coach was fitted with the very latest soft cushions and the springing was so light that, despite its heavy appearance, Georgia realised that they were moving at a fast pace down Carlos Place towards Berkeley Square.

She saw Lady Carrington's jewels flashing in the lantern-light from the linkman and leaping flares fixed outside the doorways, and thought to herself how incredible it was that she should be travelling in this luxurious coach, accompanied by three members of the *beau monde,* when only a few days ago she was being slapped and humiliated by her stepmother.

Georgia hardly dared to move lest she should spoil the elegance and the beauty of her new dress. It, too, glittered in the passing lights, and she could see as she glanced up that the Duke, sitting opposite her, was looking at her with what she felt was a strange expression on his face. Because she suddenly felt embarrassed she turned her head quickly towards the Dowager.

'This is all very new and exciting for me, ma'am. I only hope that I shall not embarrass you, for indeed I am not used to such exalted company as I shall meet tonight.'

'You need not be afraid of the Prince,' the Dowager replied. 'He loves a pretty face, and will undoubtedly say the most complimentary things to you. The only danger will be Lady Hertford, who becomes more and more possessive of His Royal Highness. Indeed, though I dare not say it outside this coach, I much preferred the reserve and dignity of Maria Fitzherbert.'

'I think it is you, Grandmama, of whom Lady Hertford will be jealous,' Pereguine said. 'You know that the Prince is one of your flirts.'

The old lady laughed.

'To tell the truth, Pereguine, I am as excited tonight as a young girl going to her first ball, not on my own account, but because I have someone young and attractive to chaperon. I always have detested the cronies of my own age, they bore me to distraction. But I've often wished that I had a daughter to present at Court, it would have given me much satisfaction.'

'You would have been the most inveterate old match-maker in the whole of London,' Pereguine teased her.

'And I should certainly have won the matrimonial stakes,' the Dowager said. 'Had I a daughter, Trydon, I assure you that by now I would have forced you up the aisle with her.'

'Had she been like you, ma'am, I should have needed no forcing,' the Duke replied.

The Dowager was delighted.

'Flatterer!' she exclaimed. 'But it is indeed sad that my sweet Georgia is married, and therefore I cannot plot her future.'

'And I can assure you,' Pereguine said, 'the fact that your schemes cannot be put in operation makes both Trydon and me heave a sigh of relief. I told you years ago, Grandmama, that when I wed it will be to someone of my own choice, not yours. And Trydon, after his last experience, has forsworn women altogether.'

'What experience?' the Dowager asked curiously.

'Pereguine is talking nonsense,' the Duke interposed hastily, 'I beg you not to listen to him, ma'am. He's a gabster, if ever there was one.'

'I'll tell you in secret what occurred, Grandmama,' Pereguine said mischievously, 'but I assure you a very pretty trap was set for our Ducal friend, only with great astuteness he avoided it by playing coward and showing a clean pair of heels.'

'You are not going to call me a coward!' the Duke exclaimed angrily. 'Hang it, Pereguine, talk about your own affairs, not mine.'

'I was but funning you,' Pereguine said half apologetically, realising that he had gone too far.

'Pay no attention to this loud-mouthed joker,' the Duke said, speaking not to the Dowager but to Georgia.

If she heard him she gave no indication of it. She was

looking through the window. The night was suddenly dark and damp, and some of the gaiety and excitement had evaporated. She did not know why she felt as though a cloud of depression had settled upon her. She only knew that her spirits were low and that for a moment she wished she were back at Four Winds with Nana, with no social or-deal ahead of her.

She kept seeing the face of the French spy as the light from the lantern had shone on his face. Would she recognise him again? Was she sure that a dozen, or perhaps more, men would not look very much the same, with the collar of a dark cape almost obscuring his chin, and his hat pulled low over his forehead?

Georgia felt a moment of panic, and had she been brave enough she would have begged the Dowager to stop the coach, or turn it round and take her back to Grosvenor Square again.

'I am an impostor,' she thought. 'I am here under false pretences, for I swear that when the moment comes I shall not recognise the man.'

Almost as if he knew instinctively what she was feeling, the Duke bent forward and his hand covered hers. For a moment her fingers fluttered as though they would escape, and then, almost without thinking, she returned the warmth of his clasp.

'It's all right,' he said softly, 'there is no need to be afraid, nothing will happen tonight; and even if we go to Almack's it is very unlikely that he will be there. Enjoy yourself, think of other things.'

The Dowager watched them with sharp eyes that missed nothing, but she was silent and so was Pereguine. For a second Georgia forgot the others were in the coach and felt that she was alone with the Duke, and that he was talking to her quietly and consolingly, as he had done at the little inn they had visited on their way to London.

'It is just that I am afraid that I shall not know him again,' she said in a voice hardly above a whisper.

'You will,' the Duke answered. 'Memory is a strange thing: at times one is sure that something of importance is forgotten, and then a look, a gesture, a word, will bring it back in a flash.'

'And supposing we do not find him?' Georgia said.

147

'We will,' the Duke said, and his voice was confident. 'And remember not to let him realise that he has been recognised. It is unlikely that he will remember you.'

'Very unlikely,' Georgia agreed, and now despite her worries she smiled.

'That's better!' the Dowager said sharply. 'I won't have my evening spoilt with all these tiresome intrigues. If you ask me you are just a trio of theatrical dramatists. I do not credit for one moment that anyone would want to assassinate the Prince, unless he were a lunatic, and certainly not in Carlton House, where His Royal Highness is surrounded by all his special friends. Forget all the tiresome twaddle these sap-skulls have put into your head, Georgia, and enjoy yourself. Remember you will be far the most beautiful person present.'

The Duke released Georgia's hands and sat back. Her fingers were warm from the contact with his, and she no longer felt depressed or indeed afraid. The Dowager was right, it might all be a lot of dramatic nonsense, and dressed as she was now and in such company, it was hard to believe that she had indeed braved the darkness and dangers of the Channel to carry one of Bonaparte's spies into England.

The horses drew up with a flourish at the porticoed door, and Georgia, feeling as if she was in a dream, had a vivid impression of a huge pillared entrance hall and a majestic curving staircase; of painted walls and gilded panels; of niches framing busts, statues, griffins and urns! There seemed to be an entire army of flunkeys in gorgeously gold-laced and gold-buttoned uniforms. Then she was moving up the stairs in the wake of the Dowager and into a drawing-room hung with yellow Chinese silk and furnished in the Chinese fashion.

When the Prince was at home to his intimate friends he dispensed with a formal entrance and was already in the drawing-room to receive his guests as they arrived. Beside him was Lady Hertford, plump and curved, covered with lace, ribbons and an inordinate amount of jewelry. She had a young unlined face, which was almost incredible for a grandmother, and she had fat white hands, which seemed irresistibly propelled towards the Royal personage. She was for ever patting or playfully slapping the Prince's arm to show the intimacy of their relationship.

As the Dowager sank in a very low curtsey before the Prince he raised her hand to his lips.

'It's delightful to see you, my lady,' he said, 'it is far too long since we had the pleasure of your company.'

'Your Royal Highness is exceedingly gracious as always,' the Dowager said. 'I am only so delighted to see you in such handsome looks, and more elegant than I remember.'

Georgia had heard that the Prince could never resist a compliment, and if she had not been so frightened she would have been amused by the expression of gratification on his Royal Highness's rather bloated face. Already she had caught his attention.

'And is this the new beauty you promised me?' he asked, his large protruding eyes looking her over as if, Georgia thought to herself, she were a horse at a fair.

'May I, sire, present Mistress Georgia Baillie,' the Dowager said.

Georgia sank to the ground in a curtsey that she had been practising assiduously in her bedroom while she was dressing for dinner.

'Charming, charming!' the Prince exclaimed. 'You are right, Lady Carrington, as you always are, she is indeed a beauty. She will give the gossips of St. James's something to chat about tomorrow.'

'Undoubtedly, since she has your Royal Highness's approval,' the Dowager said with a twinkle in her eye.

To Georgia's astonishment she felt the Prince's fat fingers tickle her palm before he released her hand.

'We must see much of Mistress Baillie,' he said, and almost, it seemed, with an effort turned to the Duke who was standing beside her.

'Nice to see you, Westacre,' he said. 'Where have you been hiding yourself these past weeks? Or does Carlton House no longer meet with your approval?'

There was almost a peevish note in his voice; for the Prince could not bear to think that his friends should have any interest which did not directly centre round himself.

'I had to leave London on matters of business, sire,' the Duke replied. 'It is not something I can speak of in company, but I have matters of great import to convey to your Royal Highness later.'

'Matters of import, aye?' the Prince asked. Having been deliberately excluded from all affairs of State by the King for so many long weary years, he was always intrigued and delighted to think there was something of importance which required his attention.

'Good, good,' he said putting a heavy hand on the Duke's shoulder. 'You must tell me about it later. I shall not forget.'

'Thank you, sire,' the Duke said respectfully.

Pereguine was greeted, and as other guests began to arrive the Prince stepped forward to greet them. Georgia looked round, searching the faces of the people who were already there, when a name announced by the major-domo made her start and turn trembling towards the Duke.

'Lord Ravenscroft.'

The name seemed to echo round the room, and Georgia felt for a moment that she must run away, though where and how she had no idea.

'Steady, he will not recognise you.'

It was the Duke who spoke, his voice sharp, almost as though he were on the parade-ground. She raised her eyes, dark and frightened, in a white face from which the colour had drained away.

'Are you sure of that?' she whispered.

'Quite sure,' the Duke answered. 'He will not expect to find you here. Even if he does know you, what can he do except be polite and keep his distance? I will see to that.'

'You will . . . will protect me?'

It was a voice of a frightened child, frightened by the dark and of bogeys that were almost more real than reality.

The Duke smiled, and the twist of his lips was suddenly very tender.

'I will protect you, Georgia,' he said softly. 'You know that don't you?'

She raised her eyes to his and once again something passed between them, something which brought the colour back into her face, which made her heart turn over in her breast and her breath came quicker between her parted lips. For a moment everything faded; they were alone, two young people in a world that was suddenly golden and enchanting, filled with a strange music which seemed to come from within themselves.

'Georgia, I want you to meet Lord Denman.'

The Dowager's voice broke the spell, and Georgia

turned her eyes away feeling as if she had dropped from a mountaintop down into the valley.

She stared a little blindly at a middle-aged man, resplendent with medals, whom the Dowager was introducing to her. She said something conventional, and gave apparently the appropriate reply to a question he asked of her. But she knew that something momentous had happened, which she could not even explain or express to herself. As if in a dream she was introduced by the Dowager to a dozen other people. Then, almost as though they made a full circle, they arrived back at the Prince.

'You know my old friend, the Comte St. Clare, don't you, my lady?' Georgia heard him say. 'He must meet your pretty Mistress Baillie—the Comte Jules St. Clare.'

Georgia dropped a curtsey, and as she did so felt as though a thunderbolt had struck the room. She felt the man to whom she had been introduced raise her hand to his lips, heard him murmur *'Enchanté,'* knew as his eyes flickered over her casually that she remained unrecognised.

For one moment she felt that her legs would not carry her. Then, as the Comte exchanged a few words with the Dowager, she managed, without in any way seeming evasive, to reach the Duke's side. He was talking to a distinguished-looking man wearing the uniform of a General, and for a moment she stood quietly at their side while the General finished what he was saying.

'Forgive me,' Georgia pleaded, and forced her stiff lips into a semblance of a smile.

'Yes, what is it?' The Duke's question was only a murmur, for he knew by the expression on Georgia's face that something had occurred.

'The man standing with the Dowager,' she said, forgetting all the plans they had made.

'The man in grey?' the Duke asked, and without waiting for Georgia's confirmation he knew there was no doubt as to the man's identity.

It was the man in grey he had seen at Four Winds, through the tiny shutter in the staircase. It was the man in grey to whom Caroline had announced that the crossing had been arranged for the following night. Of course this was the man, why had he not thought of him before? Someone who had wormed himself into the Prince's favour,

151

someone who perhaps had been in England for many years. In the brief second, as the Duke looked across the room, he saw the whole plot fall into place.

The man in grey, already *persona grata* with the Prince, already accepted in the best Society, was in the pay of Napoleon. He had crossed the Channel, using another gang of smugglers to convey him to France, he had seen Napoleon and made plans for the Prince's assassination. It may have been his idea, for who better than anyone else knew of the King's madness, the crisis in the political situation and what chaos such a deed would bring in its wake. He had then returned to England with Georgia's crew to wait for further instructions from the Emperor.

'You see him?' Georgia's voice broke in on the Duke's reconstruction in his mind of what had happened.

'Yes, I see him,' he replied. 'Act quite naturally. I must introduce you to someone.'

Without waiting for her to agree he turned to the person nearest, and discovering it was Lady Hertford he raised the lady's hand to his lips.

'I declare, ma'am, you grow younger and more beautiful every time I see you,' the Duke said. 'I am beginning to believe that you have sold your soul to the devil in exchange for the secret of eternal youth.'

Lady Hertford giggled. It was the same flirtatious giggle that entranced the Prince.

'There must be a touch of the blarney in the Westacre blood,' she said, 'but I am glad your Grace is back. The Prince misses you when you are not in attendance.'

'I am indeed honoured,' the Duke said with a little bow, 'and may I present to your Ladyship Mistress Georgia Baillie, who is here under the chaperonage of the Dowager Lady Carrington.'

'I am delighted to meet you,' Lady Hertford said, but the tone of her voice was cold and her eyes as they rested on Georgia's little pointed face were hard.

'It's just a small party tonight,' she said to the Duke, as though Georgia was an interruption that had been speedily dealt with. 'His Highness was anxious to entertain only his intimate friends. Indeed, we shall not be many more than twenty-five.'

'Then it is a great privilege to be present,' the Duke said formally.

Of what was said in the next five minutes before dinner was announced Georgia had no idea. She was only conscious of the presence in the room of two men who made her shiver even to think of them: Lord Ravenscroft and the man in grey. Lord Ravenscroft had not seemed to look her way; but, as the Prince offered Lady Hertford his arm to proceed towards the dining-room, she heard the thick oily voice that had haunted her dreams for a whole year say:

'Surely I'm not mistaken—it is Georgia, little Georgia Grazebrook.'

She thought for a moment that she would faint with the sheer horror of seeing him again. Then a courage which she had not known existed came to her rescue.

'You are mistaken, my Lord,' she said, 'I am no longer Georgia Grazebrook, I am married.'

It might have been her fancy, but she felt she saw an expression of annoyance on His Lordship's dissolute face.

'Your husband is here?' he asked.

'He is at sea,' Georgia answered. She felt as soon as she had spoken that it was a mistake to have given him such information, for the look she most dreaded in His Lordship's eyes returned.

'You are even lovelier than when I last saw you,' Lord Ravenscroft said. 'Now you are in London, we must see something of each other. I will call on you tomorrow.'

'I . . . I shall not be there,' Georgia said incoherently. Her pose of being assured and sophisticated was breaking under the strain.

'I shall find you,' Lord Ravenscroft said.

She felt the terror that had possessed her for so long sweep over her. She could not answer him, she could only look at him with an expression of loathing on her face, feeling like a small rabbit mesmerised by a snake. Then someone came between her and the man she hated.

'I have been instructed to take you into dinner,' Pereguine's voice said suavely. 'I have the good fortune to be sitting on your right.'

She slipped her arm into Pereguine's and felt as though it saved her from falling.

'You look a bit queer,' Pereguine remarked with the frankness of a brother. 'Are you feeling all right?'

'It is . . . that . . . that man,' Georgia managed to murmur.

'What man? Is he here?' Pereguine asked.

'Yes, he is here,' Georgia said, 'but it is not he who is troubling me. It is Lord Ravenscroft.'

'Oh, that outsider!' Pereguine answered. 'If ever there was a man who is yellow and not up to snuff it's His Lordship. Why the Prince should include him in his parties I have always failed to understand.'

They were moving in slowly towards the dining-room. Georgia felt her confidence return as they moved further away from Lord Ravenscroft, for Pereguine's gay inconsequent voice seemed to make light of everything that she found serious and terrifying.

'Don't put yourself in a pucker over the chap,' he said. 'Trydon will deal with him. Tell me about the other one, which is he?'

The last words were uttered in such a conspiratorial whisper that Georgia could not help smiling.

'The man in grey,' she had replied.

'What! the Comte St. Clare?' he exclaimed. 'You must be mistaken! Why, he is accepted as *bon ton,* and a lot of chaps think he's quite a decent fellow for a Frenchman.'

'He is the one,' Georgia asserted grimly.

'By Jove!' Pereguine ejaculated as the full implications of what she was saying percolated into his mind. 'Does Trydon know?' he inquired as they reached the dining-room.

'I told him,' Georgia replied.

The dining-room was walled with silver and supported by columns of red and yellow granite. It was fantastically colourful and unlike anything that Georgia could have imagined as the décor of a royal palace. She found herself seated at the side of the long dining table with Pereguine on her right, and the elderly General, to whom she had been introduced by the Dowager, on her left.

The Prince sat at the head of the table with Lady Hertford on his right, and the Dowager on his left. At the other end Lord Ravenscroft was in the place of honour with two rather attractive women on each side of him. As the meal progressed, however, Georgia could not help feeling that the ladies failed to hold his attention.

As course followed course served on gold plates, she knew that His Lordship's eyes were on her. Whatever delicacy she placed in her mouth, it might as well have

154

been sawdust. She felt with the sick horror she had known for so long that he would make good the threat he had whispered to her through her bedchamber door that night. He was like some loathsome animal, she thought, utterly confident of his strength and his cunning, and knowing that however long he remained, his prey could not get away.

In search of consolation she looked across the room. The Duke, as befitted his rank, was higher up the table, and separated from the Comte by a lady wearing a tiara of opals set with pearls. Lady Hertford might call it a small party, but there were twenty-eight people seated round the long polished table, an innovation introduced by the Prince, who had dispensed with the damask tablecloths which had invariably been used until the beginning of the century.

The table was decorated with enormous gold ornaments and a mass of tiny white orchids, speckled with red. For a moment Georgia fancied they looked like drops of blood, and she felt herself shiver. Could she have made a mistake? Could the man in grey, the Count they said that everyone liked, really have been the passenger she had carried across the Channel that dark night some three weeks ago? Could she have been mistaken? She knew that she was not.

There was something about the lines running from his nose to his lips, the shape of his strange face, that was unmistakable. She had thought there might be other men like him, but now she knew that she would have recognised him in a crowd of hundreds.

Course after course was served accompanied by special wines that were poured into long engraved crystal goblets, bearing the royal insignia. Then, as they reached the dessert and Georgia thought with relief that the ladies would soon be leaving the room, the Duke bent forward.

'May I be allowed, sire,' he asked the Prince, 'to tell you a story which I think will interest everyone in this room?'

'A story, aye?' the Prince inquired. He had been whispering some coy aside to Lady Hertford, who had raised her fan to her face as if to hide her girlish blushes.

'Yes, a story, sire,' the Duke replied, 'and one of great import because it concerns your Royal Highness.'

'Concerns me, does it?' the Prince echoed, delighted at

the thought of hearing something about himself. 'Go ahead, Westacre, but don't make it as long as the sermons my chaplain preaches at me. I keep meaning to speak to the fellow.'

'I won't take long,' the Duke promised. 'The story begins, your Royal Highness, in France where Napoleon Bonaparte received in audience some three weeks ago a visitor from England.'

'He did, did he?' the Prince asked, sitting up in his chair. 'How the devil did he do that?'

'I will tell you,' the Duke answered, 'but first let me explain what was said at this secret and very important interview with Bonaparte. The visitor from England had a plan. It was a plan, your Royal Highness, to dispose of someone extremely important and extremely valuable to his country. That person was you.'

The Prince's jaw dropped. 'Dispose of me? In what manner? Who told you this, Westacre?'

'Allow me to continue, sire,' the Duke replied. 'The plot was considered an excellent one because it was believed that your death, at this particular moment'—he paused and everybody present was thinking of the King—'would have caused political chaos and a great deal of unrest in the armed services, especially in the Navy, which has a great affection for your Royal Highness.'

'Yes, they have, indeed they have,' the Prince agreed. 'But to assassinate me, good God! I have never heard of such a thing!'

'I feel faint at the very idea,' Lady Hertford cried, but seeing that nobody else was interested in her feelings she leant forward like everyone else at the table with her eyes on the Duke.

'The visitor to Bonaparte returned to England,' the Duke continued.

'And how the devil did he do that?' the Prince interjected. 'What is Collingwood doing, if people can pass backwards and forwards across the Channel as though it was Piccadilly.'

'The gentleman travelled,' the Duke said, choosing his words, 'with the smugglers, who, as your Royal Highness knows, conduct their trade with an impudent disregard of the Revenue officers who fail regrettably to apprehend more than a tenth of the contraband traffic that plies the English Channel.'

The Duke paused and looked round the table.

'Of course, the gentleman in question had his mode of travel made easy for him. He had a friend in England, someone of authority and influence, who has organised a great deal of the smuggling trade—in fact, one might almost say the larger part of it. It was simple, therefore, for this spy of Bonaparte's, for he is nothing less, to ask his friend for transport to the coast of France, and in the same manner for his transport back again. What is more, once in France, the spy from England arranged for another Frenchman to bring him a message from Bonaparte with instructions whether the assassination should take place immediately or at the gentleman's leisure. You see clearly, sire, how useful this controller of smuggling-boats could be.'

'Good God, I have never heard such a thing!' the Prince ejaculated, and there were similar murmurs round the table. 'Who is this chap?'

'He is an Englishman—in fact, he is someone your Royal Highness knows well—his name is . . .'

There was a sudden shuffle at the far end of the table as a chair was pushed back and thrown to the ground, and Lord Ravenscroft, his face contorted to an expression of almost diabolical evil, drew a small pistol from the inside pocket of his coat.

'Stand back,' he threatened, 'stand back and do not touch me. I will kill the first man who lays a finger on me. Curse you, Westacre, for I cannot conceive how you fathomed it was I. Damn you, and may you rot in hell!'

He was backing as he spoke towards the door, but Pereguine, moving with a swiftness of which Georgia would not have believed him capable, was there before him.

Lord Ravenscroft, his eyes fixed on the faces of the astonished company, seated as if petrified at the table, did not realise until he was almost there that his exit was barred. Then, as he turned and fired, Pereguine ducked and the bullet smashed into the wood of the door, shattering the panel.

There was a shriek from the ladies, and the gentlemen,

suddenly released from the spell which had kept them seated like statues, sprang to their feet. But even as they moved there was another shot, and Lord Ravenscroft crumpled to the ground. Pereguine, still with his back to the door, was holding a smoking pistol in his hand.

There was a babble of voices as the gentlemen hurried forward. But the Duke was not looking in the same direction: he was watching the man in grey, seeing him insert his hand into the inside pocket of his grey brocade evening coat. There was a shriek from Lady Hertford, a petrifying moment when the Prince saw the long thin stiletto move towards his heart.

Then the Duke had seized the hand holding the weapon, twisted the Count round and caught him on the edge of his chin with his fist carrying the punch of a man who had learnt boxing from the greatest experts of the ring.

The Count seemed to shoot into the air before he fell to the floor unconscious, the stiletto glittering on the carpet beside him. The babble in the room was incoherent until Major-General Lord Darlington took command.

'Remove these creatures immediately from his Royal Highness's presence,' he commanded the panic-stricken servants. 'Please resume your seats, gentlemen, the noise is unseemly.'

His words, like a douche of cold water, extinguished the chatter. Everyone looked towards the Prince, who, crimson in the face, sat gasping at the end of the table, while Lady Hertford, putting her head against his shoulder, was weeping emotionally into her handkerchief. Only the Dowager sat bolt upright, a smile of amusement on her lips and a twinkle in her old eyes.

'Your Highness is unhurt?' a gentleman-at-arms asked somewhat needlessly.

'Quite all right, quite all right,' the Prince replied.

His Royal Highness, the Duke thought, had behaved with admirable courage and composure.

'May I beg your Royal Highness's pardon?' Pereguine asked, standing beside his chair.

'For what?' the Prince inquired a little testily.

'For carrying a weapon in your royal presence,' Pereguine answered. 'I am well aware that it was an offence, but I had reason to think that something like this might occur.'

'You did, did you?' the Prince exclaimed.

'Not from Lord Ravenscroft, that was a surprise,' Pereguine replied, 'but I knew as we came into dinner that the man in grey was the tool chosen by Napoleon for your assassination.'

'You are with Westacre, I see that,' the Prince said, 'but why the hell, if you knew who he was, didn't you arrest him before he threatened me?'

The Duke smiled.

'Would your Royal Highness have believed us?' he asked. 'Besides, I had no idea he intended to make the attempt tonight. In fact, I am sure it was not in his mind when he came here, it would have been too public, too obvious that he could not escape. But in the confusion over Lord Ravenscroft's death he thought he saw an opportunity of vanishing before anyone would realise who had killed you.'

The Prince took out his handkerchief and mopped his sweating brow.

'You saved my life, Westacre,' he said heavily, 'I shall not forget it. And now will someone give me a glass of brandy? I damn well need it after what I have been through!'

Brandy was produced and Lady Hertford, still weeping, led the ladies into the drawing-room, where they sat talking excitedly of what had occurred, everyone wishing to relate what they had seen, what they had heard and what they had felt.

Georgia found after a time that she ceased to listen: she was thinking instead that her job was now done. There would be no reason for her to go to Almack's tonight, or any other night; no reason for her to come to the reception at Carlton House tomorrow night; the clothes the Dowager had ordered for her would not be needed; the Duke would escort her back to Four Winds and that would be the last she would ever see of him!

As these thoughts coursed through her mind, she knew what she had felt when the Duke had risen from the table and seized the man in grey just as he was about to strike the Prince. She had been afraid not for the Prince but for the Duke and she knew now that she loved him—loved him with an overwhelming love that seemed to burn through her like a fire.

She loved him with her whole being so that she was certain that she must have in fact been loving him for a long time. That was why she had felt so safe and secure in his presence; why she had wanted him so desperately to accompany her on that trip to France; why that ride across country to London had been amongst the happiest hours she had ever spent in her whole life.

Sitting in the Chinese drawing-room of Carlton House, while the ladies chattered around her like an aviary of colourful birds, she slipped into a world of her own and felt again the Duke's lips on her cheek and on her hand. She must have known at his touch then that she had loved him but dared not face it even to herself. She had known it was love she felt for him when he had bent forward in the coach to hold her hand and reassure her.

Even as her love seemed to evoke within herself an ecstasy that was beyond words, she knew it was hopeless. It was a love that she could never express because they could never, never belong to each other. She felt the tears prick her eyes, and for one appalling moment she thought that she might cry. Then, as had happened so often before in her life, pride came to her rescue. She loved him, but he must never know it.

She was conscious of nothing else all the evening. The Prince showed her some of the treasures that he had accumulated in Carlton House; she stared at the priceless examples of Chinoiserie, the pictures and the statues, but she didn't see any of them.

She didn't even realise that the Prince was standing rather closer to her than was necessary; he was touching her cheek and once again as she left he had tickled her palm with his fat fingers. She was conscious only of one person, the Duke: calm, composed, talking and laughing he was moving with an easy manner among his friends, and yet inevitably coming back to her side.

The evening came to an end, the good nights were said. The Prince thanked the Duke once again, then admonished the whole company:

'Nothing is to be learnt of this by the newspapers,' he said. 'I trust you all not to relate to anyone what has happened here this evening. Let Bonaparte wonder what has happened to his plot, to those he sent to assassinate me. It will be more tantalising for him to be uncertain of what has occurred than to know that he has failed. Can I trust you?'

They all assured him that not a word of what had happened would pass their lips.

'Thank you all for your fortitude and your continued friendship,' the Prince said.

Georgia followed the Dowager down the wide, marble staircase. As they reached the hall with its pillars of porphyry, an officer in the uniform of the Hussars came hurrying through the entrance door.

'Good Lord, it's Arthur!' the Duke exclaimed. 'I heard you were a prisoner; what the devil are you doing here?'

'Hello, Trydon. I've come to see the Prince,' the officer replied. 'I've just arrived home. I was exchanged for two of Napoleon's Admirals, never thought I should have such a piece of luck. I imagined I was going to rot in some stinking French prison until the war had ended.'

'Then you are indeed a fortunate young man,' the Dowager interposed.

'I apologise!' the Duke exclaimed. 'Lady Carrington, may I present Colonel Arthur Goodwin, an old friend. We served together in the Peninsula.'

'Until I was such an idiot as to get myself captured,' the Colonel exclaimed. 'It was a clever ambush, I must admit, but I have kicked myself every night for a year for having ridden into it.'

'I want to hear all about it,' the Duke said. 'Lunch with me tomorrow.'

'I can't,' Colonel Goodwin explained, 'I have to see the Prince tonight, and then tomorrow I must go to Sussex. I have to find a place called Little Chadbury. Ever heard of it? I'm calling on a girl called Georgia Grazebrook. I have a message for her from her brother.'

The Colonel bowed to the Duchess and started to run up the staircase. It was Georgia who found her voice first:

'Stop, please! I am Georgia Grazebrook. Oh, tell me about Charles! I did not know he was a prisoner.'

The Colonel stopped in his stride and came slowly down the stairs again.

'Charles was taken some months ago,' he explained, 'while trying to save the life of a seaman who had fallen overboard in a storm. The French picked him up before the British could get to him, and he is in Calais Castle.'

Georgia put her hands to her breasts.

'How awful for him! Is he well?'

'As well as can be expected,' the Colonel answered, 'but frustrated and infuriated at the thought of being a prisoner and out of the war.'

'You must tell me everything about him,' Georgia said.

The Colonel looked at the Duke with a look of appeal on his face.

'Listen, Georgia,' the Duke said quietly, 'the Colonel must see His Royal Highness first. But when he has finished here at Carlton House perhaps he would be so obliging as to come to Grosvenor Square—that is, if Her Ladyship will permit it?'

'You know as well as I do that I am as impatient as Georgia is to hear the rest of the story,' the Dowager said.

'I will be with you as speedily as possible,' Colonel Goodwin promised.

'Carrington House,' the Duke said, 'I will send the carriage back for you, or do you have one of your own?'

'I am not so grand as that, old man!' the Colonel replied with a grin, 'and you couldn't afford one either in the days when I last knew you.'

'I couldn't indeed,' the Duke laughed. 'But hurry to His Royal Highness. You know that he will be infuriated if he thinks you have seen anyone else before you have related to him the details of your adventure.'

'That's just about the right word for it,' the Colonel said, already halfway up the staircase again. He stopped as if he suddenly remembered his manners.

'Your servant, ladies,' he said with a bow, and then was bounding up the next flight of stairs two at a time.

The Dowager led the way outside to where the coach was waiting.

'Charles is a prisoner,' Georgia said almost to herself, but the Duke heard her. 'What shall I do now? I cannot bear to think of him in the hands of the enemy.'

'Perhaps we can think of a solution,' the Duke said quietly.

'You can?' She turned to him, her eyes shining in the light of the flaring torches outside Carlton House.

'I don't promise anything,' the Duke said, 'but I have an idea.'

'I believe that you could do anything,' Georgia whispered impulsively. Then afraid that she might have betrayed herself she got hastily into the coach.

11

THE four horses pulled the phaeton at a spanking pace down the Brighton and Dover Road. Georgia, feeling the wind on her cheeks, was certain that no one had ever journeyed at such a speed before. There was no moving this time across fields and by twisting lanes as she and the Duke had done when they came to London from Four Winds; now they were returning in style.

Dressed in a new travelling-coat of coral red with a bonnet trimmed with feathers of the same colour, and seated between the Duke and Pereguine, Georgia thought with a sudden pang in her heart that this was a moment she would always remember.

She would, she thought, have been happier than she had ever been before, had she not had the thought of Charles's imprisonment hanging over her like a cloud. And another more ominous depression lay at the back of her mind and haunted her however much she tried to avoid it—the knowledge that this was almost the end of her association with the Duke. If only he had been someone ordinary, she thought, perhaps they could have continued to be friends; but a Duke must live in a world into which she could in future have no entry. She must go back to Four Winds and try to salvage enough money to pay the people on the estate, and to keep the house open until such time as Charles returned.

Her first thought on waking, after a night of very troubled sleep, had been what her stepmother would think of all that had happened. But when she had timidly voiced her fears to the Duke, he had replied:

'Forget her, she will trouble you no more.'

'But why not? She will come to Four Winds.'

'She will never come to the house again,' the Duke

answered, 'I had a word last night, after I left you, with the Controller of His Royal Highness's household. He has promised to deal with Lady Grazebrook, and I assure you that you will never see her again.'

Georgia should have been confident, but somehow she could not credit that what the Duke said was the truth. She had the feeling that as soon as he went out from her life Caroline Grazebrook would come creeping back, that she would punish her for what had occurred and hold her directly responsible for the death of both her closest friends.

As if he sensed what she was feeling the Duke said quietly:

'We will talk of this later, in the meantime forget it. It is, I promise you, of little consequence.'

That was the truth, Georgia knew, for there were far more important plans afoot. The night before, when they had returned to Grosvenor Square, the Duke had merely outlined in a few words what he intended to do, and when the morning came Georgia, hurrying downstairs long before the Dowager had been called by her lady's maid, found Pereguine dressed and waiting for the Duke's arrival.

'Did Trydon really mean what he said last night?' Georgia asked, forgetting in her anxiety the courtesy of bidding her host good morning.

'Good morning, Georgia. Do sit down and have some breakfast,' Pereguine suggested, rising from a table laden with silver dishes.

'I do not think I could eat anything,' Georgia said.

'You must,' Pereguine insisted, 'no one can go adventuring on an empty stomach. That's one of Trydon's rules, by the way. He said he learnt in the Army that men fight better and march better when they have eaten, and so he insists on us all doing the same.'

'You really mean that we are g . . . going into b . . . battle today?' Georgia asked, stammering a little because she could feel the excitement rising within her.

'You heard what Trydon said,' Pereguine answered. 'He is not given to bubble-dreams. If he said he will do something, then he will.'

'But to rescue Charles, how could he?' Georgia asked.

Pereguine gave her a little frown and glanced towards

165

the flunkeys hovering near the sideboard, where there lay a cold collation and othet delicacies, just in case someone was hungry enough to eat them.

'Yes, yes of course,' Georgia said quickly, 'I was but funning.'

Because she knew that Pereguine was right when he said that if the Duke had said he would do a thing, he would, she forced herself to eat a dish of eggs and to sample a comb of honey, which Pereguine told her came from the Dowager's garden in Surrey.

Pereguine devoured several lamb cutlets and sampled one or two other dishes, while Georgia waited with a growing impatience for the servants to leave the room. At last Pereguine waved them away, telling them to have fresh dishes prepared in case His Grace required breakfast when he arrived. As the door closed behind the butler, Georgia bent forward eagerly.

'How is he going to do it?' she asked, her voice barely above a whisper.

'You will have to ask Trydon,' Pereguine replied. 'If you ask me, I think he is to let in the attic! But that's Trydon all over: he suggests something which seems crazed, and yet when one does it, it seems comparatively simple.'

'But how could this be simple?' Georgia asked, 'Charles is a prisoner.'

'That won't stop Trydon!' Pereguine asserted. 'And now, if you will forgive me, I'll see to my duelling pistols. It strikes me that we may be needing them.'

Georgia gave a little shudder as she remembered how he had used one the night before. Then she said:

'I would like to thank you. I tried last night, but you would not listen. Now that Lord Ravenscroft is dead, I feel as though I were free and no longer overshadowed by fear.'

'Then it's a good thing the old rattlesnake is out of the way,' Pereguine said lightly. 'Don't thank me, thank Trydon. If he hadn't impressed on me how dangerous the Count might be, I would not have been carrying a pistol. It was a pretty risky thing to do, it might have got me into very bad odour with His Royal Highness, but as things were it turned out differently.'

'You were wonderful,' Georgia said rapturously, 'you both were.'

As if he appeared because she was thinking of him, the Duke came through the door.

'Still eating?' he asked. 'It's time we were off.'

'Off?' Georgia and Pereguine echoed.

'I have my phaeton outside,' the Duke replied. 'Hurry, Georgia, and get your coat. I presume you have packed what you need for a night or so?'

'I told my maid what I shall require,' Georgia answered, 'but I thought we would be leaving later, when Her Ladyship is awake.'

'One female is enough on this trip,' the Duke said with a smile. 'Convey my respects to Her Ladyship and my regret that I cannot pay them in person.'

Georgia ran up the stairs. When the Dowager heard of their journey she made no protest about being left behind but only said wistfully:

'I wish I were twenty years younger! You young people are lucky. However dangerous an adventure may be, it is better than being left behind.'

Impulsively Georgia flung her arms round her and kissed her.

'You have been so kind to me,' she said, 'I can never thank you enough.'

The Dowager reached up and patted her cheek.

'You are a pretty chit,' she said, 'and I am sorry I shall not have the pleasure of showing you off at Carlton House tonight.'

'I would have liked it too,' Georgia said, wishing suddenly that the meeting with Count Jules had not come so swiftly. If it had taken several more days to find him, it would have meant that she would have more time with the Duke.

All night, when she had not been thinking of Charles, and worrying about him, her thoughts had been with the Duke. She could almost see his face in the darkness, and she could still feel that warmth and strength in his fingers as they had held hers. She touched her cold cheek where his lips had rested.

'I love him,' she whispered into her pillow, 'I love him, I love him, I love him.' And she knew with a sense of despair that she would be saying these words alone in the darkness every night for the rest of her life.

She had awoken at dawn because it brought her nearer to seeing him again, and now glancing up at him under the brim of her bonnet, watching him tool the reins of the horses with confidence and skill, she felt her heart turn over in her breast. He was magnificent. There was something commandingly autocratic about him, and she wondered how she could have ever believed that he was a fugitive, or that it had ever been necessary for him to go into hiding.

The Duke took his eyes momentarily off the road and looked down at her.

'Enjoying yourself?' he asked with a grin.

'It is wonderful,' Georgia said, and the wind seemed to whip the words from between her teeth because of the speed at which they were travelling.

'By Jove, Trydon!' Pereguine ejaculated. 'I envy you this horse-flesh. If we go on like this, we will beat Prinny's record to Brighton with ease.'

'I should hope we would,' the Duke said, 'but there's more important things afoot at this moment than gaining records.'

'I wish to God you would tell us what you are up to,' Pereguine grumbled, but he knew there was no point in talking at the moment and lapsed into silence.

They stopped at a smart coaching inn just before noon. The ostlers hurried to the horses' heads, and the landlord bustled out to welcome His Grace and his friends and lead them to a private room. Wine was brought and rounds of cold beef, legs of mutton and ham, and a boar's head tastefully decorated. The landlord pressed them to sample the cooking in the inn, but the Duke said firmly that they were in a hurry and must be served immediately. In fact Georgia felt that no amount of time could have improved on the cold lark and oyster pie which was her choice, although the two men preferred something more substantial.

She was taken upstairs by the innkeeper's wife to wash her hands in the best bedroom. Staring at her reflection in the mirror she thought that, despite a comparatively sleepless night, she looked fresh and wide-eyed with excitement. She was also feminine enough to appreciate that her bonnet was becoming, and her tiered travelling-coat was very different from the shabby, unfashionable velvet riding-habit she had worn when she travelled north.

Now she appeared a lady of fashion, but she knew that in her heart she was still the frightened girl who had been forced by circumstances into an illegal act. What was more she was still alone in the world, save for Nana who was getting old and should be retired, and a brother who was a prisoner in the hands of the French.

If she felt pathetic she certainly showed no sign of it when she came back to the private room and the gentlemen rose to their feet to greet her.

'A glass of wine, Georgia, and then we must be on our way,' the Duke said a little while later.

'You have given us barely half an hour's rest,' Pereguine complained.

'There is work to be done,' the Duke answered.

'Will you not tell us what you intend to do when we reach Brighton?' Georgia asked.

'We are not travelling to Brighton,' the Duke answered, 'our destination is Four Winds.'

'Four Winds?' Georgia was astonished. 'But why? What can we do there?'

'I will tell you when we reach your home,' the Duke said. 'I have no desire to talk here, or anywhere else where we might be overheard. I have learnt one lesson from the events of last night—trust no one! His Royal Highness's Controller was saying the same thing. The Prince is often very indiscreet in front of his closest friends. Heaven knows what secrets Bonaparte has learnt from his careless conversation about our military prowess or our naval strategy.'

'You are right,' Pereguine approved. 'Keep your silence, Trydon, although I am convinced that Georgia and I will die of curiosity long before we reach Four Winds, whenever that may be.'

The Duke merely smiled.

'You are not too tired?' he asked Georgia.

'Tired?' she echoed. 'You know that the comfort in which I have travelled this morning is very different from what I am accustomed to.'

The Duke's eyes twinkled at her, and he knew they were both thinking of those exhausting trips across the Channel.

'Good girl,' he said lightly, and once again she felt a warmth spread over her because of his approval.

They set off once again and four and a half hours from

the time they left London they turned in through the lodge gates of Four Winds. The house was basking in sunshine, its mellow red brick encircled with verdant woods making it appear like a precious jewel in a velvet box.

'By Jove, that's an attractive place!' Pereguine ejaculated.

'It is my home,' Georgia said a little shyly.

'Then I congratulate you,' he answered.

'The only thing is,' Georgia said hesitatingly, 'I am afraid you will not be very comfortable. It is . . . it is not what you are accustomed to in London.'

'Trydon and I often slept on the hard ground when we were on the Peninsula,' Pereguine answered. 'I assure you that any bed will seem luxurious after that.'

Georgia looked at the Duke as if for reassurance.

'I dare say Nana will not let us go hungry,' he said. And at that she could not help laughing.

They drew up at the front door in fine style, and it was some time before old Ned emerged from the stables to take charge of the horses. As Georgia entered the front door, she thought how shabby the house looked in comparison with the elegance of Carrington House.

Nana came hurrying through the hall from the kitchen quarters. Her face was anxious and apprehensive as she had thought it might be Lady Grazebrook arriving. But there was no mistaking the warmth in her welcome as she held out her arms towards Georgia.

'Miss Georgia, my dearie, I was never a-dreaming it could be you. And what have they done to you? You look so different, but smart and beautiful as I wished you to appear.'

She looked towards the Duke.

'So you kept your promise, sir, you brought her back to me safe and sound.'

'Safe enough,' the Duke said, 'but we have work to do that is of import, Nana.'

'And what may that be?' Nana asked.

Georgia put her arms round the old woman.

'Listen, Nana,' she said in a low voice. 'Charles is a prisoner, and there is a chance, though I do not know what it is yet, that we may be able to rescue him. Help us all you can.'

'A prisoner! My baby!' Nana seemed to reel under the

170

shock. 'Those dratted Frenchman—is no one safe from their devilish tricks?'

'Perhaps His Grace can help Charles,' Georgia said. She had forgotten as she spoke that Nana did not know the real identity of the stranger they had kept hidden in the priest hole. But as she spoke she looked towards the Duke, and the expression in her face was very revealing to someone who had known and loved her since a child.

'His Grace!' Nana said slowly, 'then I was right. I guessed you was of noble birth, sir. I've been brought up in gentlemen's service, so it would not be like me to make a mistake.'

'I am still the same person you wouldn't let go hungry, even though you called me a rapscallion,' the Duke said.

Nana blushed and looked a little discomforted, but Georgia gave her a hug.

'I'll tell you all about it later,' she promised. 'Please, Nana, some wine for the gentlemen, and a cup of chocolate for me if you have time.'

'I will get it right away,' Nana answered, muttering as she left the hall: 'A Duke, I was sure he had noble blood in him!'

Georgia started laughing and the two men joined in.

'Now, Georgia,' the Duke said. 'I want you to get together your crew, every one of them. And also the local steeplejack.'

'The crew!' Georgia ejaculated, 'but why? I don't understand.'

'You will,' the Duke said briefly.

He drew some maps from the pocket of his riding-coat, and walking into the library laid them on the big flat-topped desk which stood in the centre of the room. Georgia followed him looking bewildered.

'Please hurry,' the Duke said, 'and perhaps it would be best for you to change your clothes. Your people will be somewhat surprised to see you as you are now.'

Without saying any more the Duke proceeded to spread out the maps on the desk, and Georgia, after standing for a moment irresolute in the doorway, went to do as she was bid.

She found the gardener and sent him to the village to summon as many of the men as possible. She trudged down the narrow dusty lane to where one of the foresters

171

lived, finding him at home and sending him in search of several other employees. She remembered to ask for the steeplejack—there were two of them, father and son. She had suspected they might be away since they repaired the steeples all round that part of the countryside. Luckily, they were both at home.

She then went back to the house and, woman-like, changed once again from the old clothes in which she had gone to summon the crew to one of the elegant crisp muslins she had brought with her from London. As she put it on and glanced at herself in the mirror in her bedroom, she thought that perhaps this would be the last time she would wear it: all her clothes would have to go back to the Dowager. They had been given her for one purpose only, and now that had been achieved they were really no longer her property.

Because she loved the Duke, she could not bear that he should see her in the shabby garments she had worn for so long. She had seen the admiration in his eyes when she had appeared in the sparkling dress the Dowager had bought her to wear at Carlton House, and she knew that, before he left her for good, she wanted to see that same look in his eyes again.

She came down the stairs to find that already half a dozen men were standing awkwardly in the hall.

'You wanted us, mistress?' one of them asked. 'Be we a-crossing tonight?'

Georgia shook her head, greeted them by name and without answering any questions crossed the hall to the library.

'The men are here,' she said to the Duke, 'where will you see them?'

'Ask them to come in here,' the Duke replied as though he owned the house.

The men shuffled into the room holding their caps in their hands, and the Duke welcomed each one with a handshake. Georgia was amused to see that they were pleased to see him. He had been their comrade in a tight corner; they knew that he must have disposed of the body of the Frenchman and was now one of themselves. They trusted him.

Other men, panting a little from the haste in which they had obeyed the summons, came crowding into the library.

172

Georgia crossed the room to shut the door, having a quick glimpse of Nana's angry and affronted face, as she realised where the men were being entertained.

'Are you all here?' the Duke asked.

'Yes, sir.'

'And here are the steeplejacks,' Georgia explained bringing them forward. 'Ernest and Ben Farrow. They are quite famous in these parts and I was fortunate to find them at home.'

The steeplejacks smiled sheepishly at the compliment.

'I have news for you men,' the Duke said. 'Mr. Charles, your master, now that the Squire is dead, is a prisoner of the French.'

There was a chorus of exclamations and one man let out a hastily repressed oath.

'Now I know what you feel about your young master,' the Duke went on, 'I wish to ascertain if you are all prepared to come with me in a desperate attempt to rescue him.'

For a moment there was utter silence. Then, as if on a word of command, every man moved forward impulsively towards the desk.

The wind blowing from the south was warm on Georgia's face as they set out on the edge of dusk. She had spent two hours of furious argument with the Duke as to whether or not she should accompany the rescue party. She had won in the end simply and solely because she had sworn that if the Duke would not take her with him she would order the crew not to sail with him.

'I shall tell them you are not to be trusted,' she stormed, 'I will tell them any lie, but you will not go without me, I will not be left behind!'

' 'Tis not a woman's task,' the Duke said.

'It was not a woman's task to smuggle cargoes across the Channel as I have done a dozen times or more,' Georgia snapped, 'and I commanded the men well enough to bring them home to safety. In fact, it was only when you were with us that we nearly failed in our quest.'

'A female is notoriously illogical,' the Duke smiled. 'Very well, Georgia, you win, but I carry you under protest; there are too many people in the boat as it is.'

'We shall have no cargo,' Georgia retorted, 'and there is plenty of room, as well you know.'

'Who could ever argue with a woman!' the Duke said throwing up his hands.

Now she had won her point she was ready to forgive him. It was the first time that she felt embarrassed in her high boots and full-skirted coat, the first time she wished she could wear something more becoming. She had not listened to all the instructions the Duke gave the men, she only knew that he had been closeted for a long time alone with the steeplejacks, and that they carried on board all sorts of equipment.

They moved swiftly and easily over the smooth water. It was not a very dark night, and a pale moon was peeping through the clouds. The Duke and Pereguine conversed together, but otherwise they rowed in silence, and after a time the Duke started to give directions.

'Starboard a little,' he said to Georgia, 'keep a steady course now for the next hundred yards or so.'

The moon came from behind the clouds, and they saw the coast of France ahead of them.

'Heave to,' the Duke ordered. 'What time do you make it, Pereguine?'

It took some time for Pereguine to kindle a lantern, and having looked at his watch, he instantly extinguished the light.

'It's about four o'clock,' he said.

'And dawn should begin about four-thirty,' the Duke replied. 'Start rowing, men, we have got to time it exactly right.'

'What are we going to do?' Georgia asked. She realised that in all the hustle and bustle of getting everything arranged and changing her clothes she had still no idea of the details of the plan ahead.

'You will see,' the Duke answered.

As if he sympathised with her curiosity Pereguine whispered:

'Colonel Goodwin told Trydon that the prisoners are exercised on the battlements at dawn and dusk.'

The boat moved on, and now the Duke took the tiller from Georgia and told her to settle herself low in the boat. As he took over his hands closed over hers, and he gave her fingers a quick squeeze.

'You must be brave,' he whispered into her ear. 'Whatever happens, we shall have made the attempt.'

'I know,' she answered, 'and I shall be grateful, even if we fail.'

She slipped to the floor of the boat and for a moment let her face rest against his knee. It was an instinctive gesture that he did not notice; for he was intent on steering towards the great fortress which rose sheer out of the water just ahead of them.

The night was still dark as they came up to it, hardly moving their oars. With hardly a sound, the two steeplejacks jumped ashore carrying their equipment with them. Georgia straining her eyes in the darkness waited breathlessly for some sentry to give the alarm, but there was only the splash of the waves to be heard. The whole castle was in darkness, and she guessed that the French would not be expecting an invasion of men from the sea, only guns and perhaps ships thundering against the impregnable stone walls.

There was no sign of the steeplejacks, and after a short wait the Duke handed the tiller to Pereguine and stepping across the boat went ashore. Georgia saw him go, and with an effort prevented herself from putting out her hands to hold him.

He was going into danger, he might be killed, and she knew if he was it would torture her always that he had not said goodbye. She wanted to go after him, wanted above all other things to be beside him, but she knew it would be the wrong thing to do and she could only wait, holding her breath as she tried to listen to what was occurring.

Nothing appeared to be happening, and then, almost imperceptibly, as the sable sky lightened a little, she saw on the great walls of the castle two tiny figures, edging their way up, a rope dangling from their waists. It was the steeplejacks. They were making footholds and moving up to the first battlement. Below, staring up at them, stood the Duke.

Pereguine drew out his watch.

'What time is it?' Georgia whispered.

'Four-twenty-eight,' he answered.

The boat was rocking in the waves, and one man stood in the water to hold it steady. Georgia tried to think, but her brain felt as if it was numb. She could only watch

175

fascinated those tiny figures climbing, climbing, and the dark figure of the Duke watching from below.

'Four-twenty-nine,' Pereguine whispered, and then a minute later, 'Four-thirty.'

In a window at the very top of the Castle there was a light, then a light appeared lower down, and another lower still by the battlements. Georgia's eyes ached from the strain of watching. Suddenly she heard a tune being whistled, and she knew who was whistling it. She had remembered that as they were driving from London the Duke had turned to her and asked:

'Has your brother a favourite tune? Most people have something they connect with their childhood.'

'Of course,' she answered. 'My mother always played "Charlie is My Darling". We used to stand round the piano and sing it. Afterwards she would catch my brother up in her arms and say, "You are my darling, my darling Charlie". I used to feel very jealous.'

The Duke had said no more and it was only now she remembered wondering at the time why he had asked such an inconsequent question.

The strains of 'Charlie is My Darling' sounded shrill and clear. Nothing happened. Georgia could see now one of the steeplejacks descending the rope which he must have fixed to a part of the battlement. He reached the ground beside the Duke, and moved immediately towards the boat as if on a word of command. The other steeplejack followed him a few seconds later. Now there were two ropes dangling. No one could have seen them had they not known they were there.

The tune went on. 'Charlie is my darling, my darling, my darling, Charlie is my darling.' Suddenly a head appeared over the battlements.

'There's a rope two feet to your right,' the Duke shouted. 'It will hold you, hurry.'

For a moment the head did not move. Was it Charlie, or was it someone else? Then Georgia saw a man heave himself over the battlements, cling to one of the ropes and come slithering expertly down on to the rocks. The men in the boat gave a muffled cheer.

'Hurry,' the Duke commanded, 'and get the boat moving.'

The man standing in the sea and holding the boat

176

shoved it out to sea, so that it was already moving as Charlie and the Duke splashed through the water to reach it. The crew bent to their oars. And now there were heads above the battlements, sounds of voices and shouts of commands.

'Pull,' the Duke cried, 'pull as hard as you can! Quicker, quicker, keep your heads down.'

The boat was clear of the rocks, and Pereguine at the tiller swung her round, the men pulling with all their might.

'One, two,' the Duke began, 'take your time from me. One two—one two.'

Then almost too late to be frightening the firing began. Bullets came from the battlements, but already the boat was out to sea and the darkness encompassed them.

'Keep your heads down,' the Duke commanded, 'one two, one two.'

There was no need for him to ask the men to row harder, they were uttering grunts as they pulled at the oars with all their strength. Still there were shots whistling past them and Georgia crouching down on the wooden boards of the boat held her breath for fear someone should be hit.

Then suddenly they were out of shot and the castle was out of sight. They were in mid-channel and the dawn was breaking in the east, with the first golden flush of the sun creeping up to dispel the last evening star.

'Charlie! Oh, Charlie!' Georgia cried as her brother scrambled down the boat towards her, to hold her in his arms and kiss her on both cheeks.

'We've done it,' the Duke said, in tones of quiet satisfaction.

The men gave him a cheer, a cheer not only of triumph, but of relief, for what he had suggested had seemed crazy and impossible to all of them.

'And now for home,' the Duke said, his eyes resting for a moment on Georgia's happy face as she sat with her arms round her brother.

She had pulled off the dark handkerchief that she had worn over her hair, and her hair was soft and golden against Charles's face.

'How could you have attempted anything so crazy, so mad?' he asked almost incoherently.

'It was not me,' she answered, 'it was the Duke'

'The Duke?' he queried.

'The Duke of Westacre, he is a friend of Colonel Goodwin.'

'Then the Colonel found you?'

'He told us where you were,' Georgia replied.

'Oh my God, I don't believe it's true!' Charles ejaculated, and she knew by the sudden break in his voice that he too was very near to tears.

'It is all right,' she said, 'you are safe now, we are going home.'

'I must get back to my ship,' he answered. 'Can you imagine anything so nonsensical as to go overboard in a high sea and to be picked up by the enemy.'

'I understand you were trying to save a man.'

'I tried and failed,' he said, 'the current was too strong. He was a decent chap, too, one of the best.'

'You are safe now,' Georgia said consolingly.

It was the only thing she could say. She could not help feeling almost resentful that Charles's thoughts were already far away with his ship-mates and that he wished to return to them immediately, leaving her alone. She was more grateful than she could ever say that the brother she loved was no longer a prisoner and yet, because she knew she had no place in his plans for the future, she felt lonelier than she had felt before.

She glanced to the stern of the boat where the Duke was sitting with the two steeplejacks. She thought how handsome he looked, how elegant and unruffled, despite all they had been through. Tomorrow, she supposed, he would return to London to the social life of which he was an important part. Charles would go with him, eager to tell his story to the Admiralty, and she would be alone at Four Winds.

Quite suddenly, and she supposed it was the strain of all she had been through, she wanted to cry. 'I shall love him until I die,' she told her heart, and felt the tears well up in her eyes.

12

THEY reached the creek just before eight o'clock. Nana was standing at the point looking for them out to sea. They saw her before she saw them and Georgia knew by the way the old woman's hands were clasped that she was praying. She watched the expression on Nana's face transformed from desperate anxiety to almost incredulous joy when she saw that Charles was aboard.

The men were laughing and shouting as they dragged the boat up on to the shingle. This time there was no need for subterfuge and silence. They were almost intoxicated with the triumph of having rescued their master from the stoutest stronghold of the enemy.

Charles, having hugged Nana, was shaking hands with the crew, and they were all trying to tell him what had happened since he had been away. Georgia stood a little apart feeling lonely and unwanted. She saw the Duke have a word with Pereguine; then they brought large bags of gold from inside the cave where they must have concealed them before the boat left for France. She watched the Duke hand ten guineas in gold to each man of the crew, and she thought with a sudden bitterness that this was another debt they owed him, and one that was very unlikely to be repaid.

Suddenly she became conscious of herself, of her high boots and her shabby coat, that had once belonged to Charles, of her hair blowing about her face from the wind. Without a word she slipped away, hurrying back to the house along the rock passages, up the rickety staircase and through the empty cellar.

'This is the last time,' she thought, and wondered how, with Charles back at sea and the smuggling finished, she would ever be able to pay the men who worked on the estate.

By the time the Duke and Pereguine came back to the house Georgia had changed into her new white muslin and was laying the table in the dining-room for breakfast.

'I am hungry enough to eat an ox!' Charles announced. 'Hurry, Nana, and bring us everything you have in the house that is edible. I haven't had a square meal since I was captured.'

'My poor lad, I knew those devils would be a-starving you,' Nana exclaimed indignantly and bustled into the kitchen.

Charles seated himself at the table, and Georgia noticed with a little smile that without question he took his father's chair at the head of it. Georgia joined Nana in the kitchen and came back a few moments later with a pot of steaming coffee.

'This will give you something to start on,' she said, 'and there is a ham Nana and I have been keeping for just such an occasion as this. It was cured only three months ago and we thought, as we worked on it, that no one should eat it, save you.'

'Quite right,' Charles said grinning at her, and then, as if anything she said was of little consequence beside what he wished to hear from the Duke, he said impatiently:

'Continue, your Grace. What made you think you could rescue me?'

'Yes, what indeed?' Georgia asked, remembering what the Duke had said to her as they left Colonel Goodwin at Carlton House.

'Seven years ago, in 1802, when there was an armistice with Bonaparte,' the Duke replied, 'my Colonel took me abroad with him, and we went to France. Actually, he thought it was a good idea to have a look round and see what Bonaparte was plotting. The Prime Minister and a number of other people were convinced that the cessation of hostilities was just an excuse to gain time. Bonaparte wanted to build ships and redeploy his armies. When we arrived at Calais, in my Colonel's private yacht, we were met in a most friendly fashion by the Mayor of the town and invited to rest for the night at the castle. There were, of course, no military prisoners there but quite a number of civilian ones, and I remember asking if they ever got a chance of exercise and fresh air.

' "The more important ones are allowed a quarter of an hour on the battlements at dawn and dusk," the Mayor replied.

' "I suppose the same restrictions applied to our prisoners during the war?" my Colonel enquired.

' "Yes, indeed," the Mayor told him, "the British officers had the same privilege." '

'So that is how your Grace knew!' Charles ejaculated.

'Of course I confirmed with Colonel Goodwin that the rule still held,' the Duke said. 'And I remembered something else. We went on the battlements of the castle, and I stood looking down at the sea, at the waves breaking over the rocks below, and I thought to myself, "No one without wings could escape from here—unless he were a steeplejack!" '

'Whatever made you think that?' Georgia asked.

'I don't know,' the Duke said. 'Perhaps all our actions are predestined, perhaps all our thoughts have a meaning, so that sooner or later a good use can be put to them.'

'A good use indeed!' Charles said. 'How can I ever thank you, sir?'

'Don't try,' the Duke answered, 'it will embarrass me. Now that our adventure has turned out to be a success I am prepared to say that I enjoyed every moment of it.'

'Which is more than I did,' Georgia interposed. 'When I saw someone look over the battlements I was not certain it was Charles, and I expected every second to see the French open fire on us.'

'They would never in their wildest dreams have thought that a prisoner might try to escape by the sea-wall,' Charles answered. 'The other entrances to the castle are heavily guarded.'

Nana created a diversion by coming into the room carrying the largest dish in the house piled high with eggs and ham.

'I have four fat pigeons roasting on the spit,' she announced, 'and the garden-boy has gone down to the village for a leg of mutton.'

'A leg!' Charles exclaimed. 'Four legs is what I shall need.'

'And who's going to pay for it I would like to know?' Nana asked tartly. 'We haven't been able to afford such delicacies while you have been away, Mr. Charles, I can assure you.'

Nana flounced out of the room and Charles laughed.

'Trust old Nana to put me in my place,' he said to Georgia, 'I always feel when she's about that I am going to be put in the corner for some misdemeanour.'

'You were not punished half as much as I was,' Georgia replied. 'You always were her favourite.'

'And why not?' Charles asked. 'I was very attractive as a child.'

'That is why I used to pull your hair,' Georgia answered, 'and if you go on like this I will do it again.'

They were laughing and teasing each other, until Georgia became aware that the Duke, strangely silent, was watching her. The words she was about to say trailed away into silence, and she sipped her coffee without looking at him.

'By the way,' Charles said with his mouth full, 'I thought the men's rowing had improved out of all recognition, they never used to keep time or have such rhythm. It's a good thing they had had some practice or we wouldn't have been out of shot of the rifles on the battlements.'

'Do you really think it's such a good thing that they have had so much practice?' the Duke asked, his voice grim.

Charles looked at him and had the decency to appear embarrassed.

'No, sir,' he admitted, 'I was just talking like a goose-cat.'

'Your sister has been risking her life crossing the Channel with contraband,' the Duke continued.

'I wouldn't have allowed it had I been at home,' Charles said hastily.

'No, I presume you would have been obliged to go yourself,' the Duke answered, 'but that does not exonerate you from your responsibility towards the men on your estate who have been forced to break the law and to take the most unwarrantable risks with their lives and their freedom.'

'I didn't mean Georgia to get mixed up in it,' Charles explained. 'It's a hell of a tangle, but perhaps I might explain to you, sir, what occurred?'

'I know the full circumstances,' the Duke said, 'and your confession has been destroyed.'

'Destroyed?' Charles cried. 'You mean that you got it back from my stepmother. Oh, sir, what can I say? I can't express how grateful I am.'

'You must have had a screw loose to write anything so incriminating in the first place,' the Duke said sternly.

'Yes, I know that,' Charles said shamefacedly.

'All's well that ends well,' Pereguine interrupted, 'so stop berating the lad, Trydon, and let's make plans for returning to London. I for one need a rest before I can undertake any further journeying.'

'I will get the bedchambers ready,' Georgia said quickly.

She felt she could not bear to stay at the table while Charles was forced into a position of humiliation. She knew he deserved it and that the Duke was right in being stern with him. At the same time she thought no one would have been particularly severe on Charles if she herself had not become involved.

As she left the dining-room Nana appeared with the pigeons nicely roasted and arranged on a plate with watercress from the stream. Georgia knew that Charles's exclamation of delight was all the reward the old woman wanted. She loved to feed her children, as she called them, Charles in particular.

'I will prepare the beds in the guests' rooms,' Georgia said to Nana. 'After they have had a rest the gentlemen will be returning to London.'

'We needn't leave until about four o'clock,' Pereguine interposed. 'That will still give us enough daylight to reach town in time to enjoy a gay evening.'

His words made Georgia feel as though he had stabbed her to the heart: 'a gay evening!' And as if that was not enough Charles said eagerly:

'May I come with you? For I must be at the Admiralty tomorrow morning to tell of my return and make what plans I can to rejoin my ship?'

'Yes, of course,' the Duke said, 'you must give their Lordships your report as soon as possible.'

Georgia could bear no more and hastened from the

dining-room along the passage and up the stairs. She went into the two main bedchambers and pulled the curtains. The rooms were neat and tidy, and the sheets on the beds were of snowy white linen, fragrant from the lavender bags which she and Nana made fresh every year for the linen-room. She saw that there was water in the china urns and soap in the dishes beside them. Then she went to her own room.

She shut the door and threw herself face downwards on her bed hiding her face in the pillow. Everything was finished, they would all be leaving later on this afternoon, and she would never see the Duke again. He would go back to his world and she would remain here alone struggling as she had done before with the poverty, the troubles on the estate, the endless problem of paying for the very food that they must put into their mouths. But none of that mattered beside the fact that she knew that when the Duke left that afternoon he would take her heart with him. Fool, fool that she was to have fallen in love! But how could she have prevented it?

She had known from the very first that he was different. Even now, she could see the silhouette of him coming into the creek on his horse. There had been something in his bearing, something in his quiet cultured voice, that told her he was riding into her life, and that she would never be able to forget him.

She went back over all the times they had been together—the moment when his lips had touched her cheek; the warmth of his hands as he had bent forward in the coach. She could still see him knocking down the Frenchman and standing over his prostrate body. As he had done so, he had looked up and their eyes had met. It was almost as though he had laid his triumph at her feet.

'I love him.' She had said the words so often now that they might just have been a parrot phrase, but each time they brought a stab to her heart, a lump to her throat.

She lay there for a long time; then slowly she rose and taking her valise from a cupboard began to pack the things she had brought with her from London. She put them all in, the elegant coral driving-coat; the gauze and em-broidered dresses; the lace-trimmed underwear that the Dowager had insisted must go with her gowns; the satin

184

slippers that were so tiny that she wondered if they would ever fit anyone else.

Finally with a little sigh Georgia took off the dress she was wearing and laid it on top of the others. She looked in her wardrobe; there were only the old shabby gowns she had worn in the past—she had not realised how dilapidated they were until she compared them with the elegant creations of Madame Bertin.

Then, woman-like, because she could not bear the Duke to remember her looking anything but her best, she picked up again the gown she had just discarded and put it on. The crisp white muslin became her as nothing else had ever done, with the narrow blue ribbons over her white shoulders and the wide blue sash round the waist.

The sun was pouring through the window and she knew that she did not need the taffeta coat that went with the gown. With bare arms and neck she slipped down the stairs. The clothes must go back to the Dowager and she must write her a letter of thanks. She would send with them a big bouquet of roses from the garden. Perhaps their fragrance would express her gratitude better than she could put it into words.

The house was very still. Nana would be in the kitchen preparing more dishes for her beloved Charles and the Duke and Pereguine would be asleep. She tiptoed past the doors of their bedchambers. The sun was risen to its full height and she kept beneath the shade of the trees as she went down to the rose garden. Filling her arms with the roses that had been her mother's favourite flowers, she stood for a moment looking round the place that had comprised her whole life ever since she had been a child.

Quite suddenly she wondered what would become of her. In a few years Charles would get married; he would come here and live with his bride, and she would no longer be necessary to Four Winds or to anywhere else. Nana would retire, they had often talked of her moving into the little cottage at the end of the drive.

In whatever direction she looked Georgia thought there was nothing for her but loneliness. Nobody had really wanted her since her mother had died and although Nana loved her it was always Charles who came first. For a moment she almost resented the fact that she could no longer encounter the dangers and the anxieties of those trips across the Channel. It had at least been a relief from the monotony of her days. Perhaps it was more human to feel frightened than to feel nothing at all.

Then she shook herself out of her self-pity: it was better to have had all this than to have known nothing. It was better to love with her whole heart as she did now, even though she knew that it could bring her nothing but unhappiness, than to have never known the Duke. She thought of him going back to London, to the gay glittering crowd which surrounded the Prince. She thought of him being surrounded by women who set traps for him, the women who pursued him and the women, who, according to the Dowager, he too pursued. How she envied them!

The night before last he had thought she looked pretty, other people had called her beautiful. But she felt utterly inadequate and helpless when she compared herself with those sophisticated glittering figures who dominated the London scene. What had she got to offer anyone? She laughed bitterly to herself at the thought that she might even have contemplated competing with them.

Carrying her roses she walked back to the house and in through the open french windows of the salon, expecting the room to be empty, she gave a little startled exclamation when she saw the Duke, looking exceedingly fresh and elegant and standing by the mantelpiece.

'I . . . I thought you were asleep,' she stammered.

'I was not particularly interested in resting,' the Duke replied, 'I had other things I wished to do.'

'You wish to leave earlier?' Georgia inquired.

'I want to talk to you,' he answered.

She stood for a moment looking at him, making a picture in her white dress and with her arms full of fragrant flowers that any artist would have wished to portray. She put them down on the writing-desk and stood for a moment looking down at them.

'I have picked these for Lady Carrington,' she said, 'perhaps you would be kind enough to convey them to her with my love and gratitude. There . . . there will be my valise to go back as well.'

'Your valise?' the Duke inquired. 'Why should you wish to return that?'

'Her Ladyship gave me these gowns for a special purpose,' Georgia replied, still looking down at the roses. 'That purpose has now been achieved. I would not wish to keep anything to which I am not entitled.'

'I can imagine no one who is more entitled to them and a great deal more. Without your help, Georgia, His Royal Highness might be dead.'

'I cannot take any credit,' Georgia said. 'It was you who thought of everything, and it was you who saved him.'

'I should not have been watching the Count had you not indicated to me that he was the man you had carried across the Channel,' the Duke said. 'You must accept our thanks, we are overwhelmingly grateful.'

'I do not need your gratitude,' Georgia said. 'On the contrary, I am deeply in your Grace's debt for having saved Charles. Even now I can hardly believe it! It seems like a dream.'

'Charles is a very lucky young man,' the Duke said, 'and I have told him so in no uncertain tones.'

'You have not been harsh with him?' Georgia asked quickly, a little frown between her eyes. 'He is young, he is irresponsible, and he enjoys life so tremendously that he always forgets to think of the consequences.'

'It appears that you have not only had to think for him,' the Duke said, 'but also shoulder his responsibilities.'

'You have been unkind to him,' Georgia said accusingly, 'that was unnecessary.'

'I think your father had he been alive would have said very much the same,' the Duke said. 'But do not fret yourself, Charles is not in the least downcast. In fact, the one thing he has set his heart on at the moment is to drive my phaeton, and I am cudgelling my brains for the sake of my horses as to what possible excuse I can make.'

Georgia laughed.

'Charles is incorrigible, he was just the same when he was little, no one could be cross with him for long. And though he was really extremely sorry for some misdemeanour, he would have forgotten all about it a few moments later.'

'The best place for Charles is where he is most anxious to be,' the Duke said, 'in his ship. He has the type of high spirits of which the late Lord Nelson was exceedingly appreciative. One day Charles will make an excellent and most progressive-minded Admiral.'

Georgia laughed again.

'You are looking too far ahead,' she said. 'I can only think of Charles as a rather naughty little boy. You already see him as an old man.'

'And how do you think of yourself?' the Duke asked.

The smile died from Georgia's face. 'I know not what you mean.'

'I think you do,' the Duke said. 'But must we talk with half the width of the room between us? Come here, Georgia.'

There was a little pause, then Georgia said hastily:

'I am sorry, but I cannot stay here conversing with your Grace, for I have too much to do.'

'Indeed?' the Duke asked, 'and it cannot wait?'

'No . . . I . . . No . . . I have a l . . . letter to write.'

'Stop trying to run away,' the Duke said quietly.

'I am not—I mean . . .' Georgia tried to look at him but failed.

'If you will not come to me then I must come to you,' the Duke said, and moved across the space which divided them.

At his nearness Georgia could feel herself trembling, but she continued to look down at the flowers, picking them up one by one and arranging them on the desk.

'I think,' the Duke said in a quiet voice, 'that it is time we talked together about your husband.'

Georgia's fingers no longer moved and her whole body stiffened.

'My . . . m . . . my husband?'

'Yes,' the Duke said, 'I am a trifle anxious about him.'

'There is no need,' Georgia murmured.

'But indeed there is,' the Duke said, 'for no one seems to have knowledge of his whereabouts. In fact Charles informs me that he has never heard of the gentleman!'

'I was m . . . married when Charles was . . . at sea,' Georgia explained. 'They have not m . . . met. In fact, , . . Charles knows . . . very little about my . . . my marriage.'

'That is obvious,' the Duke said.

There was a silence until more quietly still the Duke said:

'Tell me one thing, Georgia, has any man ever possessed you?'

Georgia's eyes widened and Lord Ravenscroft's evil face came to her mind. She turned her head sharply as the blood came flooding into her pale cheeks.

'No! no!' she exclaimed passionately. 'How could you ask such a thing?'

The Duke's lips twisted in a tender smile.. Reaching out he took her left hand in his. He looked down at it and very gently drew the gold wedding-ring from her third finger.

'In which case,' he asked softly, 'isn't this rather unnecessary?'

At the touch of his fingers Georgia felt herself quiver. Too late, she snatched her hand away, leaving the wedding-ring with him.

'It was a sensible pretence,' the Duke said. 'And perturbed me greatly until I realised it as a lie.'

'You guessed?' Georgia asked.

'I knew,' the Duke answered, 'that no one could have looked or seemed so innocent and not been a maiden.'

She blushed again and began to gather up the roses.

'It was a subterfuge to deceive my stepmother's friends,' she said. 'Now I can be myself.'

'Which you have always been to me,' the Duke said. 'Georgia, must you go on pretending that nothing has happened between us? You have fought me for long enough and I cannot tell you how much I have suffered, thinking you were unobtainable, believing you belonged to someone else.'

She dropped the roses and turned round to stare at him.

'I made you suffer?' She hardly breathed the words.

'One day I will tell you how much,' the Duke said. 'You see, I believed, little Georgia, that my love was contraband.'

She stood looking up at him, her eyes shining like stars, her lips trembling. She felt as though the whole world was suddenly golden. The birds were singing outside the window and there was a strange warmth creeping over her, a flame rising within her heart. Then she looked away from him and broke the spell.

'You are merely playing with me,' she said harshly. 'Go back to London to the people you know and to whom you belong. They are waiting for you.'

'No one is waiting for me,' the Duke said, 'except, I hope, one person.'

'And who is that?' She could not prevent herself from asking the question.

'You,' he replied.

'It is impossible,' she protested. 'Can you not see how impossible it is? There are all those women and . . . and . . .'

'And the fact that I am a Duke,' he finished with a little smile. 'Could you not perhaps overlook the fact that quite inadvertently and without any connivance on my part I inherited a title?'

'You are mocking me,' Georgia said fiercely. 'Can you not see that we live in different worlds?'

'On one or two occasions,' the Duke said, 'I had reason to believe that those two worlds were bridged because we were close together. That night in the library, Georgia, there was only you and me, and last night, when I let you, against all my better judgment, come with me on that dangerous journey, I thought that if we should both die it would not matter much because we were together.'

She looked up at him then, and he saw the tears well up into her eyes.

'Did you think that?' she asked. 'I thought the same, and I knew as I watched you standing looking up at the battlements, that if anything happened to you I should not wish to remain alive.'

He looked down into her eyes with an expression of tenderness on his face that no one had ever seen before.

'Then why, darling?' he asked very softly, 'are you arguing with me. I love you, do you want me to say any more?'

'But you cannot! It is impossible!' Georgia cried. 'What have I got to offer you, and I am so ignorant, I do not belong to the smart world of elegant people, of Princes and Dukes, of balls and routs and assemblies. I am just Georgia of Four Winds. Just an ordinary girl.'

'But someone who is to me the most wonderful, the most beautiful and most exciting person in the whole world,' the Duke answered.

He put out his arms and drew her very closely to him. For a moment she hid her head against his shoulder. Then he put his fingers beneath her chin and tipped her little face up to his.

'So small, so vulnerable and so courageous,' he said. 'Could any man ask for more?'

'You are making a m . . . mistake,' Georgia told him. Trying to fight against the wonder and glory which seemed to be overwhelming her. 'There are all those other w . . . women, have you th . . . thought about th . . . them?'

'I never want to think about any of them again,' the Duke said. 'Oh, my little love, you are so foolish. Can't you understand what has happened to us?'

She drew a deep breath, and then his lips were on hers, holding her captive and making it impossible for her to speak. She could only surrender herself to the wild ecstasy which awakened within her was leaping higher and higher like a burning fire. She felt as if they were indeed one person joined together for eternity. He held her closer and closer until she knew that never again would she be lonely, never again would she be unwanted. . . .

What seemed an eternity later, the Duke raised his head and looked down at her parted lips.

'I never thought to convince you,' he said softly, 'that a Duke could, after all, be a very ordinary man.'

She gave a little gurgle of laughter, instinctively reaching up her arms to put them round his neck and draw his head down again to hers. For a moment he resisted her.

'Wait,' he said, 'you have not yet told me why you are marrying me. I want to hear it from your own lips those words I have longed for but which I thought I would never be entitled to ask you to say. Tell me, Georgia.'

And softly, so that he had to bend his head to hear, she whispered:

'I love you . . . Trydon . . . I love you with all my heart.'